The Shining City on the Hill

by Caroline Collier

A Universal Language Trade Paperback Original

Printed in the United States of 'Merica

Published by Universal Language

UniversalLanguagePublishing.com

TheShiningCityOnTheHill.com

Cover design by Clare Dolan
www.claredolan.co.uk

Interior photographs by Vishal Malhotra

The exact figures are unknown, but even by the most minimal estimates, more than 100,000 human beings lost their lives as a result of the 2003 U.S.-led invasion and subsequent occupation of Iraq. This book is dedicated to them ... and to everyone on the planet who has made a commitment to honor life through nonviolence and compassion.

Stage One: Unraveling

1 Life on the Hill   1

2 The Transgression   23

3 Grandmaster Fury   43

Stage Two: Dreams of Perfection

4 The Lovers   66

5 Elevation   87

Stage Three: Deliberation

6 Enchantment   113

7 Temptation   136

Stage Four: Transit

8 Salvation   162

9 Two Worlds   186

Stage Five: Visions

10 Attempting Redemption   212

11 Karma   236

Stage Six: Rebirth

12 Full Circles   260

Caroline Collier

What would you do

If the world broke in two?

Would you run, or fight,

Or destroy what you knew?

Would you take a look around,

Try to block the attack,

If you knew where to go

When you couldn't turn back?

With something to read

On apocalypse eve,

Will you cut the trees down?

Will you save me a seed?

STAGE ONE

UNRAVELING

CHAPTER ONE

LIFE ON THE HILL

The news is always distressing, and Karma Hill hates herself for watching while the world takes a turn for the worse. The television news anchor prattles on about record unemployment, increasingly violent protests around the country, and the astronomical gap between the ultra-rich and everyone else.

The disheveled young woman picks and chooses the words she can stomach to hear. Witnessing the unraveling of modern America on a high definition screen has its advantages. No matter how lousy things get out there, she always feels insulated in the cold comfort of her living room.

Karma, deep down, wants to raise her voice in protest, but she feels helpless, defeated. Her student loan bills still arrive regularly in the mail, but she has long since stopped paying them. She can't. At least she can't pay those *and* her broadband bill, so she chooses the latter. She makes enough by doing odd jobs and selling odd things to scrape by, which is thankfully satisfactory, because the prospect of legitimate employment is diminishing by the day.

Karma intuitively knows when to look down at her cell phone. She has the special sense to know in advance when someone is trying to communicate with her. As expected, the screen lights up with a picture she took near Machu Picchu. She feels the high-pitched ding of the ringtone reverberate throughout her floral couch. A contact aptly named "Michael Casual" has sent a text message - "Cool if I swing by? In the neighborhood," it reads.

She, as usual, is hoping the messenger to be her on-again, off-again flame Christian, but, as usual, she is receiving a business call. From experience, she knows "in the neighborhood," from the fingers of Michael Casual, means right down the street. She yawns in her dimly lit living room before typing the curt reply of "sure."

Though Michael has, on more than one occasion, expressed his interest in the slight, and equally casual, Karma, she has a true lover's obsession with Christian alone. Regardless, as she passes the mirror in her dining room, she takes a moment to run her fingers through her shoulder-length brown hair (which needs a trim), though no measure of manual labor can change the fact that she hasn't shampooed in several days. En route to her bedroom, which sits at the end of the long hallway running down her side of the duplex, she grabs an empty storage baggie from the kitchen cabinet.

During these hot summer months, the sunset hours are brutal, even inside with the dim hum of the air conditioner. The Texas heat can penetrate the sturdiest layers of insulation, which her '50s-era house doesn't have in the first place. Everyone in her Texas town spends the late summer days harboring the deep burn of an angry soul. After 29 years in the same town, she has grown inured to the hot and stagnant summer boredom.

From experience, she knows how much pot Michael wants to buy. Her stash of sweet island skunk is brittle and running low, which means she has a useful reason to call Christian - to ask for more. As she picks out the tightly curled buds and weighs enough on her digital scale to make an eighth of an ounce, the possibility of some other form of employment crosses her mind. Alarm clocks, though, don't exactly fit with her lifestyle. Her cum laude degree in physics surely qualifies her to do something meaningful, but she isn't looking.

Karma wonders if the extended Hidalgo family - all eight of them living on the other half of her duplex - speculate about what she does for a living. While the Hidalgo men work two jobs apiece, and the women - Flor and Esmeralda - clean houses while alternating care of the three kids, Karma spends almost all of her time ensconced inside of her tapestry-laden house, which has become equal parts sanctuary and prison. She hears the happy cry of the littlest Hidalgo, Nicolas, and imagines having a child of her own.

"Christian would be a terrible father," she says to her cat Tank, who yawns lazily from the foot of her bed. The only single Hidalgo, Javier, he would make a capable father. She chuckles at the thought; he doesn't speak much English. As the odors of cooking oil, corn, and baby powder waft over to her side of the house, she thinks about just how different she is from her neighbors.

The Hidalgos, like most immigrants from Mexico, live decidedly practical lives. They found spouses without fretting too much over the process, went to work and made babies. They ate together as a family on the rare occasions when each of them was temporarily free from the bonds of labor. They send money orders back to their mother in Jalisco religiously. Karma doesn't share shit with anyone, except for with Christian, to whom she would give anything. The way she bends over backwards, literally and figuratively, for that man has driven everyone else out of her inner life. This disgusts her more than all the rest of the world's perils combined.

"He doesn't even care about you," her mother's voice echoes in her head. Her mother, who moved to Denver a few years ago, is right. Christian would tell her that he loved her while in the throes of passion one night, only to disappear in a cloud of marijuana smoke the next. Though they have now been casual lovers for years, he batters her increasingly fragile emotional state without any concern for her wellbeing. He talks about his other sexual conquests in her presence. He laughs while telling stories about how he makes women cry. He brags at length about his trust fund - a legacy of his oil baron grandfather - but never gives her anything. He even charges her full price for the quarter pounds of hydroponic weed she regularly buys off him.

Christian Cantrell is the American dream. He is the guy that strangers argue deserves his vast wealth. He is the one anchoring the economy, creating jobs. He deserves the birthright of his millions, and people across the country argue on his behalf that taxing him more would be unfair.

Karma hates herself for loving him, but Christian is her obsession. A permanent union with him would erase her problems, she believes, and this is the only scenario that offers her any measure of hope for the future. She desperately wants to be super-wealthy while devoid of all responsibility. "Doesn't everyone?" she asks Tank, who has drifted back into naptime.

A familiar rap at her door interrupts the muted sounds of the Hidalgo clan sitting down for dinner on the other side of the wall. Karma slowly makes the well-worn trek to her front door, whose paint peels outrageously, where Michael Casual stands with a friendly smile. "Whatcha doin?" is his eternal greeting.

"Nothing much," always her reply. She hands him the bag in

4

exchange for three crisply folded twenty-dollar bills, just as they have done a hundred times before in this ritual of subversive capitalism. Like clockwork, he breaks a brittle top off a piece of his expensive dried plant (more expensive by weight than gold), and she stuffs it in her blue glass pipe, which needs to have the thick resin scraped from the side of the bowl.

Karma only smokes pot these days to be polite to her customer-friends. After a solid decade of inhaling and enlightening herself, weed has ceased to do much of anything to her. Nothing can dispel the cloud of boredom and bitter disappointment, but Karma keeps trying. As they quickly pass the pipe back and forth, Karma and Michael Causal make small talk - about the band he is drumming for these days, so-and-so's love life and etcetera. In a matter of minutes, Michael says thanks and leaves her to the quiet and lonely house she swears she prefers.

Infiltrated by the numbing mist of pot, she unmutes her colossal HD television and changes to a more calming channel. As she watches cooking guru Rachael Ray mix a spinach salad with wilting mushrooms, she thinks about the only thing for which she truly cares - Christian.

His cruelty has become too much to bear, and she doesn't want to feel it, so she reaches underneath the cushion at the far end of the sofa and pulls out a label-less orange medicine bottle. Mindlessly, she pops off the cap, fishes out a shiny white hydrocodone tablet, and swallows. Only when the pill sticks in her throat does she think to run to the kitchen to pour a glass of water. Standing still over the sink as the lukewarm water (it never gets any colder this time of year) escapes the tap, the whispering word "restless" runs in an out of her inner ears.

Karma shuts off the water and wanders in a circle around her modest castle. She keeps her music gear, most of which is collecting a layer of diaphanous dust, in the large spare bedroom. If she cared enough about the world to write a song for it, she has all the pieces in place and even knows how to use them. Instead, she picks up her favorite acoustic guitar and starts to play her sad tale of heartbreak. If she can only get deep enough into the emotions of loss, emptiness, and despair, she can find her way out, she believes. If she can figure out how she really feels, at that point, she can start to write the song for her future with Christian.

Somewhere during the second verse, she gets bored and stares at herself in the large mirror mounted on the wall. She leans closer and inspects the corners of her eyes, where the telltale signs of age are beginning to manifest. Still, for 29, she looks remarkably young. If she paid more attention during the occasions when she graced the outer world with her presence, she would notice she still turned heads. Karma has an effortless, almost ethereal, glow and misleadingly innocent brown eyes. As she stares as deeply as possible inside of herself, she only sees the flaws.

Another ding-ding from the phone interrupts her reverie of imperfection. Marian Smythe this time, also known as the most annoying friend in town. "Can you bring a CD up to DL," it reads.

"Sure," again, Karma curtly replies.

Karma and her customer-friends have developed code-speak, because although she is indubitably foolish, she is not so stupid as to flaunt her illegal activities for the interwebs to see. CD, in Marian's case, also means an eight of an ounce. Although Karma prefers pick-up to delivery, she relents. DL is the venerable neighborhood bar Dragon's Lair, or the only place in the vicinity seedy enough for Christian's regular presence.

She grabs her phone and another baggie then meanders back to her bedroom, where she has carefully hidden the expensive weed in the top drawer of the dresser. She plugs the phone into a speaker dock and cues up the song she was just playing: Jeff Buckley's "Lover, You Should Have Come Over." As she picks clothes from the pile at the foot of her bed, she attempts to get back into the emotions she felt as she was just strumming the song. The hydrocodone begins to dull the sharp edges of her perpetual heartbreak, so instead of finding sadness, she swings into the opposite moods of false pleasure (overload of synthetic chemicals) and ice-cold anger (her soul's reaction).

Noting that they still smell passable, she settles on a pair of low-cut jeans with flared legs. She looks in another mirror and takes stock of the woman she has become. While others might see beauty, she focuses on the slight sag of her skin and the barely perceptible soda bulge in her belly. She slumps, purposely. Because it just doesn't matter, she convinces herself, she grabs a t-shirt from the plastic shelf in her closet. Satisfied by the way her grey New York Jets shirt blends into the wall behind her, she cocks her head at a flattering angle and gives herself an intimidating look in the mirror.

Just then, the phone dings again. She crosses her fingers and is happy to see Christian has finally stepped from her imagination into her reality after a five-day absence. "At DL," she reads with a quickening heart.

Her reply: "Nice."

Ding ding: "Sorry I'm a sociopath. I ruined my life. Need to talk."

Not good, she thinks. Although moody self-criticism is a bond between them, Christian is not one prone to histrionics. Though, technically, he *has* sort of ruined his life, he doesn't usually see things in this particular light. Christian had been born with everything - the money, the loving family, the looks, and the smarts - and he still has a substantial chunk of his blessings left.

7

Though a thousand voices have warned him along the descent, he has never admitted to nearing the bottom of any hill.

Karma and Christian were classmates and casual acquaintances in high school, and both had gone to private colleges. He, with the help of endless funds, went to Vanderbilt, and she, with the help of a scholarship and a few student loans, to Trinity University in San Antonio. He now lives in the guest house on his parent's fading (but majestic) property. He claims to be writing films, and he *has* discussed plenty of ideas, but he has never made anything resembling an actual movie.

He imports large quantities of marijuana from California -- not because he needs to, but because he can and doing so is a thrilling risk. She, on the other hand, earns a modest income by bartending for catering events and supplements that income with her entrepreneurial niche. She pays her own rent for the duplex, which is either 15 minutes or a world away from Christian's guest house home, to which she is rarely invited.

She ruminates about the American dream as she hears one of the Hidalgos make a quiet ruckus on the other side of the wall. She imagines the children, Miguel, Eduardo and Nico, working hard, going to college, and returning home to live in laziness with madre and padre.

She laughs. Have she and Christian attained the dreams of their forefathers? Did their ancestors cross oceans, make every sacrifice, put their lives on the line in foreign wars so that their progeny could learn everything in God's encyclopedia but choose to work in illegal trade? Are Karma and Christian the culmination of American excess? She thinks about warning the Hidalgos, but she isn't cruel enough to dash their grand hopes for the boys.

Now in a semi-stupor, Karma flings herself on the bed, which sits directly on the wood floor surrounded by piles of wrinkled clothes. She stares at the ceiling, which needs to be repainted. The cruel contradiction of being lost inside the safest, most bountiful place on earth hovers dangerously close to her conscious mind.

Tank, the cat, looks up and yawns. She contemplates saying fuck it all and throwing the covers over her body, but she gets up, grabs Marian's bag of skunk, takes another hydrocodone tablet from underneath the couch cushion and heads to the Dragon's Lair.

Karma drives the 13 blocks from her house to the Dragon's Lair without paying attention to where she is going. The bar sits at the moderately bustling intersection across from Dale's Taco Shop and catty-corner from the gas-and-vice convenience mart. Along the way, she refrains from adjusting her Honda's radio, which is stuck on a tired grunge rock song from the '90s that she has heard thousands of times.

She remembers the days when she would have stopped to pick up a pack of smokes before entering the Lair, but she prides herself on the fact that, when she became a pill junkie, she dropped her other compulsions like the bad habits that they indubitably were.

She parks and checks her eyes, which are glassy and oddly pinched. She can hear the noise from the bar escaping out into the parking lot. Despite the darkening hour, the heat is still despotic. She absently fans herself with her shirt.

Incubus' angsty hit "Pardon Me" greets her as she nears the Dragon's Lair, which is downstairs from a coffee shop. Several mug-toting patrons curiously eye her from window seats. The bar doesn't really get going until at least 11, but at this hour, a handful of evening drinkers sit in a haze of cigarette smoke sipping on brown beer bottles whose silver labels bear the colors of the American flag. Christian is not at the horseshoe-shaped bar, but she finds him, alone, on a couch in the back room with the pool tables. His hair fuzz is newly shorn; his balding head drooped.

"I'm sorry I haven't called lately," he says without looking up. "I've been really busy."

The anger of rejection starts to burn up through the skin of her face, traveling from jaw to forehead. She tenses while searching for a witty, piercing response.

When he does allow his gaze to meet hers, she softens. She falls right into his inviting green eyes every time. In them, she sees all those nights when she thought she couldn't be any happier than she felt in his arms. She forgets the problems, the reality, and the fact that she cannot outrun the past.

She falls out of herself and sits down next to him on the gray vinyl barroom couch, which has to be at least 30 years old. She ignores the stains whose sins she doesn't care to visualize. With her similarly colored t-shirt and submissive demeanor, she nearly disappears into the torn vinyl.

"It's just," he continues, "A weird time for me, you know. I just need to figure all this out. I just need..."

"Space, I know," she answers for him. As though they had ever had anything but space. Their intoxicated embraces happened randomly, always in the mysterious hours of the night - those in which nothing good ever happens. Recently, their passion extended late into the early daylight hours, when the earth was turning to face the sun, but the gentle sunlight had shocked Christian, who left without so much as a goodbye. He didn't reappear at her house for nearly two months. She pushes this memory away from the barroom.

"No," he says. "I have a lot on my mind, you know. There are all these things. I just need to understand what's important to me, what I need. I've been focused on everyone else for too long, and I really need to make this all about me and what I want." He speaks quickly and emphatically, as if some force bubbling up inside him can no longer be contained.

"Okay," she says, but inside, she reels in the furor of hearing his selfish words. In truth, she never expects anything else from him. Over the years, he has demanded everything from her, promising to give it all back and deliver her to the innocence of her dream, but his promises always evaporate. Suddenly, she doesn't care. A switch in her heart has flipped, and she decides that she doesn't have the capacity for loving him anymore.

Christian takes the last swig from his bottle of Miller Lite then kicks it across the dirty floor. The speaker back here has long since cracked, but the Nirvana tune is eternally recognizable, stuck on repeat for the least 15 years, Cobain's lessons not learned. "We need to talk," he goes on, as if he has not already made his point.

"Is it about the sociopathy?" she asks, then sighs.

"No, it's about fucking Marian," he says, his eyes suddenly dark and unattractive. He balls his hands into tight fists, making his forearms expand frightfully. "She got busted selling coke at the fucking F lounge and is going to swing a deal to take us down. That fucking bitch.

"I knew it. You've been selling to her, haven't you? Just be fucking straight with me. What does she know about me?" he asks, as he starts pacing, hulk-like.

Karma breathes deeply, trying to ignore the dull ringing in her ears. Marian, yeah, she thinks. I knew I couldn't trust her, but Christian is being extra delusional. Has he finally tipped the scale over into the deep end? She fingers Marian's eighth, which is cramped inside the front pocket of her jeans. The soft touch of the worn denim calms her. She takes a deep breath and swears silently that everything will be okay.

Karma still has herself convinced that she is on the right path in life. She has always treated people with kindness and respect (well, somewhat), so she assumes that, partly because her parents had named her Karma, she would be okay. Being arrested for selling drugs, whether or not pot should even be illegal, would be a large and expensive obstacle to overcome. She decides that her risk is minimal and that Christian is flat-out crazy. He paces a few feet from her, apparently forgetting that he is waiting for her answer to his question.

At that moment, she hears Marian's distinctively tinny, loud voice at the bar in the other room. Her heart drops along with the temperature in the room. In a rush of paranoia, she readies to stash the sack into one of the pockets of the pool table, but Christian grabs her by the arm and drags her toward the bathroom.

Christian and Karma skirt the edge of the barroom unnoticed and make their way down "the hall of shame" to the women's restroom, which is roughly twice the size of the men's. Once inside, Christian carefully closes the latch and pulls out a generous little baggie filled to the brim with cocaine.

"I just need to calm down," he says. "Do you want any?"

Finally finding her spine and words, Karma retorts, "You know I quit doing that shit. I told you not to bring it around me."

He regards her disapprovingly as he pours out a mini-anthill and arranges it into a fat line with a credit card. His gaze mocks her, daring her as he rolls up a well-used dollar bill.

"A dollar bill," she comments. "Times must be *really* rough, Christian. 'Member when you refused to snort coke out of anything less than a hundred? 'Member that street bum bacteria you didn't want to get in your nostrils?" She turns up the corner of her mouth in a sarcastic scowl and makes a rude 'tsk-tsk' sound.

"What's happened to you? You treat me like shit, like I

don't even matter, asshole. Do you have any idea how bad you make me feel? You really are a fucking sociopath," she says to him, the hiss in her voice swirling about each consonant.

He laughs like he enjoys her commentary as he bends over the counter. Christian pays no attention to the unsanitary tile surface as he inhales a rail the size of a fingernail file. He holds the bill up toward the fluorescent white light as he relaxes, temporarily sated.

As soon as he opens his eyes, he grabs her and holds the back of her head in his hands. He draws her very close to his face, watches her squirm. Christian is on top of the world, and he knows she will never say no to him. She has mouthed the word in the past, but she's never meant it. He knows he can fully control her for life -- not because he particularly wants to and not because he cares about her, but because of the thrill of total spiritual domination. She tries to maneuver her head out of his grasp, and her fruitless efforts amuse him.

"I'm sorry. I love you," he murmurs. He kisses her, softly at first, then with an invasive push of his tongue.

For the first time, he repulses her, even more than the stench of shit and vomit in the ugly, black bathroom with a chipped mirror. She can taste the residue of the line he just snorted. By extension, she feels the numbness invading the tip of her tongue. She is so horrified about where she is and whom she is with, she inhales sharply like she has just been punched in the stomach.

"It's over between us," she says. "This wasn't what I wanted from you. From life. This was not the way I wanted to create my experience. We're both losing ourselves. Look at us."

She looks at their combined reflection in the cracked bathroom mirror. She sees nothingness. She sees futility, and waste, and collapse. She is out of tears, though, so her eyes remain glassy and disinterested. She has one more bullet to put through their once pleasant connection. "I don't even know you anymore," she tells him.

He scoffs, finally awake to what is going on and incensed by her betrayal.

"Me?" he yells. "Who the fuck are you anymore? You sit in your house all damn day and never want to do anything. Never want to drink, never want to fuck, act like you don't even want me around. How the fuck is that supposed to make me feel? Huh?"

He clenches his fists but flattens them out before directing his anger on the wall behind the exposed pipes of the toilet.

He makes a finger and wags it threateningly in front of her eyes, but she does not flinch.

They both stew in frustrated silences while the questions they just raised scramble for answers. They think back in time, define themselves in terms of snapshots from the past, and arrive at conclusions about who they were and who they had turned into. Independently, they both come to the conclusion that everything has changed.

Karma, while she has not openly admitted it to her conscious mind, knows this realization has been on its way. She is not stunned by the finality of the decline they have experienced. In her own quiet way, she has already come to accept it. The air of waste swirls around her, and she feels the environs appropriate. She is lost, probably permanently, and lost in a world by herself, but this does not matter.

Christian, on the other hand, still believes in his fairytale. He once possessed the most power, so his loss is greater, while Karma is simply free to float around in the murky nothingness.

As he tries to fight off the facts, the vein in his forehead starts bulging and turning odd shades of bruise. A rage addles him from deep within then explodes all around him. He begins convulsing, his violent tics an extension of the fury he has been waiting to express his whole life. He falls, hitting his head on the side of the toilet right in the bulging vein. Blood erupts onto the floor, and Karma sits on the black-and-white tiled countertop. She takes extra measures to ensure her tan cloth shoes don't get dirty.

As she regards the scene with an air of detachment, a wallop hits from the bathroom door.

"Police, open up," a gruff voice yells from the other side.

"Bitches," Marian's loud voice chimes in.

Karma carefully reaches into her pocket and pulls out Marian's share of the sweet island skunk. She can almost see her heart beating through the thin cotton of her shirt. That cunt, she thinks, I can't believe it. Still guarding her shoes, Karma reaches over the unconscious Christian, drops the plastic bag in the toilet, and flushes it.

She looks in the mirror, checks that the part on the left side of her head is straight and turns around to meet her fate. Her mood shifts back and forth between annoyance and panic.

Karma closes her eyes as she slowly opens the door, ready to smile and talk her way out of a fairly foreboding situation. A picture of her in an orange prison jumpsuit crosses her imagination, but she chooses not to dwell.

She unhinges the latch, expecting guns and mustaches, but all she sees is Marian and a short dude in a black t-shirt, black skinny jeans, and a chain linking a belt loop to his wallet. "Great, a fucking hipster," she whispers imperceptibly.

"Where's my sack, beyotch," Marian asks, with flair, before she notices Christian slumped in a pool of blood on the floor. Her tone changes from one of coolness to one of genuine concern. "Omigod, what happened?" she blurts out in a forced valley girl voice.

"He was doing blow, and he passed out," Karma replies as succinctly as she can.

Out of reflex or pure stupidity, Marian and her friend, who awkwardly introduces himself as Dave, walk into the small bathroom and lock the door behind them. Dave bends over Christian and lifts his head. The movement causes Christian to stir, and Karma doesn't even feel a pang of relief.

Over the next few minutes, Christian wakes up and sits against the wall, his face and white button-up stained with browning blood. He doesn't say a word, except to convey that he is "fine."

Karma contemplates giving him the hydrocodone pill in her pocket (which she had conveniently forgotten when she thought that her arrest was imminent), but she decides against it. Convincing herself that her actions are for his benefit, she covertly swallows it with a handful of water from the sink as she is making a show of cleaning him off. Marian finishes the job, though, because Karma stops short of dirtying her hands.

Someone has reported the locked bathroom to the owner of the Dragon's Lair, who is now knocking. Everyone in the bathroom knows Matt, the stingy tall guy who has owned the bar for years, so they let him in to help. Instead of lending a hand, Matt asks Christian to leave immediately.

"Sorry man, but you can't be in here like this," Matt says. "It's not good for the bar, you know. And now one of the bartenders has to fucking clean this up." He shakes his head, incredulous at the stunts people pull in his business.

Christian, with Dave's help, makes it to his feet and limps out the door. Karma does not follow him. Instead, she joins Marian for a drink at the bar. Marian promises the bartender a generous tip for having to clean the blood out of the bathroom and orders three Bud Lights and three shots of Jagermeister. Dave returns sans explanation.

"I don't want a Jager," Karma says. "I don't really even drink anymore."

Dave and Marian split the extra shot. They make small talk for all of about 60 seconds before Marian launches into a story about how she got caught with blow at work but how it really isn't a major deal. Her mom knows someone who specializes in that sort of thing or something, she explains, then she goes on and on about the dynamics between her and her mother.

To Karma, Marian's words begin to disassociate. The syllables morph into clouds and rearrange themselves between mouth and ear. Karma loses the story, and it is lame at any rate. She briefly wonders if Christian is okay, but decides she doesn't care. She excuses herself to go to the bathroom, leaving her Bud Light half finished as she walks upstairs into the hot Texas night.

She sits down with her back to the building and watches the kids in tan shorts and Polo shirts walk into Dale's Taco Shop, which is open until three in the morning. She never eats there, abstaining from the thick queso sauce and greasy fish tacos thanks to several previous Dale's-inspired bouts of stomach sickness.

One of the kids, this one sporting a Ducks Unlimited baseball cap, wobbles across the street and to the window of the upstairs coffee shop. He doesn't notice Karma siting a dozen feet from him as he opens his mouth and retches all over the window, which is by now dark and empty. The kid laughs, somehow pleased with himself for the sickness he is creating. He thinks the whole thing is funny, but she is annoyed. And bored.

As the kid stands there laughing drunkenly, her handsome neighbor Javier Hidalgo drives by in his shiny yellow Mustang. She sometimes spies on him from her bedroom window as he washes it on Sunday afternoons, so she would recognize the bright yellow car with the white pinstripes (which he applied) anywhere. He notices her and idles by the sidewalk.

"Hola, Karma," he calls through the car's open window.

She musters the energy to go talk to him. Javier's car smells like the kitchen of the Italian restaurants in which he works six days a week. Still, he always manages to smile. His handsome, square jaw with the thin covering of a black beard invites joviality and confidence. The stench of food and oil emanating from his checkered kitchen pants slightly offends her, but she makes an effort to be affable because he is her neighbor.

"Que tienes, Karma?" he wants to know what is wrong. His eyes are perceptive, she thinks.

"Porque estas sola?" he asks why she is alone. "No me gusta tu novio."

She has mentioned her boyfriend Christian, although Javier might have his doubts since he rarely sees him around the house. Javier wonders if his neighbor is a prostitute, as many guys come and go to and from her side of the duplex, which smells like strange vegetable food and incense. He wonders if perhaps she is merely uncommonly friendly.

Javier has only been in the States for three years, and the 21-year-old accepts that social customs in America must be decidedly different from the ones to which he was accustomed in Jalisco. He likes his neighbor. He thinks she is pretty and intriguing. Probably not a prostitute, he thinks, probably a wholesome girl in need of a good man. He wants to be direct and honorable. He asks why she is not married.

"No quiero," she answers, meaning she doesn't want to be.

Poor thing, Javier thinks. These American men are rats. He will take care of this girl. He asks her if she would like to come to his half of the house and eat some pozole stew his sister Flor has prepared.

Karma's stomach makes a noise, suggesting its hunger. She says yes, then gets in her own car and follows him to the house that, technically, they share.

18

*　　　*　　　*

Javier takes Karma's hand and leads her through the door so perpendicular to her own. Candles light the front room, which contains a sofa, made into a bed for Javier to sleep, a television with a digital antenna, and a tile picture of the Virgen Maria.

Flor Hidalgo sits in the adjacent dining room at a folding table covered in a yellow and white vinyl tablecloth. Her boys, Miguel and Eduardo, sleep in the room they all share with her husband Carlos, who works the late shift at Dale's Taco Shop and won't be home for a few more hours. Javier's brother Adolfo and his wife Esmaralda sleep in the smaller bedroom in the far corner of the house with their baby Nicolas.

Because the candles only carry a small amount of light, and she is programmed only to see what she wants to see, Flor does not notice that her brother is leading their strange neighbor into her living room. "You must be tired and hungry," she tells him in Spanish. "I made both pozole and your bed."

"Gracias, Flor," he thanks her. "Say hello to our vecina, Karma." He rolls the 'r' three times on the tip of his tongue as he says it.

Flor's heart pops up and seals the bottom of her throat, but she straightens her back, smiles with pursed lips, and welcomes the lazy puta who has no husband, no children. "Bienvenidos," she says to Karma. As if this skinny girl hasn't annoyed them enough by chatting in fractured Spanish, now she shows up to eat their food.

Flor, in a show of generosity, offers them both a bowl of pozole -- a spicy green pork stew she made with hominy. On her day off, like this Wednesday, she likes to make traditional Jaliscoan dishes to bring comfort to her family members, who work so hard. To Flor, family means everything. When the five of them plus baby Miguel paid a coyote to transport them across the Rio Grande river, they made a vow to guard and protect each other at all costs in the unknown wilds of the United States.

While she re-warms her stew in a green skillet on a stand-alone "Magic Chef" range, she frets over the fact that her noble but impressionable little brother has brought the unfriendly neighbor into their sanctuary. She can literally smell the trouble in this woman's heart, and she mixes her growing anger into the stew.

She stirs more quickly and with a violent force as Javier asks Karma again why she is not married.

"I would like to be married one day. I will have many children," he tells her with a flicker of shyness. This phrase he tries to repeat in English, to show off his intelligence and adaptability. She finds his pronouncement a tad disingenuous.

Unlike his sister Flor, who has remained culturally chaste in her Mexican mountain ways, Javier had plans to explore the American culture. He bought the Mustang because he believed it signified money and virility. He wanted to get inside the mindset of these Americans, and how better than with a fancy car? He had noticed Karma peeking through her tilted window shades as he fussed over his vehicular pride, and at that point, the seeds of fascination had been planted.

The last few months, as everything grew anew after the spring rains and into the primal heat of the early summer, Javier imagined himself to be in Karma's inner world - the group that came and went with easy regularity but did not stay long. He wondered if he could disappear next door and sample the loose pleasure of America. He blamed her for his fascination.

As he looks at her over the candlelight, he decides that she can't possibly be a whore. Her eyes, he thinks, they convey such kindness and pain. She certainly wants to connect with someone, he thinks. And even if she is a whore, I can convert her. She can still be saved.

Conversely, Karma absently regards Javier. The language barrier eases many of the demands of communication. After her blow-up with Christian, she only wants a little calm comfort. She has been alone with her longing for Christian for so many dozens of months; Javier seems like a perfectly rational alternative. Out of the blue, she imagines having a child with him - a little coffee colored, smiling thing. Waves of sleepy contentment lather her. Her eyelids fall halfway down across her eyes, and Javier takes this as a sign of arousal. The energy in the room shifts.

Flor places two steaming bowls of pozole down on the table, glares at Javier, gives Karma the stink eye to ward her off, and announces she will be retiring for the evening.

Javier and Karma are both distracted - he by the rushing blood in his loins and she by opiatic bliss, so neither notices the heavy, bothered footprints Flor leaves as she stomps off.

The commotion wakes little Eduardo, whom the Hidalgos call Lalo, and he walks out of the bedroom to hug his tio Javi. He says hi to Karma before his mother hisses for him to return to bed.

The mix of oxytocin (the mothering hormone) and hydrocodone prevents Karma from finishing her bowl of soup. Besides, it tastes like hate. "Tengo sueño," she tells him that she is tired.

She allows him to follow her next door; they tiptoe down the long hallway, wordlessly step over the piles of clothes, and lie down next to each other on her disheveled bed. In silence, Javier thanks the Virgen Maria for granting his prayer of bringing him close to his neighbor while Karma drifts off into la-la land. Tank the cat looks up and yawns. At least he isn't that Christian asshole, the cat thinks.

In her final thoughts of the day, Karma wonders if Christian is okay, but she doesn't actually care about that or anything else at the moment. She was been traveling in between sleep and wakefulness for years, and no one has seemed to notice.

Javier feels her tranquility and assumes it is a sign of something good that will happen. His mind races forward into the future.

CHAPTER TWO

THE TRANSGRESSION

When Flor's eyes open the next morning, she immediately looks down to her fat belly. Before she has a chance to remember her name in this world, she feels the fury of inadequacy. In Mexico, her paunch might have signified beauty, at least her being a proud mother, but here, in Texas, her extra pounds, placed right around her middle for the world to see, remind her again of her status as a second-class citizen. Every time she walks out of the damn door, she sees these skinny women who never cook and, ostensibly, never eat. Being a member of the first world's forgotten caste is not the dream Flor envisioned in her untroubled, pastoral childhood.

She also hates her long, shiny black hair, which falls off the pillow and spills over onto her husband Carlos, who has his back turned to her in their double bed, as usual. His softly sobbing body greets her along with the quiet morning light. The temperature is already infuriating.

Disgusted, she reaches out and pulls Carlos onto his back. Tears roll down his face, and she wants to spit on this pitiful excuse for a man. Carlos is not the husband she thought she wanted, and she knows he does not appreciate all the cooking and cleaning she does for him, the way she rears their two sons. Yes, Carlos gave up the comfort of his homeland when he followed Flor and her family to Texas, but he never stops to consider how much she has lost, too.

Flor and Carlos grew up in neighboring villages in the mountains of Jalisco. She could recall snippets of memories of her now-husband as a little boy, but she never truly noticed him until a large gathering to celebrate the end of an agave harvest season. One fateful night, in a tent lit by clear, sporadically burned out Christmas lights, he held out his hand and asked her to dance. Although he was only 16, he looked so handsome in his shiny cowboy boots and wide hat. His short stature and general rotundness struck her as solid and reliable then; now, she sees him a soft loser.

Still staring at him with disgust in her eyes, she shakes her head in an overly dramatic manner, regretting those long-ago trysts in the stables where his father housed the two horses. Flor is the second youngest of twelve children, and until the day she announced she was pregnant and getting married, her family had never known her to do anything rebellious. They still haven't wholly forgiven Carlos for deflowering her.

The arrival of their little Miguelito ruined any delusion of living an idyllic life in the mountains of Jalisco. What once looked like simple, natural beauty then resounded emptily of poverty and lack of opportunity. She could accept this fate for herself, but not for her perfect little son.

Carlos, having heard story after story of the cruelty of the American ways, resisted fiercely, but when Flor announced that her oldest sister had paid a coyote to deliver three Hidalgo siblings, Miguel, Carlos, and her brother Adolfo's wife Esmeralda to Texas, he reluctantly agreed to the trek.

The Hidalgos, after making their way north to the border, loaded themselves in the back of a semi trailer. The awful heat of the cramped space should have been a clear omen. After a few years in north Texas, the heat of that night has hardly abated.

At first, they all shared the living room in her oldest sister Maria's small house. After the better part of a year, the three Hidalgo adults, their two spouses, little Miguel and his new baby brother Eduardo rented half of this pitiful duplex.

She hated the peeling paint and tacky appliances from day one, and she didn't expect to wake up in the same miserable house two years later. Although the road on which the duplex sits is not busy enough for streetlights, it does see its fair share of traffic. She can hear the motion from her bed this morning, and the cars driving by make her mad, remind her of the endless obligations that define her every living moment.

Flor usually cleans houses for rich white folks with big, fancy televisions, but her sister-in-law currently has the better paying client, so Flor has been stuck at home with her two boys and Esmeralda's baby Nicolas. She hates the United States. Hates being stuck in this damn ugly house on this damn busy street. She despises living in constant fear of being arrested or deported. She has only driven the car she technically shares with Carlos a handful of times. Although she can walk down the block to the grocery store, for all intents and purposes, Flor feels like a captive in her home, in her life. Everywhere she goes, she sees hatred in the white people's eyes.

Still not speaking to her morose, whiny husband, Flor walks to the bunk beds on the opposite wall of her bedroom and gently wakes her sons. Despite all the ire she has accumulated in her heart, Flor genuinely loves her boys. They are her raison d'etre (if she knew such phrases). She does everything in her power to conceal the disillusion that plagues her every breath.

Yawning but happy, the boys roll out of bed and follow her back to her spot at the stove, where she pretends to enjoy frying eggs for the whole family for breakfast. She warms the corn tortillas, which Carlos brings home every night from Dale's Taco Shop, and throws the whole mess on the table.

She notices that the couch-bed she made for her baby brother Javier has not been touched. Immediate fury spits out of her eyes and navel. She clutches her fat midsection to contain the emotion so that her bitter disapproval will not spray all over the boys. Javi used to be the only person in the world she trusted, but if he wants to consort with that whore next door, she thinks, he will be dead to me like everyone else. She presses down the remaining tortillas hard in the skillet, imagining them to be the neighbor-puta's face.

Carlos, who is now softly singing to his sons at the dining room table, notices. He can feel the anger emanating from his wife, and it makes his ribs rattle. Were it not for the boys, Carlos would have returned to Jalisco the minute he saw the reality of life in the Unites States. Or the minute he picked up a shovel to help fix a hole in the decaying American roads. Or the minute Flor first swung at him.

He can't stand another second of life in this godforsaken place. He feels like a prisoner, confined to 80-hour-a-week work details and a strict, uncaring wife who refuses to comfort him when he cries to bemoan his hopeless fate. He looks at the green and white plastic clock on the wall and notices he doesn't have time to eat. If he and Adolfo are late to the job site, they will get the dirtiest, hardest jobs, which are awful on any day, but today, his armpits are already drenched and odiferous, and he has no time to shower. He says a small prayer that he can make it through another 24 hours of this travail.

Carlos, agitated despite the early hour, storms back to the bedroom and surveys the small corner of the closet that holds all of his worldly possessions. Working in filthy environments, he relies heavily on both his wife and Esmeralda to keep him clothed in rags that don't reek of his constant sweat. He finds a clean pair of jeans, which are ripped above both knees, and a pair of clean and ironed black work pants, which he will change into when he arrives at the taco shop after his street repair shift. The hangers that should hold his shirts, however, are empty. His pendeja wife has failed again.

What will he wear to work, he wonders? He grabs yesterday's red t-shirt from the top of the hamper, but he cannot stomach bringing it closer than a few inches from his nose. Shaking, he tears the shirt right down the middle. It rips cleanly between the a and the c advertising Dale's Taco Shop. The precision of his fury calms him a bit.

He tries to hold it in, but he gives in, bellows, "Floooorrrr." For all her constant nitpicking, how could she possibly neglect something so essential as his work laundry?

Her insolent feet plod slowly, tauntingly down the hallway, and he is past his breaking point. She opens the door, smirking. Carlos stiffens his palm, then launches across the room and plants it directly on the left side of her face.

This is not the first time physical violence has erupted between the two, and Flor weighs nearly as much as her husband. She charges into Carlos, but he sidesteps her as she tumbles onto the empty bedside table. A glass devotional candle, replete with a picture of an emblazoned Virgen and the words "La Milagrosa," bounces off the wood floor with a rude thud.

"Now you have really done it," Carlos yells at her in Spanish. "You have destroyed the things I worked *hard* to earn." He tenses the muscles in his hand again, reels back, and implants his hand directly on the reddening mark he had just left on his wife's face. "How dare you?" he roars.

"You pitiful man," she retorts in real protest. "I bought that candle for one lousy dollar, and what miracles has it brought us? I regret that I ever met you. You are a worthless excuse for a man. You have given me nothing. My life is bleak and miserable. You go to work, but you never provide anything for my sons and me like we deserve. You are no lover. I have never once been satisfied." Her tone is calm, emboldened with the vapors of the ice living in her soul.

She charges again, this time catching him in a moment of disbelief. They both topple onto the bed, where he regains control and throws her into the wall. Her back hits and cracks the drywall. He spits directly in her right eye, which she then raises, defiant.

Carlos picks up the unbroken candle and silently prays for the miracle of not killing his wife right now. More than anything, he wants to grab her fat neck and snap it. "How dare you speak to your husband like this?" he yells.

He then throws the candle, hitting her squarely in the shoulder. Her gaze has yet to leave him or to relent with its nail-gun accusations. He reaches deeper into the hamper and pulls out a soiled chambray shirt. He will get another at the taco shop, he thinks, angry that Jefe Dale will probably charge him 20 dollars (nearly four hours worth of work) for the replacement. Ending the fight, he spins, shirt in hand, turns his sticky back to her, and files out of the house behind Adolfo, who recently joined him on the street repair crew.

Flor picks up the Milagrosa candle and says a prayer of her own. "Maria," she asks. "Please, I never want to see that man again."

After Adolfo's car engine fades into the buzz of the passing cars, the mouse-like Esmeralda comes in the room with a babbling, year-old Nicolas on her hip.

"Are you okay?" Esmeralda asks.

"Fine," Flor replies.

"Adolfo and I fight, too," Esmeralda says in hopes of pacifying her always-angry sister-in-law. "Marriage is a difficult thing. My parents fought, too. I guess our dreams of love were not meant to come true." She laughs nervously.

Flor just looks at her, still too paralyzed by anger to talk or move. Miguel and Lalo, wearing terrified faces and pajamas, sheepishly move to the doorway. Flor cannot look directly at either; she understands that her tension deeply affects the otherwise happy children. She tries to drive her guilt away and replace it with her maternal instinct, but her anger obscures all else.

"You know," Esmeralda offers, "My boss told me last week that I could bring Nicolas when I come to clean her house. Her children are grown, and I think she is lonely. She's a nice woman. I don't think she'd mind if I brought all three today."

Esmeralda turns to Flor's boys and asks them if they would like to go watch the big television at the old lady's house. Miguel, the explorer, nods, but Lalo crawls to his mother's lap. He has always been the more emotional of the two, and despite his young age, he intuits that his mother needs his comfort. He says that he doesn't want to go see the big television at the lady's house.

Flor and Lalo sit still on the bed for the entire time it takes Esmeralda to ready herself and the other two boys for a day of cleaning houses.

Flor supposes she should be grateful for her sister-in-law's kind offer, but instead, she smarts at the mess left in the sink from the breakfast she made but never got to eat. Miguel hugs his mama and leaves with Nico and Esme. Flor gets up and returns to the kitchen to begin cleaning the dishes.

Her face stings, commanding all of her attention, until she notices that Carlos has left his car keys hanging on a nail by the door. He must have shared a ride with Adolfo today, because usually he takes the car to work just so Flor can't use it.

For the second time in her life, Flor feels like doing something that has not been approved. She jingles the keys and manages a real smile.

"Lalito," she asks her sweet son. "Would you like to go to Plaza Mall and buy some candy?"

The drama from earlier in the morning is now forgotten, and Lalo smiles, exposing the white nubs of baby teeth that line his gums. "Si, mama," he answers with a touch of thrill.

Flor tries to scrub Carlos' handprint from her face, but the redness only glows brighter. She ties her hair neatly behind her head and throws on her favorite outfit - a pink velour tracksuit. The thought of escaping the confinement of her house eases the morning's climactic trauma.

Driving down the road, Flor starts to feel empowered. She is flirting with danger by breaking free of the routine expected of her, and her insubordination is truly liberating. Lalo looks up at her; his eyes are as wide as smiles. Together, they feed on the excitement of doing something fun and dangerous.

For the first time, Flor considers herself an actual American. In a car. Going to the mall. She has nothing but a carefully folded 20-dollar bill in her pocket - no cell phone, no license even. She did have a Mexican identification card at one point, but she suspects Carlos confiscated it as he had the rest of her. If he ever finds out I took this car, she thinks, he may murder me.

As she drives by the houses with the dead and yellow grass, she wonders if all the husbands in these mini-castles beat their wives. The neighborhood she lives in is full of older white people. A few houses proudly display the country's flag. Some show off erect flowers and flourishing bushes. Others have saved the excessive water it would take to maintain a happy garden during the brutal summer and let their property succumb to the natural decay of the seasons. Some houses have new paint. Others, like hers, are dull and peeling. Although the lunch hour is yet to arrive, the heat prevents any outdoor activity. The streets are empty of pedestrians and bicyclists. Carlos' car is without air conditioning, but with the windows rolled down, the ride is bearable.

Although Flor has little experience driving and navigating, she has paid careful attention in preparation for a day like today, in which she would be the captain. She knows she only needs to make four turns to get from her house to the Plaza Mall, and she is proud of herself for remembering them all. As she parks and unbuckles her son from the too-big seatbelt in the passenger seat, her self-esteem rises. Although her ire constantly boils throughout her interior, she experiences a flash of happiness. "Maybe America isn't so bad after all," she tells Lalo, allowing herself a deep breath.

Flor and her small son enter Plaza Mall. It was once named Seminary Mall but has now been repopulated with taco shops and boutiques for quinceañera parties. The ice-cold blast of commercial air conditioning delights them both. Although the unit at the house works well enough, they use it sparingly to save money. Walking around and admiring the leather belts and sequined denim jackets in the cool air seems like a real treat. If Flor had more than the 20 dollars in her pocket, she might buy a nice dress, she thinks. She likes the comfort and durability of her plush pink outfit (which she bought for two dollars at Goodwill), but something a little fancier might cheer her up.

Because of the early hour, Plaza Mall is mostly empty. Every conversation she overhears is in Spanish. She doesn't join in by talking to strangers, but she does feel a kinship with the people working in and wandering around the mall. For a second, she forgets she isn't in Mexico and imagines she and her son are strolling around a shopping center in Guadalajara. The ache for her homeland hurts worse than the remnant of Carlos' handprint on her face.

As they near the dome of opaque skylights that infuse the food court in the center of the mall with the sun's glow, Flor notices a small crowd gathered around a large flat screen television in front of an electronics store. She leads Lalo over to experience the excitement of high definition vision. The television is rebroadcasting the previous weekend's game between her favorite team, Chivas, and the Monarcas from Morelia. Although she, Esmeralda, and the boys had watched the game live the previous weekend, witnessing the high definition broadcast is truly spectacular. Flor feels like she is on the sidelines staring into the eyes of the players.

Lalo, entranced, lets go of her hand and walks in for a closer look. "Careful," she calls out to her son. Flor notices that a price tag is conspicuously absent from the television. She chuckles as she discards any notion that she will ever have a TV like this one. The inequity between her and the people who can afford such entertainment rekindles her rancor. The young man standing next to her feels the heat and slinks away.

The distinctive smells of roasting peppers and sizzling barbacoa distract Flor from the game and the electronics store. She looks over at a place in the food court with a hand-painted sign advertising "Taco Heaven." A tall, happy-looking guy with glasses and thick, curly hair leans over the counter and hands cartons of tacos to a mother and her daughter. Flor remembers her lack of breakfast and calls out to Lalo to join her for some comida. She walks up to Taco Heaven and surveys the menu.

The place offers everything from menudo to asada burritos to horchata. She is ravenous; she wants to order one of everything.

As she is deliberating, she hears an eruption of glass and the collective intake of a group gasp. A fully dressed police officer, who sits to her left over a flimsy foam plate of meat and beans, rises and hurries toward the electronics store with a look of annoyance on his face.

She hears Lalo call out to her in tears. "Mama," he cries, audibly scared. Flor is afraid to turn around and look, and when she does, she finds the exact scenario she feared. The officer in his haughty starched uniform jerks her little son by his hand and leads him away from the broken, formerly expensive television. The crowd gives him a wide berth, not wanting any more involvement in the accident than they already have.

"Whose child is this?" the officer asks in English. "He broke this television."

Flor does not understand the words, but she catches the meaning.

The tall officer, with his forbiddingly square jaw, rudely holds Lalo's arm, frightening the child. The condescension in his face mirrors the countenance she aimed at her husband earlier this morning. He pities her and her miserable life, Flor knows.

He is a Hernandez, according to his metal nameplate, and Flor hopes that his Spanish surname will inspire a little empathy. Lalo drops his head in shame then furtively gives his mother a pleading glance. She reaches out for his small hand, and the officer lets him go.

"How do you plan to pay for the ruined property?" Officer Hernandez asks her in English.

Flor does know the word pay, having heard it at the grocery store. She thinks of the lone piece of paper money in the left pocket of her pants, and she freezes then gives off a nervous laugh.

"Disculpe," she begins.

"Stop. We do not speak Spanish here," Officer Hernandez warns her with a fast, deep breath. He is having a horrible day and has already pulled over three drivers without U.S. licenses.

"This neighborhood's gone to shit," he murmurs under his breath. He is tired of showing clemency to anyone. These people are like deer, he thinks. You have to control them somehow. "How do you plan to compensate for the ruined property?" he asks her.

This time, Flor is unable to translate any of the words he uses. She sees where this is going, and she imagines jail and the terrifying experiences that accompany it. Without giving her options too much thought, she picks up Lalo, who borders on too bulky to be carried, turns, and runs in the direction of the parking lot.

Officer John Hernandez stands with his thumbs wrapped around his belt loops and rocks slightly backward on the balls of his feet. "Unbelievable," he says to no one in particular. She rounds the corner, and he begins to pursue. He does not notice as she cuts through a stall selling spices and tea mixtures, and when he reaches the store, the sympathetic shopkeeper (also sitting there sans documents) smiles and points in the opposite direction. He looks where she designates, surveys the path for side exits, and breaks into a run.

Even with Lalo in tow, Flor is fast enough to make it to her car by the time he has put her in his sights again. He yells at her, "Stop. Parate. Ahora."

She throws Lalo over the driver's seat, turns the key in the ignition, and heads to the adjacent freeway. In the haste, neither buckles with the seatbelt.

Flor has never driven on the freeway in Texas, but she

figures this is her best chance to blend in with the other dark-green sedans and escape into the traffic. Maybe I'll go all the way to Jalisco, she thinks. She revs the engine and merges onto the freeway, avoiding an accident only because the oncoming SUV sees her rapid, erratic descent down the ramp. She is going so fast, she feels like she is flying. Lalo manages to buckle himself in without being asked, though the belt is too large to do him any good in the event of an accident.

Lalo is unsure about what is happening, so he starts singing along to the radio. For the first time since the adventure began, Flor notices the music coming from the car's speakers. To calm her son, she turns up the volume. Vicente Fernandez is her parents' very favorite and the voice of all she considers Mexico to be. With a range of liberated feelings in her voice, she chimes in to his anthemic song "El Rey."

Flor takes the appearance of the song as a sign that the Virgen has answered her prayer by urging her to drive away from Texas (and Carlos) and back into the comfort of her mama's waiting arms. She feels guilty about leaving Miguel behind, but with one son remaining, she hopes Carlos will be less inclined to follow her back to Mexico and kill her. It has to be this way, she repeats to herself.

Flor drives for several minutes before seeing the dreaded whir of a police siren and the offensively flashy lights in her rearview mirror.

Lalo notices the reflection and has seen enough television to be concerned. He looks up at her, wordlessly demanding an explanation.

"This is a parade, mijo," Flor tells him, as the tide of her angry seas begins to invade the shores of her voice. "Just like when I was a girl, the whole village comes out to celebrate and make noise. It was a surprise for you, mi amor."

The answer appeases the three-year-old, and he asks his

mother to tell him more about Mexico. Transporting herself back to the place where she had once felt safe eases the panic she is experiencing. She doesn't notice the tears that well up on the lower lid of her eye and softly begin to escape in slow streams. She tells him about the brown eggs she and her sister Maria used to pick up every morning over the ridge by the back of the house; how the chickens would carry on with their never-ending tales of drama but were actually happy to see the girls. "Rich brown eggs," she tells her son, "Not like the watery ones they have here."

She has been driving for at least 20 minutes, and she can now hear several police sirens behind her. A massive black SUV is also following her closely. A helicopter starts hovering overhead, and she never stops to consider that her trip back to Mexico might be currently broadcasting to several million homes in the immediate area. In high definition. The unforgiving sunrays bounce from the gaudy beige pavement back into her eyes, temporarily blinding her. She sees a sign with a word comprehensible to her: Alvarado. The familiar syllables comfort her, but only slightly.

Other cars are on the freeway, and some drivers stare and ridicule, but others shoo her to the side of the road, as if they can make the difference. Lalo, sensing that something is terribly wrong, holds his mother's hand. She looks down at him and smiles with vacant eyes. She has closed the windows, so both labor a bit to breathe through their coats of sweaty skin. She doesn't notice the heat -- or the squad car planted on the shoulder by the side of the road -- as the car drives over a large metal grate.

The parked police car flashes its lights at her, and she realizes she probably isn't making it back to Mexico. At least, not today.

*   *   *

Flor expects to hear a loud pop from one of her tires, but she is able to continue driving. Almost immediately, the car starts to slope downwards and to the left. She opens the window a finger's width and can faintly hear the defeated hiss of air as it escapes out of one of the tires. The anger she has built for so long vanishes from her heart. The tires on the left are starting to feel wobbly, and she has no choice but to slow down. That or wipe out. Two police cars flank her on each side, and the black SUV maneuvers in front of her.

Flor imagines she is not only in a parade but that she is the guest of honor -- the princess of the whole fucking United States of America. She laughs and cries, her mood resembling one of happiness. "Isn't this fun," she squeals to Lalo. He is holding it together for Mom's sake, so he nods, though he has picked up on her crazy vibe.

Her laughter evaporates, and Flor is left with the sadness of her mistake. She pauses to consider the unfavorable situation in which she has placed Carlos. She has defeated all of them. Contrition washes through her as she thinks of Miguel and Lalo, who will grow up without a mother. Esmeralda will care for them, she thinks with regret.

Her mind wanders to the near future, when she will be arrested, the pink suit ripped off her back. The only stories she has ever heard about American prisons are exceptionally nasty.

"You will be raped every day," unseen voices chant in her head. She imagines that tall officer Hernandez holding her down on a concrete floor and raping her until she bleeds. She thinks back to his eyes and remembers a lecherous malice.

She imagines his placing her, naked, on a bus to the border town of Matamoros. She can feel the asphalt beneath her bare feet as she envisions her unceremonious return to Mexico. She sees a picture of her older self, broken and worthless. The drug traffickers will still want me, she thinks. They'll kidnap me and sell me into slavery.

So this is my American fucking fairytale, she thinks as she resumes her laughter. Her current reality brutally contrasts with the one for which she had hoped. If she could do it again, she never would have ventured beyond the borders of her family's land. Mexico, baby.

She holds Lalo's hand again, though it feels much heavier this time. The perceptive little boy has realized the gravity of the situation. He sits slumped, swallowed by both the seat and the accompanying belt. He grips her hand and cries, not wildly, as such a young child should, but resignedly. She wonders what will happen to her boy. He has an American birth certificate, she thinks. Maybe somehow he can grow up and buy one of those televisions. Maybe, if he works hard, he can marry a nice girl and live the dream I had for myself.

Flor can hardly bring herself to look in her child's eyes. She is now driving on the rims of her two left wheels. She knows that the gaze they share could be their last. She finally gathers the courage to fully regard her enchanting little boy. He has such innocence and forgiveness, she notices. I wonder where he got those qualities. She says one more prayer to La Milagrosa: that her boys would be provided for.

She then does one last motherly task and pulls the dark green Saturn to the side of the road. As several hundred thousand bored Texans watch in HD on public television, Flor Hidalgo slows down and veers to the shoulder, puts the car in park, and turns off the ignition. She hopes her son will not always have to feel like a second-class citizen and a criminal. She really hopes.

A bevy of police officers surrounds the car with pistols drawn. Excessive, she thinks. They yell at her as they approach, but she does not move. A pale-skinned guy with dark glasses and a blond flattop opens her door and gently lifts her out of the car with his hands. From behind this officer's back, another jumps and tackles her, throws her face-first onto the pavement, and cuffs her hands behind her back.

Lalo waits in tears in the front seat. The officers' shouts subside; the helicopters punctuate an otherwise eerie silence.

A female officer pulls Lalo out of the passenger seat and carries him off to the black SUV, where he is given a stuffed bear to take his mind off the trauma. He stares at it, names it Loco.

Flor does not resist at all. Her eyes can't take another second of the sunshine, so she closes them, resigning herself to the fate that was hers from the beginning.

Her eyes remain closed as she is led to the back of a squad car. She only opens them when she hears a recognizable voice - that of officer Hernandez.

"Puta," he whispers through the car window. "Watch who you're fucking with."

He could be a rapist. His eyes are evil and beady, she thinks. She shivers with revulsion.

Flor accepts the possibility that the last of her honor is about to be stripped. She deserves it, she thinks. She has always been a wicked woman.

After the scene along the highway is under control, all but three squad cars leave to go about protecting and serving. The blond officer, Phelps, announces that the city ambulance is right up the road. Standard procedure, he explains, in the possibility of a kidnapping. He has yet to make a positive identification on the woman who had been driving, and he figures he will wait to process her until he is downtown at the station, where a court-approved translator would be waiting.

Officer Phelps looks at his comrades, Officers Hernandez and Holligan, and expresses his sympathy for the mystery woman and child. "Life isn't always easy," he laments. "This heat here's enough to drive anyone crazy. I sure hope these two have someone out there that cares about 'em."

He shuffles his foot along the ground and sighs. Phelps has been a cop for 13 years, and he has seen a lot of sad and lonely situations. He tends to have as much mercy as possible on those he encounters.

Officer John Hernandez tilts his head and scoffs. "What'd she expect?" he asks, not waiting for an answer. "Sheesh. I hope she realizes what a pig she is. Probably shouldn't even be here, but no, gotta get on the road and disrupt life for everyone else."

The extraordinarily intense midday sun now rules from overhead, and Hernandez blames the heat itself on Flor, who doesn't even deserve a name as far as he cares. Hernandez and his colleagues, by regulation, have to wear long-sleeved black uniform shirts. Thick cotton shirts, at that.

"This is her fault," he complains, accusingly, at Phelps. "She put us here on the side of the frigging highway at the end of August in Texas. Other drivers could've been hurt. Did she even think about her child? I wouldn't feel sorry for her even if I heard she had been beheaded by La Familia."

The dissonant attitudes hang like a shadow between the two men. One lives in a world of light while the other festers in fumes of hate and rhetoric. Officer Phelps shuts his mind off to Hernandez, telling himself to ignore anything out of the mouth of this one and not to associate with him any more than he has to.

Phelps contemplates mentioning Hernandez' odd behavior to the supervisor. Phelps has been with the department long enough to remember all the trouble cops have caused in the community. One stole a computer containing sex tapes from a robbery victim's house; several have been arrested for spousal abuse; one particularly boneheaded kid had driven after having way too much to drink and killed a young mother on the southwest side of town.

The problematic offenders, Phelps thinks, have this attitude that they are better than everyone else. Those guys let the illusion of power overtake them. It's like a drug, he thinks, and some succumb, complicating the task of civilization for the rest of us.

The ambulance pulls up, siren on for no ostensible reason, and a paramedic jumps out. Holligan leads the uniformed young woman to Lalo. She asks him, first in English then in Spanish, what his name is.

Lalo holds up the bear and answers, "Loco." She checks him, looks in his mouth, and asks him if anything hurts. He looks up at her with sadly flirtatious eyes. She concludes that he has survived the chase unscathed.

Next, the paramedic looks in on Flor, whose tears are falling freely in the back of a separate patrol car. She will not reveal her name, but, between sobs, she asks the woman to please care for her son, whose name is Eduardo Jesus Hidalgo Cortez. The paramedic promises that the boy will be okay. After her perfunctory check, the paramedic informs the officers that suspect and child are in sufficiently satisfactory condition to take downtown.

Phelps' radio cackles. Dispatch is communicating that the boy's aunt, Maria Hidalgo Vasquez, saw the car on television and will take responsibility for him. The dispatcher identifies the perp as possibly Flor. "What a waste of a beautiful name," Hernandez tells the paramedic.

Phelps and Holligan, who have Flor and Lalo, respectively, in their cars, ready to leave. Hernandez waits for the tow truck. Lalo, belted into a car seat in the back of the SUV, still stares at the bear. He almost looks mortified. Hernandez takes one look and shakes his head, mentally writing the kid off from having a productive future. "False hopes and bad parenting," he firmly states into the scorching air as he shakes his head.

Looking at Lalo causes him to reflect on his own lack of offspring. His mother Patricia says the family's Salvadoran ancestors have turned into spirits and cursed John for marrying a black woman. Patricia is a second-generation American citizen, but she has managed to hold onto her traditional family ways. When John brought Shastilynn (Lynn) home for the first time, his parents froze. They are even unhappier about the union five years down the road, with no grandchildren at their feet during family get-togethers.

John Hernandez loves his wife, though. They are really living, he imagines. Lynn, who is an accountant, is probably at home right now preparing him dinner -- something healthy, like chicken Caesar salad. He would never have married a Latina woman, he thinks. They're all crazy like this bitch.

Officer Holligan drives off next with Flor, whose eyes bore holes through him as the car merges with the traffic.

"I hope you walk through the gates of Hell," he mouths after her.

Inside the patrol car, Flor feels as if she already has.

CHAPTER THREE

GRANDMASTER FURY

Filing paperwork at the station is an aggravating task for Officer John Hernandez. By the time he makes his way to the parking garage, where his maroon pickup waits, the fingers of night are pulling away the blue sky. John turns on the ignition and hears his favorite sports radio personality discuss the college football season, which begins tomorrow.

The officer is a Longhorns fan -- always has been and always will be. He has only been to Austin once, but he imagines the state capitol to be the greatest city in the universe. The person calling in asks what sort of season the Longhorns should expect, and both hosts agree that the team will rebound and at least qualify for a bowl game. Everyone is enthusiastic about tomorrow's season opener.

Pleased, John allows himself to drift into fantasy. During patrol hours, he must be hyper-vigilant, so he eyes each and every soul he encounters with mistrust and a presumption of guilty behavior. He can turn that attitude off after hours, he thinks. His mind turns to "Legs," as he calls her, the mystery woman whose movements he watches carefully. He imagines his hand making its way up those long, pale white legs. He imagines her surprise, and the worried pleasure she can't help but moan as he enters her from behind. The background of his fantasy is bland (and probably borrowed from a porn movie he had seen sometime). His imagination seems overly forced, but this doesn't stop his erection or his hand going down to mollify it through his pants.

Fantasizing about "Legs" makes John giddy like a hormonal teenager. In his vision, he is muscular and sweaty, his ass pumping up and down like an oil derrick. In reality, the 29-year-old officer is starting to go a little soft around the edges. The borders of hair on the top of his large, protruding forehead are slowly receding, and the pinched corners of his eyes are starting to spew a small web of wrinkles. John's member, too, is not as large or as hard as he imagines, having been tamed to the reality of the sex life of a married person.

The pleasurable vibration of his Blackberry stirs John back to his Hernandez persona. A smiling photo of his wife, Lynn, announces her incoming call. John removes his hand from his pants and presses talk.

"Hi honey," she greets him. He expects her to inquire about the televised chase from the afternoon, but she makes no mention.

"Are you anywhere near home? Dinner's almost ready. I made mayo-crusted chicken, spicy slaw, and creamed spinach and cheese. I saw the recipe on that new show on the Food Network. I think you're going to like it."

"I'll be there in less than ten," he answers. "Sounds delicious, sweetheart."

Their conversations have always been economical and direct, and this forthright, time-conscious responsibility makes them an excellent match, he thinks. They met initially on eHarmony. According to the software, John and Lynn were matched well in 27 of the 29 compatibility indicators. They followed the prescribed communication, milestones, sending must haves and can't stands, then e-mailing back and forth a few times about expectations of a good relationship before agreeing to meet in person.

At first, the passion had been overwhelming. John and Lynn could relate to each other because both sported a can-do attitude and threw a substantial work ethic at life. After several years of marriage, theirs had become the sort of love to which one becomes inured. The heat of those first embraces faded as they acquired a house and a garage full of expensive material possessions.

John feels guilty about his secret obsession with Legs, and this emotion manifests as a rash on his throat, which is displaying the rude fuzz of his afternoon beard. He scratches at his guilt while he swears, partially aloud, that he will not hurt the wife swore to protect. In fact, "I will guard you eternally" was the lone vow he wrote for his wedding ceremony. Even in the hypocritical white dress, Lynn had looked so serious and business-like.

His drive to the new-build neighborhood on the south side of town ends quickly. He parks the truck next to the curb and takes notice that the square shrubs standing guard next to the white faux-stone walls of his house are still verdant, even in the ridiculous heat. He straightens the hose and the watering spout into a symmetrical coil then walks in through the open garage. He makes a mental note that the shelves housing his enormous collection of rarely used tools could use a dusting, though the coat is gossamer to the point of being undetectable.

He stares at the doorknob leading inside, consciously connecting the visual with his need to remember to re-hang the speakers on the back patio, which are producing a slight dissonance by being at an imperfect angle. Deliberately compartmentalizing and associating these thoughts allows him to accomplish more than your average Joe.

The door opens to the kitchen, where Shastilynn is cracking pepper into a saucepan full of green vegetables. She says hello without looking up at her husband. He walks over and kisses her on the back of her neck, which is always exposed thanks to her perpetually ponytailed hair. He sees her oven dish full of crusted chicken and salivates. The whole car chase scenario has famished him.

"How was your day?" he asks.

"Fine. Normal," she answers. "And yours?"

John notes the angle at which his wife's slender stomach tapers into a substantial backside. He appreciates how Lynn always wears practical, form-fitting clothes. She turns, wooden spoon in hand, but her eyes don't rest on his for terribly long.

He tells her about Flor's ill-advised flight down the freeway, and she joins in his disapproval, shaking her head while ladling slaw onto two white porcelain plates.

"I just don't understand people," Lynn says. "If this woman is so bored, why doesn't she go get a job? I'm *telling* you, people think they can come here and rely on the government. People just do not value hard work anymore. I hate to say it, but so many Mexicans are this way."

She guffaws in her quietly feminine way as she carries the plates to the adjacent dining table. Lynn still wears the starched white shirt and grey skirt from her workday. The leather heels she has placed neatly next to her chair. He uncorks a bottle of chardonnay, pours it through a decanter into two glasses and follows her to the rectangular oak table.

The chicken is delicious, if a bit rubbery, but the spinach is bland and milky. They make comfortable small talk as the neighbors' kids holler in the backyard next door. The silence between them is rotund and hollow like a balloon, and he attributes this to the fact that they have been unable to conceive.

Because marital silence usually bodes badly for the man, he asks his wife what is wrong.

"I'm just worried about my mother," she says, slumping her shoulders while shifting her weight in the chair.

"She asked you for money again, didn't she?" he wants to know. He purses his lips and draws his eyes close together. He already knows the answer, so she doesn't give it to him.

John despises his mother-in-law. She is no better than the runaway driver, he thinks. He imagines beating that waste of a woman; he can taste her blood on the back of his hand. He would never do that, though. He may see violence in his mind's eye, but he feels uncomfortable inflicting it. He would like to be a warrior, a punisher, but brutality is not his nature, he tries to convince himself.

John internalizes his discomfort but cannot come up with words to continue the dinner conversation. He wants to leave the bigger problems inside, forgotten. After he finishes eating, he reaches for his phone and pretends it has been vibrating.

Though the screen is blank, he thinks on the fly, shaking his head left and right as he lies, "Dammit. They want me to go down to the station tonight and give a deposition about the chase. Some directive of Homeland Security." He feigns annoyance but feels relief. "I guess I should leave in a minute."

She looks up at him, uncaring. "That's okay," she says. "I didn't make dessert."

John brushes his teeth forcefully because he is fastidious about dental health. He feels both powerful and lucky tonight, so he pulls his favorite burnt orange Longhorn shirt over his head. After saying a polite goodbye and kissing Lynn on the top of her head, he gets in his pickup and hears a commotion on the radio. The announcer -- the same one from before dinner -- mentions Texas coach Mike Black, so John turns the up volume. After a worrisome exchange between the host and a caller, John hears the awful development. According to some online source named Burntblood, Mike Black has been implicated in a large point-fixing scandal and would announce his resignation the next morning.

John is apoplectic. His Longhorns are above the law when it comes to misdeeds. His mood flips instantly, so much so his incisors press dangerously down on his lower row of teeth. He snarls as he realizes that if this story is true, UT's fine football days are gone for a good long while. The fate of his team carries him through the fall months, and without his faithful beacon of Longhorn success, he will just be madder. John knows that he cannot lose this reliable source of pride and happiness in his life. His emotional containment methods are currently operating past capacity.

John is disproportionately furious; he presses the radio's off button so vigorously it leaves a dent in the tip of his finger. He glowers and salivates in a futile attempt to swallow the venom rising from the pit of his stomach. This paroxysm is familiar territory for John. In fact, it seldom abates. He can keep the direct experience at bay when he applies will, but the buried rage escapes routinely in judgmental comments and cruel appraisals of others' words and behavior.

Because he is so full of hate for people in general, John also despises himself. Rationally, he knows his reaction is out of line, but he can't help it. He has always been this way. He chose to be in the police force because it seemed like an acceptable outlet for his strong emotions. He thought he could direct it at the bad guys, but hate is pervasive. Unlike his thoughts, his feelings cannot be compartmentalized.

Thanks in part to Mike Black's dirty dealings, John nearly has a stroke when someone in a small silver Nissan with darkly tinted windows cuts him off. He curses under his breath because he is not in his patrol car and, therefore, can't officially ruin the scumbag's night. "An eye for an eye, yo," he says to the empty seat next to him.

He swerves and accelerates, threatening to run the Nissan off the road. It brakes furiously, almost careening into a concrete pillar, and John keeps driving. Instead of quelling his mood, the cut-off shenanigans have stoked the fire, which now threatens to incinerate something. John feels the loss of control, as he can no longer operate from his human mind. The baser elements of his brain begin to call the shots. He wants to bark and howl at the moon. He rocks in the driver's seat of his truck and tries to calm himself.

He thinks of Legs, and the source of his stimulation shifts. In anger, his arousal is a mix of hormones and imaginary violence. He wants prey as much as he wants love. He imagines ripping Legs' blouse right off of her. He imagines putting his hand over her mouth as she struggles underneath him. His temperature of his crotch rises several degrees. He chews on his lower lip as he pulls up to the parking lot behind the Fallout Lounge.

It is a crowded night, and the pickings are slim as far as parking spaces go. When he finds an empty spot, another driver in a black pickup cuts across him and occupies it. John jumps out of his car, pulls the pickup's door open, undoes the male driver's seatbelt, and pulls him up by the arm.

When the driver, a thin, scruffy-looking young man in a black t-shirt, dares to come at him with the phrase "What the fuck," John grabs his throat with both hands and gets off on the fear in the guy's eyes.

John doesn't say anything as he stares right at the kid. Without using words, he wants to communicate that a move like that could cost someone his life. John Hernandez' eyes are terrifying talkers.

After releasing his grip and unceremoniously depositing the kid's feet back to the ground, John does have one phrase to offer: "Get the fuck out of here," he growls. The driver quickly complies, and John takes his parking space.

Before exiting the truck this time, he checks to make sure all the hairs on his head are gelled correctly into place. He is fastidious about his neat appearance. He is still beyond angry. He breathes heavily and audibly. He takes in his reflection and gives it a stern warning to get it the fuck together.

The back of the Fallout (or F) Lounge is accessible from the alley parking lot. He always parks back there because he doesn't want any of his fellow patrolmen to see how often he frequents the place. The F Lounge is well known within the department as a favorite destination of drug doers and other assorted degenerates.

John takes a deep breath before he enters the lounge through the back door. Without taking the time to look around, he walks down the long and narrow bar until he sees a stool that has vacant chairs on both sides. The bar is snazzy, with lights underneath the expensive imported vodkas. He grabs the martini menu, which is folded invitingly in front of him. He tries to avert his gaze from the bar-to-ceiling mirrors behind the bottles. He doesn't want to see the way he feels right now. He's paranoid enough about being here.

He takes a minute with the menu, knowing full well that he will order a Maker's Mark Manhattan on the rocks, as usual. Pretending to read, he looks over at the guitarist entertaining from the corner. The guy, who wears a bright red shirt and a beret pulled over his eyes, sings a trite song about girls in California. A large canvas painting of a vintage pack of cigarettes is over the right shoulder of the singer. Between verses, the musician announces that his name is Aquarius.

When the bartender, a short, longhaired brunette wearing all black, asks for his order, he makes his specifications. She takes too long to return with it, and the delay enrages him slightly in his teeth. The raucous din of the crowd and the clink of glassware starts to give him a headache. He massages his temples with the heel of his hand, feeling the insistent thump of his heart where the epithelial cells abut one another.

Just as the bartender delivers his drink, he hears Legs' unmistakable, over-the-top laugh. He sees her at the far end of the bar, aflutter in storytelling and operating with triple the amount of a normal person's energy, as usual. The end of the bar is obscured by a lack of lighting, but he can make out that she is wearing a silver tank top. She is recounting some sort of drama, complete with jerky movements of her gazelle-like arms, to another, shorter waitress.

The bottom of his mouth slowly fills with warm saliva. He feels his total body arousal as he stares at her. She does not notice.

He turns his ear in Legs' direction and tries to tune out all the other frequencies in the room. John has made it his business to ascertain the subtle details of her life, and whatever happened must be juicy. He thinks he can make out the words "Christian" and "blood," but he cannot piece her story together. Too buzzed to listen to her intuition, Legs never notices that John is at the bar again, boring holes into her with his devil eyes.

Marian Smythe carefully places the shiny green martinis that the bartender has fastidiously prepared onto her serving tray. She straightens her long back, runs three fingers through her sandy, asymmetrically wild hair and walks in John's direction. As she passes, he swivels on his barstool and blindsides her with a menacing, "Hello, Marian. I'm afraid we've had a misunderstanding."

His presence startles her; she stumbles and spills some of the sticky-sweet green liquid out of the wide-brimmed glasses. She deflates and rolls her pouting eyes. Marian has a gift for sweet-talking her way out of bad situations, and at the moment, she sees this as her best strategy. This guy John, this weird introvert who has been hovering around the F Lounge for months, had revealed himself as an undercover cop a few days prior. He had caught her with coke and made an official notation into the department's ongoing investigation, or so he had told her at the time.

When he initially confronted her, he had cornered her in the back hallway of the bar and given her a stern warning. She had smiled and flirted to the best of her ability, and he had let her off with a frightening admonition.

In the interim hours and minutes, she has been fretting a bit over the confrontation, but she is only a small-time dealer. Marian is more of a cocaine aficionado than official reseller. Her friends and acquaintances who drink in the lounge regularly ask her if she knows where they could find a bag, so a few months ago, she started buying larger quantities and meeting their requests immediately. Marian has yet to make any profit on her side business, but at least she has been able to get her shit for free. Worthwhile, in her clouded manner of rationalization.

Marian has yet to sleep in the four days since Officer John let her off with a warning. She has consumed monstrous amounts of blow and has participated in a lot of long, rambling conversations. In the presence of virtual strangers, to whom she is united by nothing more than the forbidden predawn hours, she has spilled out the gory details of her life. That her father molested her for years when she was a child used to be a difficult subject to broach. Under the influence, the memories still hurt, but she can express them much more easily.

Marian doesn't say anything to John; she needs a moment to regain some sense of normalcy. She turns, suddenly conscious of just how short her spandex miniskirt is, gulps, and walks quickly to the back end of the bar. As she walks, Aquarius sings a slow, minor-chord tune about being "down and lousy." To Marian, the noise of the crowd subsides as the beating of her heart swells to fill her ears.

She reaches the silver door of the supply room, and before pulling out her key to unlock the large industrial handle, she downs the remaining two-thirds of one of the appletinis she is carrying.

Once inside the storage room, Marian allows her shoulders to relax a bit, puts her tray on one of the metal shelving units next to a row of grenadine bottles, and leans her back against the adjacent shelf. She mutters aloud, "My life already sucks. Why not make it worse," as she looks up to the naked fluorescent light bulb.

Whether she has directed the question at the bulb itself or at a higher power, she is not sure. Marian pulls out one of the small, clear plastic bags she has stashed on her person and drops it on the plastic tip tray she is carrying in her miniscule apron. As she absentmindedly dumps out some powder and straightens it with the shopper's reward tag on her keychain, she imagines that jail might actually be an improvement. She thinks of her apartment, where dirty clothes and takeout containers are strewn everywhere. She feels guilty when she thinks about her three cats, Mojo, Mojito and Ray Charles. She hasn't changed their litter box in at least two weeks, and the poor guys have started using the couch as a repository.

Between the partying and the two part-time jobs at the coffee shop and F Lounge, Marian wonders how she finds time for love. She has been with three guys since the almost-bust the other night. While she loves sex and bases her self-esteem on her desirability, she knows that her risky sexual behavior is unhealthy; as are the drugs, she thinks as she insufflates a medium-sized line. The bump cheers her slightly, convinces her she can get around to paying her bills before the utilities are shut off and that she can keep the creepy Officer John at bay for the rest of the night.

She mutters one more prayer - this one certainly to God - promising that if she can make it through this night, she will change her sinning ways tomorrow. She re-hides the bag of coke, placing it alongside the two others she is carrying in her hiding place, readjusts her silver tank top, smacks her pink lips together, smiles at nothing and opens the door to go back into the rattle of the bar.

John Hernandez is waiting in the empty hallway outside the storage room. He shakes his head at her again as he slowly reaches for his back pocket, resting his hand against the badge in his wallet. This action empowers him, dares him to carry out the plan he has long been formulating.

"Marian, Marian, tsk, tsk, tsk," he says. "We talked the other night about what a felony would do to your life. You're just not going to learn, and I'm not feeling very charitable. You need to follow me."

John's face is hard and unrelenting. Marian thinks she can see something wildly dangerous in his eyes, but he quickly hides everything except for the intimidation he is trying to convey.

He leads her to one of the two separate women's restrooms, which are right around the corner. The area is quiet in comparison to the loud music and conversation in the main room. He knocks, and both restrooms are apparently empty.

He directs Marian through door on the left. He then surveys the hallway to ensure he is unnoticed before he follows her inside and locks the door behind them.

John Hernandez and Marian Smythe look at each other in the empty bathroom. The door to the lone stall is closed because of an automatic hinge, and John opens it to make sure no one is hiding in there. He notices that the earth-colored concrete floor has recently been swept and mopped. A lone bit of graffiti adorns the side of the stall over the toilet paper holder. "Cry two tears in a bucket and run for the floor," it reads. Whatever that means.

Marian begins to sniffle. She asks for some toilet paper to wipe her nose. He obliges. The precarious nature of this bathroom meeting is an enormous gamble, he knows, but he needs to allow the snarling animal inside of him to feed.

Marian attempts to talk her way out of what is turning into a dangerous situation. "Please," she begs. "I haven't touched that stuff since the other night. I promise," she starts to pant.

John can see a faint white residue ringing her nostrils, so he knows she is lying. "This was your second chance," he tells her. "And you ruined it."

She breaks into legitimate tears, which arouses him. "Please," she whimpers again. "I've been through a lot lately. It's just not easy. I'm doing my best. Please, just let me be. You won't have to worry about me again. I promise."

John stops to consider. He now has every ounce of the power, and the saliva is freely flowing from the glands in his mouth. He realizes that he could possibly tip the scales for this young woman right now, but he feels that she is a worthless lost cause. Redemption, in her case, is a pipe dream. This conclusion liberates him to do what he really wants to do.

Although the setting is different, this situation reminds him of a video he had seen on his laptop. In it, a police officer investigates a possible break-in, and the suspect trades sex for his not arresting her for staging a robbery. Much of the porn he likes is on the violent side. Recently, he had seen a Japanese video of a group of men beating a blindfolded woman before having their collective way with her. A rush of images of crying women, prostrate women, begging women temporarily blind him. He wishes he had his handcuffs.

John's calm demeanor belies the rushing river of blood engorging him below the belt. He adores controlling and intimidating others, and this moment has the potential to be his coup de grace.

"No," he finally answers her. "Most people don't even get a second chance. I know you have the drugs, and I am going to find them. Remove your shirt." So she won't question his authority, he pulls the badge from his wallet and briefly flashes it at her.

Defeated, Marian complies, pulling the tight silver top over her head and placing it carefully beside her on the quartz countertop. She doesn't meet Officer Hernandez' eyes as he lifts one arm, then the other, running his fingers under her shoulders and pulling her slightly forward while making a show of searching down the skin of her back.

He picks up the discarded shirt and fingers it along the seams. No coke.

Marian is nervously perched on the edge of the counter. He looks as her flesh colored bra and sourly, disappointedly takes in her small breasts. He orders her to remove the bra, and she pleads not to with her darting, somewhat frantic eyes. Marian wonders if this is normal arrest procedure, but she is too high, scared and vulnerable to question him.

She wraps her hands behind her back and slowly unhooks her bra, hoping that the officer will fail to see the little plastic bags she has stuffed into the loose lining between the cup and the strap.

He notices the plastic seal of the bags as she carefully folds the bra, but he makes no mention of this. Marian is terrified now; her shoulders slump as she brings her forearms together over her midsection. John is as aroused as he has ever been. He looks at her discomfort and imagines that she is the blindfolded girl from the video. To him, Marian is no longer another human being, but a subject that he needs to control.

"Take off your shoes and hand them to me," he says.

She does as she is asked, and he takes the shoes and makes a grandiose motion out of trying to empty them. She notices the distinct shape of the bulge from his fly, which is sticking straight up at her under his belt, furious. Marian gets a sinking feeling in her stomach and considers screaming, but she calculates that the strange and unauthorized search procedure will provide problems in any possible prosecution for the drug charge. She is trying to see the long-term benefits of what is happening. She cannot decipher whether the thumping in her ears is from inside or outside of her.

John grabs her shoulders and spins her around so that she looks squarely at her face in the mirror. She thinks that she needs to reapply lipstick to her thin lips. She watches his reflection push her down onto the countertop while she feels his rough hands slide her skirt and thong underwear off in one fell swoop. Instinctively, she lifts one leg so that the jumble of cloth falls into a single puddle around her bare foot.

She can't escape her own eyes, which are moving frantically around the reflection of the room when she feels his fingers inside of her. Insistent, probing, he is trying to push his digits as far into her as he possibly can.

While he continues to wriggle his fingers, he unexpectedly shoves a finger from his other hand into her butt, which hurts at first. Her body is blocking the picture of what he is doing in the mirror, but she can see his face, which is both furious and excited. She realizes she is being victimized again, but as she did as a child, she imagines herself on a beach. To the best of her ability, she tries to feel the sand underneath her toes and the warmth of the sun on her cheekbones. She can almost hear the waves break against the shore. She closes her eyes and feels something bigger enter her.

While she does everything in her power not to think about the here and now, he slaps her bare butt cheek and starts thrusting himself in and out of her violently. He looks at himself in the mirror over the sink. He is still clothed from the waist up in his burnt orange shirt. His brow glistens with sweat, and he imagines his expression is the same as it would be in the middle of a heated basketball game.

Instead of satisfying his dark urges, the rape fuels his anger even more. Before he finishes, an image of coach Mike Black crosses his mind. He imagines punching coach Mike in the face and bloodying his nose during tomorrow's press conference. He curses aloud as he angrily spills himself inside Marian, whose eyes are closed.

The movement stops, and Marian knows she is safe to return her mind to the shore and wander back through the sand into reality. She takes a minute to come back into her body and readjust to the scene around her. Her insides ache with shame. She hears him breathing and looks up at the room through the mirror.

John has his back to her. He collects his breath while facing the door of the toilet stall. He thinks about how much he hates Marian, how she is a whore who makes life difficult for decent people like him. He had warned her, he tells himself; she is lucky he was so lenient. She would not fare well in prison. On some level, he also hates himself, and somewhere, he realizes this, but with the words his mind uses to build thoughts, he cannot verbalize the intense self-disdain.

Marian, too, is infected with anger. Her entire life, she has striven to please everyone else. She has adjudicated conflicts between friends; she has worked so very hard. She has mopped up more of other people's messes than she cares to count. She treats people with kindness, she thinks, she didn't deserve for this pig to rape her.

Every rotten thing that has ever happened to her and every insult she has stored deep inside her subconscious meld together and rush out of her. Marian springs up from the counter and launches her torso on John. She jumps on his back, yelling, kicking and trying to grasp the short and oily hairs on his head.

He turns and tries to push her into the wall. She opens her mouth to a superhuman width and bites him on the neck. Bright red blood appears instantly in the holes her teeth leave. She is now the animal, the predator. Feeling that she has gained control, she glowers at him with devilish ferocity. Hate permeates the air; it has a particular metallic smell. The force of their unspoken threats to kill one another is strong enough to take down the building.

John strides over to her bra, which is still folded neatly on the counter. He pulls out the coke bags and spreads them out in his palm. As he holds them out so she can see his cards, he triggers the automatic towel machine.

After it spits out its inches of brown paper, John states the obvious. "Evidence," he says. He contemplates flushing the whole mess, but he wants to keep the illusion of an evidence file, though he doubts, even in her anger, that she has the balls to say anything to anyone. He gives Marian's naked body another once-over then calmly unlocks the latch, walks out of the bathroom then out of the back door of the bar.

Marian immediately re-locks it and dresses quickly. Drops of blood appear in spots on the top of her inner thigh. Her insides feel torn and furious. She pulls up the corners of her eyes as if she were going to cry and considers filing a formal complaint. She doesn't give the option much weight, though, as she remembers that a half dozen former lovers, including her boss, are on the other side of the wall. "No one will believe me," she cries into the empty air. She imagines the mistrustful looks and ridicule that would assail her from every whispered conversation.

Marian reconstitutes herself to the fullest extent possible, even turning on the faucet to try to tame her always-unruly head of hair. Her eyes are unnaturally yellow. She shrinks in the sight of the number of red veins clawing toward her pupils. She looks terrible. Badly needing sleep, she is at the point of no longer being able to cope.

She walks back out, grabbing her serving tray and its remaining two-thirds of an appletini. She assumes her waitress posture, trying to carry herself normally. Her boss, Emmanuel, is waiting for her at the end of the hallway where it meets the main room. She can't see his face clearly, but he is holding a hand on each hip. His tone is one of incredulity. His fat jowls shake and redden as he demands to know where in the hell she has been.

"Two customers walked out. You're losing me money. Happy?" he snaps. He has never actually liked or respected Marian, and this may be the last straw.

An angry customer walks up behind him. The woman, complete with fake breasts and long, bleached hair, has a grating voice, matched by her impossible, fake orange tan. "Um, excuse me," she whines. "You took my credit card and disappeared. I thought about calling the police." She holds out her hand as the wrinkles on her face emerge and preen. She then rudely demands her "fucking credit card."

"You cunt bitch," Marian says as she throws her whole waitress book on the floor. "You want your fucking credit card. Fucking take it."

Marian tosses her tray to the floor, and the glasses shatter into a hundred shards. She unties her apron as Emmanuel yells at her to get out and never set foot inside this fucking bar again. He is more incensed that anyone has ever seen him. Marian is not the only employee looking on and wishing that the rage would result in a fatal coronary.

Marian holds off on the tears until she throws open the back door of the bar. She flings herself on the brick wall adjacent to the door and beats it until the sides of her hands are raw and bleeding. She turns the spout to high and lets a lifetime of pain escape through her wails and fists. The brick wall is impenetrably thick; no one inside the bar can hear her.

"Why," she howls at the wall. "Why, why, WHY? What the fuck did I ever do to you?"

Her sobs resound throughout the parking lot onto the unoccupied metal frames of cars. Her prayers and questions, as usual, are unanswered, her Oscar-worthy hysterics a show for one man alone.

John Hernandez stands in the shadow of his truck, again unnoticed. Her pain is turning his fury into alarm.

Officer John is cognizant of his shifting mood. What transpired between him and Marian has sucked the prana right out of him, and he nervously looks around, wishing he had left before witnessing her meltdown. He does not, however, feel any shame or guilt.

Instead, John starts to panic. The reality of a cop in prison is an ugly thing, he knows. He surveys the parking lot for surveillance devices but doesn't see any. He tries to ignore the gripping sensation in his guts, but he cannot disregard the intense pressure in his temples. Unlike in the more violent emotional states he experiences, John cannot function well when he's fidgety and nearing hysteria.

He breathes deeply and purposely to dispel the obsessive thoughts which have overtaken his focus. When he sees that Marian has crumpled into a blubbering mound, he quietly slips into his pickup and drives off. He waits to turn on his headlights until he is merging onto the main street adjacent to the parking lot.

Because the hour is late, the traffic has thinned to a trickle. A car that trails him too closely causes him to curse at the top of his lungs and slap the apex of his steering wheel. He no longer has an urge to run anyone off the road, though. He has caused enough trouble for one night, and he needs to try to ease back into home mode.

He parks in front of his house and quietly unlocks then opens the front door. Lynn has left the expensive glass lamp on in the living room, and he twists it off as he passes on his way to the bedroom, which is clothed in near-pitch black. The quiet plush carpet hides the sound of his footsteps. By the dim nightlight in the adjacent bathroom, John can see that Lynn is not moving at all. He can't even detect the tiny rise and fall of her side as she breathes through her sleep.

In reality, Lynn is wide awake but does not want to interact with her husband.

He remembers Lynn's overly keen sense of smell and worries that she can detect Legs' scent from where she lies. As quietly as he can, he makes his way into the bathroom, then takes off his clothes and mixes them with the dirty ones in the hamper. He slides open the shaded glass doors separating the shower from the toilet, and he adjusts the shower temperature to his preferred range.

Under the hot water, John's paranoia mixes in with the

steam. He can feel the composite weighing down his bones, and he frets that his wife will discover what he has done. He needs Lynn to hold him into a socialized world, he thinks. He would be a loose cannon if anything ever happened between them. He doesn't love his wife, no, but he loves the way their marital image portrays him as a great American dreamer. Their union provides him necessary shelter. If she discovers the bite mark on his neck, he will blame the crazy lady from the car chase.

After he finishes and wiggles into clean boxer briefs, pajama pants and an old t-shirt, he climbs into bed next to Lynn, hoping she will stir. She doesn't, and he offers a prayer to Madre Maria, the forgiving saint from his childhood. "Maria," he says to himself, "Please, do not let my wife find out what kind of man I am. She's a good woman, and she does not deserve this. Please, also, do something about her mother."

Anxiety causes him to lift his arm and rub Lynn on her exposed shoulder, which is severely dark in contrast to the white bed sheets. He shakes her once, then twice more, until she rolls over to look at him.

John gasps because of the shaken, vacant look in her eyes. Even by the extremely dim light in the room, he knows her well enough to see that something is troubling her. He starts imagining responses for any sort of questions she might ask. He is so busy thinking, plotting, that he fails to recognize the canyon-like gulf between them.

Lynn, on the other hand, can see her husband and marriage spiraling away from her. She can hear the faint trickle of what was once her love for him empty into another place. The hot summer is drying up the last of their relationship.

She jumps to the conclusion of her own guilt. He must know, she thinks, and her own disloyalty breaks her heart. When she said, "I do" to John, she had the best of intentions, but she knew she was nearing completion of her ability to be married to him. She sees the tension in the way he props himself up to look at her, and she thinks he knows about the betrayal.

Both spouses are drowning in feelings of guilt and paranoia. Both, however, are misreading the other. After five years of marriage, John and Lynn Hernandez are performing from two separate scripts. The scene between them is coming to a conclusion, but only she recognizes the finality.

When he starts to speak, she thinks he will address the failing marriage, but he attacks another target. "I don't want your mother in our house any longer," he says. "I feel like she impacts us negatively, and it's to the point that she might steal something from us, like one of our televisions."

She looks away, the corners of her mouth curled upwards. He suspects that they might argue, but she gives off an ironic laugh. He doesn't know what to think about her reaction, about what she knows. The paranoia is too intense to bear.

"Don't you love me?" he asks.

Lynn feels terrible. She decides to extend her role for one more night. She reaches for his hand and leads him on top of her. He takes a minute to get ready, and when he does, he has uncomfortable sex with his wife in the missionary position, like they always do. Neither has been hugely experimental in the bedroom. He notices that she is almost wincing.

He keeps going, not particularly amorously but with a fascination about why his wife will not open her eyes as he makes love to her. She's going to discover my secret, he thinks.

When he nears climax, John mutters one last prayer to the Virgen for the night. "Please," he repeats. "Don't expose me."

STAGE TWO

DREAMS OF PERFECTION

CHAPTER FOUR

THE LOVERS

Lynn's bedroom barely distinguishes night from day. She and John invested in thick vinyl shades, which are always drawn tight, and the morning light is perpetually tempered by a cloak of dusk. She opens her eyes to a vacuum of stillness. John's indentation still exists next to her on the mattress, but, to her immense relief, she doesn't hear his shuffle anywhere in the house. She exhales, liberated by the quiet. John often wakes early to hit the gym before his shift, and Lynn has always been thankful for the silent mornings. Especially today.

She gets up and makes the bed, pulling the covers routinely tight before completing her daily bathroom routine. Donning a sheer ivory robe, she pulls her hair into a tight ponytail as she walks into the kitchen to start a pot of coffee. John drinks juice, so the single-serving coffeemaker is hers alone. She selects a liqueur-flavored cup and maneuvers it into brewing position. As the water drips insistently into her porcelain mug, Lynn looks around her kitchen and silently says goodbye to its contents. She thinks of all the effort she has spent dusting on top of the cabinets (which she does weekly). The obsessive cleanliness seems like a waste of energy. "I have been trying too hard to hide this dirt," she says to the wall with a smirk.

She grabs a blueberry bagel from the pantry and drops it into the toaster oven. Without the overhead light, she must strain her eyes to see what she is doing. The blinds on the kitchen window, which looks out onto a covered patio, are also pulled tightly shut.

Lynn adds artificial sweetener to her coffee and grabs it and the bagel and goes to sit down in the dining room. The silence strikes her as unusual, even though she is accustomed. Lynn and John have always agreed that a pet would upset the domestic cleanliness they strive to maintain. A fake flower arrangement stands alone on the white tablecloth. John never wanted real plants in the house because he didn't like the smell of natural decay or dirt. Lynn never argued. She looks up at the ceiling, which is flecked with texture and eggshell-colored paint, and chuckles to herself.

What has she been doing with her life, her heart, she wonders as she strokes her shiny, jet-black hair. Lynn, who grew up poor, worked for everything in this house. Although the government-subsidized apartments on the east side where she grew up were not as vulgar as an outsider might imagine, her spacious house was a definite step up in life. Or so she thought.

Today, her job at the Cannifer Barnes accounting firm also seems like a waste of effort. She crunches other people's numbers because she can and she thinks she should, but the fact that she has no desire to do so pulls at her like a needy toddler. She doesn't want any of this, she thinks with slight sadness.

A framed, slightly fuzzy portrait of John and her in happier days hangs on the wall to her left. The large silver frame holds a window into the past. In the picture, both are smiling; John's arm is wrapped loosely around Lynn's shoulders. She had decided on the outfits for the photo shoot. Both wore creased white button-up shirts, new blue jeans, and leather loafers. She worked so hard for the appearance of normalcy and happiness, she thinks, but this is all a lie. She looks at her own face in the picture and says "goodbye" aloud.

She finishes eating and leaves the remnants of her breakfast on the table, for the first time since she has lived in the house. She walks to the adjoining living room and quickly surveys the furniture before bidding a quick farewell to each and every piece. After working a job for years so she could afford all this stuff, she feels detached from all of it and fine with the prospect of relinquishing custody of every last thing. Because the dark and quiet is too much for this morning, she opens the blinds and allows the hot morning light to rest where it will. She picks up the plastic cordless phone, which she seldom uses, and calls her mother.

Lynn's mom Doreen is agitated, as usual. She wants to borrow money, again. She complains of aches in her knees and her lower back. She never once asks her daughter how she is doing or what is happening in her life. If she did, Lynn thinks, she wouldn't get a straight answer. Lynn promises to come visit in a few days, tells her mom to take care of herself then hangs up the phone. Next, she calls Audrey, the receptionist at Cannifer Barnes, and explains that due to some strange summertime flu, she wouldn't be in the office for a few days. Audrey wishes her a speedy recovery.

Lynn goes back to her closet, pulls a small black suitcase from the top shelf and starts making hard decisions about what she needs from here on out. She leaves the humdrum, neutral colored clothing on the hangers but decides to wear khakis and a polo shirt today. She selects anything remotely adventurous, including her oldest pair of jeans and a t-shirt from the Sands in Las Vegas. She leaves the sensibly high heels standing straight on the shoe rack and throws her pink and white jogging sneakers into the suitcase. She next clears her bathroom countertop of the necessities. Her cellphone is charging, and she pulls both the unit and the cord from the wall.

With the electric prongs dangling from the device like a severed umbilical cord, she sets the rest of her life in motion. She makes a call, deliberately typing in each number.

A warm and inviting voice answers on the other end. "Always a delight to hear from you so early in the day," her lover purrs. Lynn's heart swells and brightens the dark bedroom. Her happiness makes her feel certain that she is making the right decision. She feels like a flower (not a plastic one) in bloom as she explains that she has taken the day off work and will be coming over. She doesn't mention that, this time, she plans to stay.

Lynn drives her immaculate sedan through the bright morning with a fresh set of eyes. She sees her neighborhood not as a function of her routine, but as a place teeming with life and change. Though all but the sturdiest plants have withered and browned underneath the sun, the patches of remaining green strike her with force today. Life can survive in these awful conditions, she thinks. It's all a cycle.

Other cars, both large and small, buzz around her. Her city mates are running errands, shuttling kids to air-conditioned venues like the library, and generally staying out of the heat. Though the clock in her car still displays a single-digit hour, the heat is already forbidding people from the daytime.

She pulls up in front of her lover's yard, which is one that remains semi-green. The Phelps kids, Emma Grace and Scotty, are frolicking in the sprinkler. A wet slip-and-slide collects beads of water and reflects the blinding sun. Lynn gets out of the car and doesn't mind when Emma and Scotty run up to hug her, leaving wet kidprints on the side of her shirt.

"Hi, Aunt Lynn," they both squeal. "Will you play with us?" Lynn feels a tinge of regret at the realization that she did not pack her swimsuit into the small suitcase in the trunk. She considers going home to grab it but decides that she has left that house -- and that life -- permanently. In a few days, when things settle, she can take Emma and Scotty to Target and buy herself a new one.

She tells Emma, who is a free-spirited nine-year-old, to watch carefully over her younger brother. She makes them both promise to come in for a drink in a few minutes. For the first time, she sees the two as her own children and cares for them in the way a nurturing mother would. "We are going to be so happy together," Lynn says under her breath.

She lifts her sunglasses off of her eyes and enters the red door of her lover's house without knocking. The sugary vanilla smell of homemade cookies welcomes her. She calls out an exuberant "Hi" and heads to the kitchen, where she figures she will find Mercy Phelps.

Mercy is cleaning up flour from the countertop. She has spilled some while making the cookies, but every mess is an experiment in good nature to Mercy, who is smiling, as always. The smell of domestic bliss is intoxicating. Mercy never makes apologies for the small piles of papers stacked in random corners of the kitchen. She is of the belief that people buy houses to live in them, and Lynn is warming up to this mindset. Instead of chaotic, she sees both Mercy and the house as a vibrant display of life.

Mercy wears a flowing purple cotton sundress. Its slightly faded color is a pleasant contrast to the oranges and reds of the assorted artwork hanging on the walls. Lynn makes a mental note to ask Mercy one day to differentiate the different Indian deities populating her walls. To complement the dress, Mercy wears a large turquoise necklace, which hangs low over her chest but not as low as her curly, sandy locks. Mercy smiles, exposing the dimple on her right cheek, as she offers to make Lynn a ginger-lemon soda. Her husband Cody, she explains, recently surprised her with one of those carbonating machines and assorted flavor bottles. "It'll give me an excuse to try it out," she says with mischief in her eyes. She sticks her leg out to a 45-degree angle to stretch it then leans over to give Lynn a warm hug. Mercy's happy presence calms everyone she encounters.

As Mercy fiddles with the machine, Lynn starts talking about how she wants to find a new career, perhaps even go back to school. She likes cooking, she says. Mercy claps and gives a little squeal, says maybe they can open a restaurant one day. With their combination of practicality and creativity, it would have to succeed. Mercy has never given a traditional career too much thought. After receiving her Bachelor's degree in English, she spent six months in an ashram in India. She didn't find herself, but when she returned to Texas, she did find Cody in a crowded downtown bar. She never imagined marrying a cop, but she followed her heart to Cody's bed, then to the delivery room where they welcomed baby Emma Grace. She would like to do more, be more, but for now, motherhood is infinitely satisfying.

The soda machine works just like it should, like everything in the Phelps house. With two syrupy, bubbling beverages in her hands, Mercy leads Lynn into the family room and onto the green couch, recently reupholstered in cashmere. The television is on at a low volume, and both women watch with mild interest as disgraced Coach Mike Black apologizes with eyes away from the camera. The ticker on the bottom of the screen announces: "Biggest sports scandal in decades." Lynn has always secretly disliked the University of Texas' athletic teams. She thinks about how angry John must be, but she pushes him out of her mind. This room contains no space for him.

Lynn thinks of the suitcase in her trunk and gathers the courage to tell Mercy about the decision she has made. The next step will be a huge adjustment for all of them, but the time has come. Lynn looks around at the dozen or so family photos scattered around the room. The Phelps are a happy, smiling bunch, and Lynn assumes the natural pleasantry will continue after the family dynamics change. She and Mercy sit and sip the lemon ginger sodas in silence. Lynn allows the house's warm comfort to permeate her being. She imagines this to be a similar experience to being stoned, though she has never tried pot.

A commotion from the television snaps her happy reverie. The screen shifts to the announcers in the main studio, who look concerned and confused. Mike Black is already a distant memory as they mutter the words "Reports coming in" and "Massive casualties feared" with looks of shock.

Mercy grabs the remote from the arm of the recliner and switches to a news station. Quickly, they learn that a suspected nuclear weapon has exploded in Jerusalem, where it is early evening. The footage the station plays several times on repeat shows a tranquil street turning into a blinding flash of screams and terrified, running figures. Although early reports are scattered, news sources have reason to believe that the Temple Mount is the epicenter of the chaos.

Lynn, who has always been an atheist, feels a mixture of sympathy and scorn for the people in both Israel and Palestine. Both have already suffered mightily, and judging by the images on television, the internecine fighting will increase before it abates. Life is too short for all this hate and negativity, Lynn thinks.

"I left John this morning," she tells Mercy. "If the world's going up in flames, I need to be with you. I love you. I want to stay here now."

Mercy smiles in gratitude. The two women lean in to each other and gently kiss.

While Mercy is receptive to Lynn's plans, she doesn't offer any explicit agreement in response to the proposal. Lynn, certain Mercy will acquiesce, leans her head back and rests it on the ponytail sticking out from the back of her head. Emma Grace and Scotty tumble in the front door, and the yellow family lab, Bartholomew, rises from his open kennel to come greet them. Mercy gets up from the couch, pretends to scold her children for dripping water onto the brown area rug then follows them to the kitchen, where they are expecting snacks.

Lynn, acting like she is comfortably in her own home, switches off the terrible news from the television, gets up and presses play on the revolving CD changer. The vintage speakers come alive with the tranquil sounds of Calhoun, a local pop band. Though the singer describes a "kick drum heart," his voice inspires tranquility. Despite the nuclear upheaval on the other side of the world and the abrupt change in Lynn's own life, she feels at total peace. Being around Mercy always has that effect on her.

Mercy, the kids, and Bartholomew return; each holds a small bowl of bite-sized pieces of summer melons. The kids giggle at the way Bartholomew begs for fruit scraps. Their happy innocence leads Lynn to believe that their mother hasn't mentioned the nuclear attack in Israel. The kids probably don't know Israel from India, Lynn thinks.

Mercy sits on the couch and holds out her plastic bowl of fruit. Lynn settles down next to her and helps herself to a particularly succulent piece of cantaloupe. Without being demanding, Lynn stares at her lover and wordlessly suggests that they continue the discussion from earlier. Mercy shuffles the kids into her bedroom and puts in a DVD of a Disney movie.

When she returns to the den area, Lynn has curled up on one side of the sofa. She is ready to talk, and she does not fear the conversation. All of her actions and words concerning Mercy come from a place of pure love, so with the utmost confidence, she asks, "Will you tell Cody today? I don't want to lie to anyone anymore."

Mercy sighs and leans back on the other arm of the couch. She straightens her arms toward the ceiling and sticks out her chest in a deliberate attempt to open her heart. "I do love Cody," she says, "And I don't want to hurt him. The kids are going to be devastated."

"But you want to be with me, yes?" Lynn replies.

"I do," says Mercy. "This is just going to blindside Cody. He has only met you a few times, and I don't think he associates your face when the kids talk about Mom's friend Lynn."

For six months, Lynn has been meeting Mercy at her house in the evenings after the police wives' yoga class. Their husbands often work identical shifts on the force, so when Lynn has an empty house, so does Mercy. The kids, being young, still go to bed early. Neither has any idea that Mom's friend Lynn sleeps in her bed sometimes. Lynn, out of respect for the family unit, hasn't shared the existence of the secret relationship with anyone. She makes a point to lie in Mercy's arms for about half an hour and make small talk when she can. She then gets up and goes home. Now, she thinks, this is all going to change. The two women have openly discussed leaving their husbands and building their own happy family, but only Lynn has taken the time to imagine the details of such an arrangement.

Mercy tries to visualize breaking the news to her husband while Calhoun sings in the background. "These are the dead days," the song begins. She feels supremely secure in her love for

Lynn; it eclipses anything she ever experienced with Cody. Her children constantly inquire about Lynn. They love her, too. Mercy can almost put herself into the mythical restaurant where she and Lynn will work side-by-side, giving food and love to all who visit. The scene fills her with gladness, and she thanks the universe for showing her true love.

She looks at Lynn and smiles. "I wonder if Cody will be okay with us staying in the house?" she says then answers her own question by concluding, "I'm sure he will want to do whatever is best for Emma and Scotty-pie."

She stands up and positions herself into a proud warrior pose while she summons the courage to jump into this next phase of her life. She wonders if the ruination of the temple in Jerusalem is a synchronous omen about the leveling of traditional ways of being. Mercy, though, is the epitome of adaptable. She considers this to be her best quality, and she knows without a doubt that no matter what pain it might cause, she needs to be with Lynn. She has never been so certain about anything, and she says so aloud.

Lynn visibly relaxes, still curled up on the side of the sofa. She knew everything would work out for the best. "I don't know what I'm going to say to John," she says. "Probably nothing. I'll write him an email. He'll be furious, but his anger's no longer my problem." She pauses, furrows her brow. "My mother will be mad, too. She had such high hopes for my American dream. She has no right to comment, though."

Mercy is now bending down to stretch her back. Without looking up, she says, "Telling the children may be more difficult. I'll buy them a book, and we can all discuss together."

Lynn agrees that this is a wise strategy. She offers to sleep right there on the couch until the transition is tolerable for everyone in the house. She tells Mercy that her suitcase is already in the car. She then goes and gets it.

When she returns to the couch, Mercy sits right next to her. Their knees touch, and they simultaneously let their hands fall into one another's. Through softly worn palms, they squeeze the mutual promise of their love.

"Let's say a prayer for the people in Jerusalem," Mercy says.

After bowing her head, Lynn asks, "Whom are we praying to?"

"Whoever will listen" is Mercy's response.

Both women pray as fervently and as broadly as they ever have. The whole time, they anchor the prayers on the intertwined fingers they are sharing. The contrast of black and white skin is lost on both. They feel unified under the flags of love and betterment for the worlds outside of them.

They hear the front door open and look at each other as Cody, unexpectedly home early from work, audibly greets Bartholomew in the entryway. Still clasping hands, they wait for him to find them.

Officer Cody Phelps, dressed in his starched black police uniform, stands in the doorway of his family room. His eyes first settle on the tidy black suitcase sitting at the foot of the sofa. He recognizes the pretty woman who is clasping his wife's hand, but he can't fit a name with the face. He thinks something terrible must have happened to this woman. Why else would she be sitting there with her suitcase, holding onto Mercy for dear life?

"Honey," Mercy says. "You remember Lynn, Officer Hernandez' wife."

"Of course," he says as the who, what, and where click together in his mind. He thinks back to Officer Hernandez' brusque behavior from the day before and assumes his cruel attitude must have caused some sort of confrontation with Lynn. He compartmentalizes his thoughts as he realizes that the "Lynn" his kids keep mentioning is the same woman now sitting on the couch. Cody didn't realize that his wife and Officer Hernandez' wife were such close friends. He remembers the officers' Christmas party from several months before, how the two women had giggled over the appetizer table, but he didn't know that they had extended their friendship through today.

Another thought crosses his mind. The possibility is pretty slim, but because of the confused emotion of the room, he asks anyway. "Lynn," he says with genuine concern in his voice, "You don't have any relatives in Jerusalem, do you?"

Lynn has briefly forgotten about the nuclear disaster. "No," she answers, with a sort-of laugh.

Cody explains that he is home early because of what happened in Israel. Any major trauma in the world can cause erratic behavior as far away as here, and the downtown office has rearranged schedules to beef up the overall number of active patrolmen for the next few days. Though the Israeli-Palestinian clash does not have deep roots in north Texas, the apocalyptic nature of the attack would bring out the crazies. Everyone at the department is a little on edge.

"It's very sad," Mercy tells him. She continues to hold Lynn's hand. His wife looks at her friend first before turning to him with pain in her green eyes. "Would you like some fresh cantaloupe? I just cut it for the kids. They're watching *Mulan* in the bedroom, but they might've fallen asleep. This heat is *so* exhausting."

The disc changer whirs after the music stops. Shortly, a meditation guide starts playing. While Cody loves these sorts of CDs (this one is probably his), he wants to know more about the developments in Israel. He asks for the remote, figuring he doesn't need to dig any deeper into Lynn's personal life, shuts off the stereo and turns on the television.

Al-Qaeda is claiming responsibility for the attack, though all three adults are aware that the international terrorist network has by now fractured into unrelated splinters. The news coverage shifts to scenes from London and New York City, where thousands of mourners are praying in the streets. The Israeli president has issued a statement claiming, "Today is the darkest day for world civilization since World War II."

The number of casualties will not be determined for weeks, if then, but the man-made nature of the disaster increases its gravity. Driving home from the station, Cody didn't see a single protester or public mourner in his town. In fact, the traffic had been normal. Maybe if it weren't so hot, he thinks, people would be seeking the company of strangers like they do in bigger cities.

He is lost in the stories from the television -- the frantic interviews with dark-haired people who are crying, talking about relatives in Jerusalem, when Mercy abruptly asks him to turn it off.

He mutes it using the remote, and for some reason, the term "fruit of our habit" sticks in his mind. He attributes the appearance of these words to the sticky melon juice still coagulating in his palms.

Mercy drops Lynn's hand and turns to him with a mix of regret and thrill in her eyes. He has never seen this particular expression on his beautiful wife's face.

"Honey," she starts then trails off. Again, she says, "Honey," and he fills with an uncomfortable sense of foreboding.

"Lynn and I are in love," she comes right out and says it. "She's moving in today, thus the suitcase, but she'll sleep on the couch until the kids are better able to understand." Lynn sits still with her back angled away from him. "I'm sorry," she concludes, almost as an afterthought.

Though the sound is muted, Cody can see the footage of the bright light over Jerusalem and feels the floor disappear from beneath his feet. "The fruit of our habit" continues to scroll across his mind. He cannot grasp the implications of what his wife is saying, as bombs and melons are all that his conscious mind can currently hold.

"Where will I go?" is the first thing he can manage to say.

"You can stay here until you find a place nearby," Mercy answers. "The kids can spend the night there sometimes, and you can come over for dinner whenever you want. We'll still be a family - just a modified one." She says all this with an air of finality, like everything has already been decided without his input.

He hasn't even had time to think about his precious Emma Grace and Scotty. He imagines their faces, crusted with sleep, as they wake up on lazy weekend mornings. Before they get out of bed, they yell for him to go get doughnuts, as is the family tradition.

Cody has been listening to an assortment of meditation tapes for years. Without consciously deciding to, he settles into deep belly breathing. His emotions range from panic to fear to anger to sadness to complacency. He does his best to consider them clouds as they cross the blue sky of his mind. He urges his tall sticky body to be still as he leans back into the leather of the recliner. He will take the chair with him, he thinks. They can't have that, too.

Cody knows he hasn't processed the situation enough to react correctly, so he says nothing. He puts the pinpoint of his focus in his belly, where his breath continues to flow in and out rhythmically, unperturbed. After a minute, he stands and walks over to the couch so that he is facing the two women.

They both look up at him as he fingers the gun, which rests on his side in its holster. They don't flinch as he unbuttons the carrying case, grasps the hard metal handle, and places the gun on an end table, right next to a smiling picture of his family in front of a Christmas tree.

*   *   *

Cody takes wide, slow steps on his way to the bedroom, where he sees his children asleep on his bed. They are huddled together under a maroon throw blanket, still wearing swimsuits. He sees peace on both of their faces. Just being in their presence is a salve to the gaping wound through which his spirit is in free-fall. The movie, *Mulan*, unfolds on the little bedroom television. They have seen it before, he remembers.

He goes to the closet and tries not to tremble as he trades his work uniform for his most comfortable khaki shorts and a Danica Patrick t-shirt. The faded feel of the cotton runs underneath his palms as he slowly straightens out any wrinkles he might accidentally be wearing. He seizes the comfort this motion brings to him. He breathes as deeply as he can and holds the air in his lungs. Empty mind, full heart.

The undesirable emotions return, and he stands still until they rotate away. Calm again, he climbs into bed next to his slumbering children and gently massages the back of each. Scott wakes first and greets his Dad with a snaggle-toothed smile and genuine appreciation. His announcement of "Dada" wakes Emma Grace, who brushes her long brown hair out of her eyes with her fists. The smiles beaming at him from both faces are an experience of unsurpassable joy. He has never felt so deeply, and tears start to flow freely and pleasurably down his cheeks. "I love you guys," he says.

Cody can be maudlin on occasion, so the kids don't make much of it. He puts an arm on each back. All three turn their attention to the warrior princess on television, who has learned that the enemy plans to invade her city and kill the emperor. She has heard the call to protect her fellow city-folk. Cody can relate.

He momentarily loses himself in the movie, but he snaps back to the reality of the change he is undergoing. His emotions circle his conscious mind at an increasingly furious pace. Self-pity takes over for a moment. He feels this completely. Fury soon overtakes the sadness. He clenches his fists so hard he breaks his skin and gasps. He wanders back into sadness for a minute, returning to his tears. With each revolution, Cody tries to be detached, not to let the changing state of his emotional body dictate his reactions. He keeps thinking about his breath. He knows he is a millisecond away from completely losing control, but he has faith in his ability to transcend the uncertainty of the environs.

Emma notices her father's odd behavior and asks, "Daddy, are you okay?"

"Yes, sugar," he responds. "I love you." And he does, with every little bit of mitochondria in his body. Cody Phelps, in the worst moment of his life, is adrift in a warm sea of love.

Consciously, he attempts to extend this magnanimous attitude into his wife, who is on the other side of the wall and who has just shattered his once inviolable reality. He imagines her and Lynn, too, in a pool of white-pink light.

Without understanding why, Lynn and Mercy feel the blessing. At that very moment, they fold into each other's arms. They fit together like basil and tomatoes, Lynn thinks. She is not just happy but also lighter, somehow. To Lynn, Mercy is more like a twin than a lover - her other half, the only way the big picture makes sense. She feels intensely sad about the hurt that others will have to bear because of her love, but she has zero remorse.

In Mercy's arms, Lynn knows she has arrived in the exact location at which she had been born to reside. She has never felt so deeply connected to any place or time. She is home.

Cody sits on what was formerly his bed, hands still resting protectively on each child. He mouths a question without making a sound: "Is she the impostor? Or am I the impostor?"

He purposely starts to create his surrounding emotions.

In the other room, the television dictates its feelings to Lynn and Mercy. They share a deep sorrow after hearing countless stories of destruction, missing family members, and the inevitable trauma of abrupt attacks. Both cry for the children who have lost a parent, for the lovers who will never embrace again in this life. Reporter after reporter is shaken to the core, calling "Sir" and "Ma'am" to Israelis walking by the cameras in a trance. Emergency medical villages have already been set up outside the city. Half the people are already wearing protective suits. The rest will not be so fortunate.

The newscaster prepares viewers for a press conference. President Shimon Peres will be speaking to the world in a matter of minutes.

Lynn and Mercy consider the possibilities of the situations -- both macro and micro. Things would be treacherous, but together, they could navigate. They both shed a few tears from the far corners of their eyes, but in each other's hold, both feel comfort and security. They will be able to persevere.

Cody, still in his bedroom, finds pacification in his children. He knows that with their beatific faces loving him, he will be able to anchor his real self and continue on to do the tasks he had been born to do. To protect and serve. "I love you guys," he tells both again. He is in the exact place he wants to be right now, he thinks. Suddenly, every book he has ever read about meditation, like *Being Peace*, makes perfect sense. He can relate to every esoteric letter in them. Cody Phelps is, at long last, in the middle of his uniquely Zen moment.

"Before zen, chop wood, carry water," he says aloud.

"After zen, chop wood, carry water."

Both kids guffaw like lame Dad has just told a stupid joke. "Silly," Scotty says as he playfully slaps him on the knee.

Cody feels alive, energized. He knows the next few days of

work might be a little tension-filled, what with the bombing and all, but he is ready to serve his greater purpose.

While the movie plays on, Cody falls into a heavy sleep full of strange portent. His dreamscape is a mix of a chaotic night in the city's center and graceful anime magic. A ninja-hooded child roams around the streets, which are full of dire proselytizers, revelers in disbelief, and thieves. The animated child swings its sword at several random people. All look shocked as they realize a cartoon sword apparating in front of them can cause literal damage. Cody, in the dream, is in work mode. As more and more people in the streets succumb to the child warrior, Cody pulls out his gun. He doesn't want to, but he has to take aim and shoot. The bullets pass right through the child, who does not so much as flinch. The bullets then find a final resting place in another onlooker, and Officer Phelps is doing more harm than good. He prays for a dragon skilled enough to fight this warrior.

Cody's dreaming world begins to deteriorate around him, culminating in the imagined sensation that his teeth are crumbling out of his mouth, incisors then molars. He jerks up in the bed, instinctively running his finger along his closed mouth. He feels relief. The teeth are all there, even if the dream had felt so real. His heart still pounds from chasing the little ninja.

The light in the hallway is on; it shines directly onto Lynn's small black suitcase, which stands symmetrically in the corner of his bedroom now. He doesn't hear anyone moving around outside the room.

Utterly alone, he stares up into the ceiling. He curls his fingers up into his favorite mudra, and he softly chants, "Om Ma Ni Pa Me Om."

He retains his pre-nap ataraxia completely. "Abundance is a state of mind," he tells himself. He has read dozens and dozens of new age philosophy books that Mercy checked out of the library. She rarely read them, so he did. Now, he blends pieces of advice that seem soothing.

Cody looks at his phone, expecting it to ring out to him. 9:42. I slept for a long time, he thinks. He takes a few more shallow breaths, to gather his energy, and then the phone does ring. Even though he expects this, the insistence of the sound startles him.

Sure enough, he doesn't hear felicitous news. Captain is calling all officers to duty immediately. The entire United States had been placed on a level red terror alert, effective immediately. Level red on the day of the Jerusalem bombing. For the second time in a day, Officer Cody Phelps feels queasiness in his stomach worse than any he has ever experienced. He asks the caller if the town has yet to experience any unusual problems.

"I'm not going to lie," the caller responds. "We've been getting some jacked up calls. People overreact, but some outrageous stuff is crossing the wires.

"Everyone in the office is on edge. An intern just got kicked, literally kicked, for spilling coffee. Half of our squad cars are investigating robberies that've been called in. Lots of calls about fights coming in, too. I just have a bad feeling about all of this."

Officer Phelps thinks about McLemore, or is it McLagan, the dispatcher who had called. Young kid, he thinks, he should know not to spread panic. Cody shakes his limbs to dispel the fear outside forces are trying to inject into him. For his kids and for everyone else he serves, Cody summons his utmost bravery.

He re-dresses in the uniform he wore earlier in the day. He doesn't care about the wrinkles, which the clothes acquired by being unceremoniously dumped onto the floor. He runs his toothbrush quickly through his mouth and straightens his tie in the mirror. Before leaving, he applies a wax product to his shortly cropped hair. He rationalizes that if he looks good, he'll feel good.

The urgency of the call has momentarily distracted him from the news that his wife has exchanged him for a black woman. As he hurries to leave, he sees that the house is empty. He debates then picks up his gun and snaps it in the holster. He thinks of the murderous cartoon ninja from his dream.

Locking the door behind him, an extra-observant Officer Phelps walks out into the night and is blinded by pure white light bouncing off the magnificent moon and crushed by the excessive heat. This must be a record, he thinks. A few minutes have crept past ten o'clock, but after 30 seconds in the moonlight, Phelps begins to sweat. The water seeping from his body weighs him down from the uniform inwards, and he visibly slumps.

His next-door neighbor, the widower Maxine, waves at him from her open doorway. Poor woman is wearing a thick robe on a hot night, he notices.

"Be careful out there tonight, Officer," she offers him.

"Thank you ma'am," he answers. "I reckon it'll be a rough one." Cody is not the type of Texan to use a word like reckon, but on occasion, he will make allowances.

Cody still has his own squad car from the abbreviated shift earlier in the day. He gets inside and allows himself a moment to adjust to the new order of being. He has never seen his car in so much detail. He notices tiny corners of dust, hidden on the edge of what the eyes can see, and wonders how he could have missed this incredible amount of minutiae. Emotions he doesn't want, like fear and anger, pop up, but he gives them no mind and waits for them to pass.

As he turns the ignition, Cody thinks about how proud he is of the way he handled his marital situation. I have absolutely evolved, he thinks. Most men would have gone ballistic, but I made the most of it. He feels he has already adapted to the changing winds that are threatening to alter the course of the world.

He encounters more activity in his usually quiet neighborhood streets than he has ever seen. Entire families are in yards, staring at the sky or bantering back and forth across the street. He lets his siren beep for a moment and flashes his colored lights. This is his way of telling his neighbors to be safe should they venture out tonight.

He stops at a light and rolls down his window. The radio rattles off and on, but not for him, so he turns it down. He doesn't go when the light turns green. Instead, he takes the time to listen to the sound of car alarms going off in the distance, of howling dogs. He feels something lurking in his normally quiet city, and he doesn't like it. Not one bit.

Gone is the drunken, happy laughter of the backyard barbecues. In its place, something eerie buzzes and crackles.

CHAPTER FIVE

ELEVATION

Officer Cody Phelps has never been superconscious until this infinitesimal shift in time. All of his old experiences are right there inside of him, but he can draw from those and many more facets of existence from a different level now. He feels as if he is observing his body and his squad car from an objective, loftier perspective. He wills his hand to the top of his head, and he can feel each individual hair twisted into a symmetrical chemical peak.

He looks outside of his car with the same quasi-amused sense of detachment. He is on one of the city's main east-west thoroughfares now, and people are everywhere. Cars are parked as far as his eyes can see. He passes that shithole, the Dragon's Lair. A dozen people mill around the outside door. The atmosphere is loud, raucous, and hungry. Across the street, Dale's Taco Shop is still open, serving quesadillas and large schooners of cheap beer. Good that people carry on as normal, Cody thinks. The last thing anyone needs is mass hysteria.

Even in his enlightened state, Cody does not want to deal with hordes of irrational people. If the situation presents itself, he thinks, I will adapt again. He is not concerned with his fate or his pain. He feels connected to each and every person in his periphery, to every star in the sky. He tries to collect the transcendence from the latter and mentally share it with the former.

Cody is preoccupied with his meditative exercise, so he doesn't notice at first when his dash-mounted radio starts calling out for him.

The sounds eventually snap him back to his duty. The dispatcher sends him to the Top Dollar Discount Electronics Store on East Thorndale Street and tells him to wait for backup. Cody is already headed in that very direction. Driving east along the crowded street, he imagines he is in a spacemobile. Each degree of acceleration causes his heart and stomach to stir like they are adjusting altitudes. Each approaching headlight is an invitation to a mystery. This town is teeming with life tonight, he notes.

He drives down a dip, under some elevated train tracks. He passes two large churches, behemoths in comparison to the old convenience stores in the next block. Cars are not regarding the rules of red and green lights, so everyone is driving in a free-for-all. After pausing for a minute to watch other drivers navigate the disarray, he decides to press on to the electronics store.

A large supermercado on the corner of the interstate and the road is still open. The lot outside is nearly full of cars and people. His intuition tells him to pull into the lot, get out, and watch what is transpiring. He feels like he needs to discover something important in the gathering. He is expectant. Someone with a large Dodge Ram pickup has turned his stereo up to the maximum and is blaring happy banda music. A crowd of nearly 100, most in some sort of work uniform, stands around clapping, dancing and stomping.

People have purchased goods from inside the supermarket and set up impromptu snack spreads on the beds of two other pickups. A woman with her head covered by a hijab eats chunks of cheese and beans that have been unceremoniously dumped into a plastic bowl. She shuffles softly to the music from the outskirts of the horde. Two little siblings play tag around the feet of the dancing adults, oblivious to the oddity of being assembled in a parking lot late at night.

He is optimistic after seeing the affirmation of life during a night like this one. He sees the gathering as a sign of a community's persevering. Heretofore, he had been afraid the bonds of people united only by geography would wilt in the brutal heat after facing a potential nuclear tragedy.

After allowing his body to sway along with the music for a moment, he returns to his car, waits for a break in the eastbound traffic, then merges with the flow. The houses get smaller as the weeds grow taller on this side of town. He runs over several potholes. The unceremonious rearrangement of his vertebrae reminds him of the jolt from an old wooden roller coaster. Gangs of people, many young and bouncing wildly with energy, walk down the sidewalks, which are flanked by dead, hay-like grass.

He thinks of his children and wishes his wife hadn't taken them out in the night.

In the park to his left, someone sets off fireworks. His body flinches at the initial sound, but he enjoys the resulting display of light and inter-related webs of smoke. The insistent pop-whizz-pop of the fireworks (someone has a large collection) sounds like an oncoming army.

The dispatcher signals him out again, sounding extremely on

edge. "Sorry about this, Phelps, but you're going to be solo on this call. Officer Turner was en route to assist you, but we started getting calls about a shooting inside the Fallout Lounge. Turner was the only one we could feasibly send."

"One officer for a report involving firearms in a public place," Officer Phelps repeats to make sure he has heard correctly. After he says them, he feels that his words were unnecessarily full of censure.

Each new development unfolds as if he is in a story, so he doesn't relate to the panic churning in the stomach of his dense body.

"That's right," the dispatcher confirms. "Listen, you wouldn't believe the kind of night we're having in here. Please get everyone to calm down and go home. I think we still have a handle on everything, but we are in the middle of a very tenuous situation."

The dispatcher pauses. Fireworks continue to detonate in Cody's left ear.

"And Phelps," he says.

"Yeah."

"Dude, just be careful out there."

"Okay," Cody promises before signing off the radio. He notices the high frequency of burned-out streetlights as he approaches the Top Dollar Discount Electronics Store. He can feel the snarling, tornadic atmosphere before he sees it. He drives by slowly to survey the situation at the store. The rectangular, freshly painted white building sits at least 30 feet back from Thorndale Street. The black asphalt parking lot abuts the street crudely; a dislodged concrete wheel bump sticks an inch into the road.

Next to the handful of people idling in front of the store is the business' name, painted in a dark color in carefully stenciled letters. "Top Dollar Electronix," it reads.

The people, who look like tall and rangy teenagers from behind, do not notice as he drives by again. All wear shorts whose tops sag far below the elastic bands of their boxer shorts. Judging by their postures, all are men who are tensed like a coil and ready to spring at a moment's notice.

On the second recon, Officer Phelps sees that the waist-to-ceiling glass walls that make up the front right of the building have been smashed to smithereens. A coating of white sand and quartz-like glass particles fans out for several feet. He sees what looks like a jackhammer, cord running into the window, resting on its side. The store's metal security gates are twisted and bent to an angle of inefficacy.

Officer Phelps parks in the street and sits still in the front seat of his cruiser, stewing the same calm undertones he has been marinating in all evening. He sees another change approaching, and he breathes in to adapt once again.

Officer Phelps switches on the red and blue lights on top of his squad car, hoping this dissuasive action will convince the looters to collect their madness and return home without any trauma. A few people, arms loaded with metal knick knacks of various sizes, scatter out of the broken window like rats and disappear into the moonlight. He can see toppled shelves and more shattered glass through the gaping hole of what used to be a display window. Top Dollar Electronix looks like it got in a bad car crash and is now totaled. He wonders about the owners, and if they have sufficient insurance.

He calls the dispatch office to check in. Considering that he is alone, better safe than sorry. In addition, the store looks more like a pawnshop than a retailer of up-to-date technology, and he doesn't want to risk hurting himself or anyone else over a bunch of old televisions. "Ten-four," he speaks into the microphone.

No answer, so he tries again. "Ten-four. This is Officer Phelps."

The radio waves are a flurry of frenetic activity. Voices, including the one he spoke to earlier, fly out of his speakers. He tries a few more times, but no one responds to him.

On his own, Officer Phelps turns on his siren in a last-ditch attempt to assuage the tense situation. This time, no one leaves. The people that have been standing, backs to him, start to turn around. He can't see individual faces, but their stances suggest a challenge. The fireworks still sparkle in the distance, and a symphony of sirens wails from every direction. The balance of power has shifted away from those cloaked in law and order, and everyone in the parking can smell the impending insurrection.

Still, he gets no communication from the office, so he shuts off the radio completely. Its clatter and paranoia are distracting him from the situation outside of his car. He can see every little movement of the small group of people facing him, and he breaks the tension by offering a friendly wave.

He catches the teenage looters off guard. They have never seen a cop wave while he could be intimidating. The east side of town has seen its fair share of police brutality. Even before the hot months descended, tensions between this part of the community and the force had been riding high. His friendly gesture confuses them, Phelps can tell, but no one makes an obvert move. Two of the guys standing closest to the building hustle off, carrying what looks like a bass amplifier between them. Phelps remains in his car, disinterested in following.

From his current vantage point, he can see straight through Top Dollar Electronix to the back wall. Several heads bob inside. In contrast to the silent standoff happening outside, the scene inside the store is chaotic. More are inside than he anticipated. They are like rodents feeding off the rotten fruits of capitalism, he thinks. And he can't blame them. They are only doing what their impulses are suggesting.

He can sense that all do not currently share his state of lovingkindness. Officer Phelps is not concerned about the outcome of this particular mission. He is ready to throw his physical body into the gusts of fate and considers getting out and doing his job the way he had been trained to do it. He almost lifts his hand to the cold metal door handle, but a razor-like thought urges him to choose his actions carefully. Each has a different consequence, an internal voice tells him.

A flash of inspiration hits, and he grabs a bullhorn from the vacant seat next to him. He rolls down the window and aims it directly into the former front of the store. The outside onlookers stand still.

"Om Ma Ni Pad Me Om," he starts. The tactic seems to work, as the kids outside un-tense and laugh. He can't hear what they say to one another, and he is surprised when, in unison, the boys make a move toward his squad car.

"No one needs to get hurt or arrested," he says with his amplified voice. They slowly keep coming, testing the waters.

"Haven't you heard," he continues. "There are bigger problems in the world. What are all of you risking by being here? Think about what is really important."

A smiling shot of Emma Grace and Scotty flashes in his mind, and he concludes with, "Aren't any of you parents? Or what about your parents? They want you safe at home."

The front kid in the group, who has an Asian face and a bandanna around his greasy forehead, stops about three feet from the car's window.

Phelps puts down the bullhorn and looks directly toward the kid's darkened eyes. He is close enough to recognize both the fright and the bravado. He speaks to the kid in a soothing voice.

"We're all in this together, you know," Phelps tells him. "What if something terrible happened in our own city? How would you feel? Consider others for a moment. Did you stop to think about who will end up paying for all these things in the store?"

The kid answers him with an odd Texan/oriental accent, slow and murky. "Yeah, we know the owner. His name is Mohammed, and he rips people off."

By the bright, full moon, Officer Phelps sees that the young man has weighted down the pockets of his cargo shorts with items small enough to fit. He holds several Xbox games in his left hand. Phelps recognizes the brand by the neon green plastic box.

"I bought a Xbox that didn't work, and that man wouldn't give me a refund. Personally, I don't care what happens to him or his store."

Officer Phelps takes a moment to consider the new perspective. Perhaps this kid is right, he thinks. Maybe Mohammed actually is an asshole. Maybe he is sitting in a lavish house and sipping liquor purchased off the hands of the working poor. He hears more commotion coming from inside the store and realizes that this Mohammed certainly didn't rip off each and every person in there. If so, he reasons, the invisible hand would have put him out of business a long time ago.

Assembling a lighting-quick pyramid of thoughts, Officer Phelps sees the difference between right and wrong, black and white. Stealing is certainly wrong, but the universe equalizes all, he thinks. He doesn't want to interfere but feels sucked into the vortex of the broken window. He tries to talk himself into inaction but instead hears the distinct sound of a gunshot from inside. A few people scream, and most, including the Asian kid, tense and run away from the scene.

Phelps can hear the kid cursing as he flees. The officer breathes deeply. As a policeman, he is alone in uncharted territory, but he refuses to let the fear overtake him.

He hears an inhuman moan from inside the store. He grasps that this is death, foreshadowed, but he chooses to make a difference. He reaches to pull his pistol out of its holder then decides to spread positivity instead, so he locks it in the glove compartment. He has nothing except for his positive imagery. He visualizes himself leaving the store unscathed and aiding whomever is inside, moaning.

The outside stragglers have all moved on to another adventure, and Cody is unsure of what may be waiting on the other side of these walls. He receives vague signals of frustration, confusion and distress. He takes off his tie, gets out of his car, and takes one deliberate step after another. The toe of his industrial boot produces a whispering sound as it slides over the powder of broken glass. He wants to approach this situation as a member of a dynamic organism, not as the prescribed role of cop. He reaches up and, without looking, unlatches his badge, which he then tosses onto the pile of shards. He repeats to himself, "We are all one." He then imagines pink ropes, made of the finest, most diaphanous light, extending from his heart region to every person inside the building. He hears a frustrated yell and the heavy clank of metal being struck by heavier metal.

Officer Phelps looks at the edges of the gaping hole made by what were once several large panes of glass. The jagged edges are far from where he will enter between two mangled stumps of security bar. He carefully hoists himself up, climbs over a broken tube television, and jumps to a dull thud on the worn red carpet. He ducks behind a shelf to his left, which has been toppled in either a rushed entry or exit.

"I come in peace," he says aloud. He hears commotion, distant conversation and moaning. Two black men with overgrown, braided hair in white wife beaters walk up to him carrying two laptop computers apiece. They eye him suspiciously, but without badge, tie, or gun, Officer Phelps is stripped of much of his power.

He greets them, as he would have if he had seen them in a restaurant. "Hi," he says. "How are you guys doing tonight?"

"Look at this nigga," the shorter one laughs. "What tha fuck?" The pair walks by. The taller one elbows Cody as he passes him. He, oddly, experiences rejection, which stirs the anger in him, but as the pair walks away, Cody lets the negativity dissolve into the air behind them.

As they are climbing onto what once was a display shelf in front of the window, Cody asks nicely if they would think about leaving the computers behind where they belong. Neither indicates that he has heard.

Cody takes a few more steps toward the moaning noise, which has softened, as if the sufferer has been defeated. Behind the glass display counter, which has been decimated, is a wooden door with a long, thin window. The door is cracked open a millimeter. He can hear the quiet tones of serious conversation. He assumes he has found the source of the pain.

He walks to the far wall of the store so that he can maneuver around the long case without having to jump over it. Vintage electronics adorn the wall above the broken display case. He sees one of those record players with an attached horn. He reaches up to touch the metal, which is an odd shade of blackish yellow and coated with a decent layer of dust.

Closer to the register begins a particleboard bookshelf half-full of DVD movies. The selection has been hastily picked over. One of the *Final Destination* movies stares up at him, the actress' exaggerated face full of fake horror. The register itself, a newer plastic model from an office supply store, is open and empty. Who knows where the usury money has gone, Cody thinks.

He approaches the door, looks up and listens. A warehouse-reminiscent tube light is on the ceiling in the middle of the store. He stares at it while straining to understand the conversation in the small room. He is sure he hears someone mention World War III. He hears swear words repeated under someone's breath. The thudding clank of metal resumes, louder now that he is closer.

He takes a deep breath and knocks on the door. Rap-rap-rap.

A stocky white guy with hideous teeth opens it and immediately grabs Cody. The guy has a hunting knife, and Cody is unarmed. The man holds his wrist tightly with his left hand, lifts his knife up, sloping down to Cody's forehead, and looks all the way through him with psychotic murder in his eyes.

"We don't want no god darn pigs in here," he says. "Jonah! Fucking pig out here."

"Is he alone?" faceless Jonah asks from the other side of the door.

"Looks that way," says the knife-wielding one whose life is rotting out through his mouth.

"Bring him in here," Jonah says.

The big-gutted guy lowers his knife and shoves Cody through the door.

Two, smaller, yet equally worn-out looking, guys stand on the other side of a metal safe, which is dented but still standing tall where it has been bolted to the ground. The one with the longer blond hair, who is rail thin and has lived some rough 40-odd years, holds a large hammer.

"Where's your buddies?" the other one asks Cody.

"First, hi. I'm out alone tonight just caring for the community," he says. He knows he sounds odd and soft, but this is the only truth he is currently capable of telling.

Although Cody has removed his badge, an embroidered patch on his left shoulder and the nametag reveal his role in society.

"I don't like cops much," the guy continues.

"I'm sorry to hear that," Cody says. "Please, let me apologize for any bad experiences you might've had, but I'm here to protect everyone from an incident like what happened in Jerusalem. Truthfully, I only came into this store to find the person who was crying. I don't figure you know where this person is?"

The bigger guy still holds Cody's arm behind his back, but he has let the knife relax at his side.

"Hmmmpf," the smaller one replies. He looks Cody up and down, from balls of the feet to crown of the head, and asks him if he knows an Officer Hernandez.

Cody says he does, but that they are two entirely different breeds of cop. "I give you my word," Cody tells him in an unworried tone. He says this casually as if he has promised to be back in ten with a pack of smokes.

"Whatever," the thinner guy says. "I don't have time for this shit."

The bigger guy lets his arm go. Cody feels the stinging remnant of the heavy-handed grip, and the brush of pain serves to re-energize him. He mutters, "Thank you and be careful," then walks back out the door.

He is in the main room again, now ostensibly alone with the moaning person. One more time, he visualizes himself safely leaving the building after having accomplished his mission to serve.

"Where are you?" he calls out. "I'm here to help."

*   *   *

The noise is full of resignation to suffering by oneself, like the sounds of a stray cat in labor. Officer Phelps calls out to the source of the moaning again, but whoever is projecting this sound either cannot or will not string together any actual words. Phelps notices the faint sound of a television and moves toward it. In the far right front corner of Top Dollar Electronix, a lone TV broadcasts, its chunky plastic antenna folded awkwardly to pick up a digital signal. The volume is turned down to a murmur, but the forceful announcement of breaking news is unmistakable. Seemingly in response to the escalating tragedy, the mystery person, probably a woman, gutturally howls again.

He moves slowly, taking in every ceiling tile, every electric outlet (and tons dot the floor, walls, and shelves). He reaches the far right wall, which is the maximum distance from the window through which he entered. He sees a still blob of black and white fabric. On top rests a paisley white bandanna. Rough fronds of black hair jut out from underneath it at odd angles. He moves closer and sees a dark, malicious wet spot spread like spilled ink on the dirty red carpet.

The blob rustles; the bandana lifts up. Officer Phelps hears dissonant screaming from the television -- a backdrop he tries to ignore.

The figure, which he now recognizes as a middle-aged black woman, sits up, slanted, against the dust-colored stucco wall. The woman can only expose the center slice of her eyeballs; thick and swollen lids cover both the upper and lower portions. The woman wears a large black V-neck t-shirt and a pair of white polyester knee-length pants, which fit snugly across her broad hips. She winces and bends then lifts the left leg up to protect her chest.

"Ma'am," Cody tells her. "My name is Officer Cody Phelps, and I'm here to help you, okay."

99

She emits a vocal cocktail of equal parts pain and relief.

"Ma'am," he continues. "Where are you hurt?"

The woman turns toward him and reveals the bleeding portion of her upper right arm, which had previously been hidden from his vision. She holds the arm gingerly, as if she is hugging herself. Phelps bends down and kneels on his right knee. His nostrils fill with an animalistic combination of sweat, blood and dust. He sees that a few droplets of blood have implanted themselves on the woman's out-of-fashion white and purple athletic shoes. Because her eyes are only open a fraction, he cannot tell if she has completely registered his presence.

"Ma'am," he asks. "What happened?"

She doesn't answer immediately. After about 30 seconds, she whispers what sounds like "Got shot" and "Accident."

Every policeman is always on the lookout for firearms. Their presence changes the nature of any situation immediately. Phelps stands up again and surveys the room. The three guys who had been in the office exit from the back room, and, without turning to look, they all jump the counter and hurry toward the broken window in the front. He trains his ears to pick up anything, but all he hears are the woman's pitiful sniffles, the low television, and the poor air conditioner trying futilely to combat the influx of the night's oven-like air.

He considers that the woman in front of him might have accidentally shot herself. She might even still have the gun somewhere near her, he thinks, but if so, she is too stunned to use it.

He kneels back down, on both knees this time, and massages the place where her shoulder turns into her neck. She doesn't move as he leans over her chest to get a better look at the wound in her arm.

The amount of blood indicates that the bullet, which probably exited through a newly bored hole in the wall, didn't hit any vital blood pathways. Poor woman must feel terrible, he concludes. Who would want to get shot on a night like this? He sees two mp3 players bulging from the front pocket of her shorts. Although he feels sorry for her suffering, Phelps concludes, silently, that the universe gave swift retribution for her sins. Instead of being in this place and time as a punisher, he wants to help her heal.

"Ma'am," he calls to her yet again, a little louder than necessary. "Can you tell me your name?"

"Doreen," she says, and the effort seems to be incredible, like giving birth to a word.

"Okay, Doreen, would you like me to try to get you an ambulance?"

She nods, moving her chin up, then down perhaps two centimeters.

Phelps has left his police radio in the locked squad car on the street, so he grabs the thin cellphone from his shirt pocket and dials the office for dispatch. No answer. He tries 911 and gets a message that an operator will be with him as soon as possible. The pre-recorded voice apologizes for an unusually high call volume and begs that he remain calm.

He finds this last bit ironic and chuckles to himself. He tells Doreen that the ambulance may take a minute, and this news causes her to awaken fully. She opens her eyes all the way, and he sees the unmistakable stupor of drink. She opens her mouth, and he smells it, too. He is surprised that he did not notice this before.

"Well, I don't wanna wait here," Doreen says. "Will you type my daughter's number into your phone and hold it up to me?" She articulates every digit he is to enter: "Eight. One. Seven. Three. Four. Three. Three. Oh. Six. Foh."

He does as asked, hears the preliminary ring then holds the phone, positioned correctly, about an inch from the side of

Doreen's face. The daughter answers, and Phelps can hear the tinny panic of the voice on the other side of the signal. Doreen tells her daughter that she needs to come get her from the Top Dollar pawn store and take her to the hospital. Apparently the daughter doesn't want to waste any time because the call is over a few dozen seconds after it began.

"She coming?" he asks.

Doreen nods her head quietly. He tells her he will wait there with her. As a peace officer, this little gesture of kindness is the least that he can offer. He asks if he can do anything to ease her suffering, and she shakes her head no. He tries dispatch one more time from his cell phone.

Emergency storm sirens begin to ring from the outside world, their warnings ricocheting over the plastic and metal objects in the store. Phelps feels fear rising up in him, but he lets it go. Doreen does not move. Phelps gets up and turns up the television, which is six feet away from where they sit.

The newscaster, from a second-rate local station, starts in on the bad news. "For those of you just joining us," he says. "By police orders, all north Texas citizens have been ordered to their homes. As a safety precaution, north Texas is now under martial law. I repeat, martial law. Any unauthorized persons out in public will immediately be detained."

Someone hands the newscaster a piece of paper. He reads it over then looks back up at the camera. "We have just received word that emergency sirens are sounding all over the area. These sirens are to alert people to the orders, not to announce a particular incident anywhere in our viewing area. Again, these actions are a result of concern over whether north Texas may be a terrorist target and whether we might see attacks like New York and San Francisco have experienced tonight. Everyone out there: do not take chances. Please be safe and calm and return to your homes. Stay with Fault Four for further news. We'll be with you all night."

Phelps wonders what is happening to the world, but he has yet to experience any panic, which he knows is simply fear left unchecked. Doreen doesn't seem particularly bothered by any of it. She is back to her stupor, still hugging her wounded arm.

The two strangers stir in the sweltering uncertainty for a few minutes. Finally, Doreen breaks the silence. "It's not looking good out there, is it?" she asks.

Phelps looks directly at her and means it when he says, "Things could be much worse."

"I guess it could be like another 9-11," she speculates. Her thick pinewoods accent has a certain naiveté. "People will be buying up water, then everything gets back to normal after a couple of days. I ain't too worried about an apocalypse." She catches her breath before continuing. "I just don't want to be in no hospital right now. Probably worse there than it is everywhere else."

Phelps concedes that she has a point. Judging by the trauma he heard on his police scanner, the hospital will almost certainly be overrun by bedlam. He tries to send a healing cloud of green energy in the general direction of the hospital district. He asks Doreen if he can take a better look at her arm. She shrugs and offers it up to his gaze.

The bleeding has slowed to several desultory trickles. He asks her to move the arm in circles from the shoulder then to flex her forearm. She does both without displaying too much discomfort, so he concludes that the bullet only glazed her flesh. She might even be capable of treating herself at home, but he is not about to suggest this. Though the lawless night has changed the rules for this police officer, he still retains some sense of ethical liability. "Where do you live?" he inquires.

"I stay on the east side," she answers. Her country voice is soft; she seems like a kind person. "Those section eight apartments. Know 'em?"

Officer Phelps has been to the complex a few times - twice for drug busts and a few more for domestic abuse calls. If she is indicating the same complex that he is imagining, then the place isn't all that miserable. Pretty much like any older complex on the west side of town, just cheaper for the residents. Poverty isn't a direct translation of immorality, he knows.

Doreen grows more alert by the minute. Phelps assumes that the dual fogs of the bullet and the alcohol are dissipating concurrently. He asks her if she is in a lot of pain. She shakes her head diagonally, indicating neither yes nor no. He asks her if she remembers how she got shot. Same reaction.

The television re-enters the conversation. Announcers are still urging calm while quoting sources from within the White House who believe that Al-Qaeda may be launching a large-scale attack on Western civilization. The anchorwoman, looking fresh in her royal purple blazer, repeats twice: "All major U.S. cities are on high alert. Again, all major U.S. cities are on high alert."

The screen morphs into footage from Jerusalem, where the sun is now rising. Cameras can't get close to the bomb's crater, but what they capture is anarchy at its worst. A reporter briefly interviews a doctor working in an emergency triage tent. His eyes look sunken, already gone.

The anchor pair comes back on screen, clarifying that the two attacks reported in the United States have not been nuclear, but, obviously, officials are concerned. Phelps wonders how many National Guardsmen have been called up, and as if he had just asked, the announcers offer this tidbit of information. All of them. From crisis training, he knows that getting the guard fully mobilized in the streets will still take a few more hours.

Helicopter blades begin to chop through the still and murky

night air. Judging by the volume, Phelps figures that the birds are over the park.

The frequency of the trembling rotors suggests that several are scouring the trees for something -- or someone -- important. The stuff left behind in Top Dollar Electronix quivers, producing a secondary rattling throughout the room. The TV starts replaying the footage they had just seen, and Phelps is tired of the negativity and worry the machine is emanating, so he shuts it off.

Despite the sirens and the choppers, the night inside is peaceful. Phelps has had a rough couple of days, he thinks, with the car chase, his wife's leaving him, and the stressful foray into this store. Doreen is the kindest, most comforting person he has come across in what seems like forever. He doesn't want to leave her side, but he has a nagging urge to return to his car and check up on the airwaves, to see if he can get in contact with anyone for an assignment. The thought that the chaos may be on the verge of escalating crosses his mind, but he ignores the shiver coursing up his spine.

He gets up and walks down the worn treads in the old red carpet, carefully sidestepping items which have been unceremoniously dumped where they do not belong. A video game console still sports a dual price tag. The higher price, in black, is slashed. To it's right, a much more generous number jumps out in red, followed by three exclamation points.

Phelps climbs back out the window to a now lifeless street. His cruiser is still parked alongside the curb. Everything looks intact, miraculously. He unlocks the door and hoists himself down into the sunken driver's seat.

His police radio is so busy, he is afraid it might literally catch on fire. Frantic voices call out through microphones across town. He ascertains that an officer is down somewhere off Thorndale. Must explain the helicopters, he thinks. He looks up through his windshield and sees three distinctive searchlights about a mile to the north. He takes in all the stimuli, detached from the danger as if he were dispassionately watching a scary movie. He wishes a large, cold root beer and a tub of extra butter popcorn would appear in the center console. They do not.

He hears his name cross the airwaves. The dispatcher from earlier is asking, "Did anyone ever get in contact with Phelps?" They haven't forgotten about him after all, but this brings no relief.

He picks up his microphone. "Ten-four. Officer Phelps here."

The dispatcher is audibly happy to hear that he is okay then asks if everything is under control at Top Dollar.

Phelps recounts his failed attempts to summon an ambulance. The dispatcher asks if he still needs one. Phelps asks if this is a possibility.

"Not anytime soon, no," ruefully admits the dispatcher, who then gives Phelps permission to break protocol and allow the wounded person to leave without submitting the paperwork. "All bets are off, tonight," he says. "Did you hear about Holligan?"

Phelps doesn't want to hear about Holligan. The news might disturb his peace.

According to reports from patrolling officers, most of the city has heeded the warning and ensconced itself within closed walls. "We're on lockdown until sunup," the dispatcher says. "The mayor and council have an emergency videoconference to explore options for tomorrow. Right now, I need you to hightail it to Thorndale and the interstate. We set up roadblocks at major intersections. We're stopping everyone and taking anyone in who doesn't have a damn good reason to be out on the roads right now."

Phelps says he'll be on his way, but instead of departing immediately, he gets back out of the car and hurries into the store. He walks over to Doreen and asks if he has her permission to leave.

She says she is expecting her daughter any minute, and he tells her about the roadblock. Doreen says that, at worst, she can walk home. He offers her a ride, but she refuses. This one seems like a nice man, but Doreen has never trusted cops and doesn't want to start partying with any tonight. She tells him to be safe out there.

"I will," Phelps promises. "And Doreen."

"Yes."

"Thank you."

"For what?"

"For being a kind person. I know you probably shouldn't have been in here, but you have singlehandedly restored my faith in humanity."

Doreen looks at him quizzically. If that's true, she thinks, then this really is the end of the world.

Officer Phelps hooks a U-turn in the middle of Thorndale street and heads to the intersection between the east and west parts of the town. He still feels observant, awake, and in awe of every molecule of his surroundings. He intends for his current enlightenment to continue indefinitely. He is human, reformed.

The streets are quiet; the air so punishing, a breeze could not even attempt to disturb it. The fireworks have stopped, but more than one of the birds continues to hover. The otherwise still night entrances him, so he, again, turns off the scanner. Were it not for the helicopter in the sky, the scene from this section of Thorndale could be happening on any summer night. All these problems I keep hearing about, he thinks, are happening in somebody else's world. I choose peace in mine. He remembers that he has left his badge on the ground outside of the electronics store, but he could care less.

He sees the police lights displayed on the thin trees before he rounds the bend that shoots straight across the bridge over the interstate, which has been shut down underneath him. One patrol car is stopped adjacent to him on the eastbound lanes of Thorndale. Phelps parks in the middle lane next to the turn-in for the supermercado where he had seen the fiesta earlier. The parking lot is now empty. He turns on his lights and pops his trunk.

Before he walks around the car, Phelps waves and calls out hello to the other officer, an older gentleman from a northern division whom he barely recognizes. He then continues to the open trunk, pulls out a stack of four reflective orange traffic cones and sets them up across the street in neat order. He has yet to see any traffic but notices a city paddy wagon parked in the shadow of the supermercado.

The other officer traverses the bridge to confer with Phelps. He introduces himself as Stephenson. The man's eyes are devoid of irises, teeming pools of ink. He looks petrified but courageous. He doesn't waste any time with small talk.

"Plan is to stop every single car," Stephenson says. "Person needs to have a damn good reason for still being out here, like going to the hospital. An American driver's license. Too many disguises, and we can't take any risks. Jones is over in the wagon. He's already got three Canadians waiting to be herded to Shantsfield."

"Canadians?" Phelps asks, thinking that no Canadians would ever venture to Texas in the summer.

"Another word for Mexicans, man. Come on, you're not that naïve," Stephenson explains. He makes a display of noticing that Phelps' badge is gone, his shirt untucked. He smirks but doesn't say anything out loud.

Phelps stares at him, unsure of whether to laugh or cry at the disparity among members of his force.

The two officers nod at one another with an unspoken complicity, and Stephenson heads back to his patrol car, shaking his head the whole way.

Phelps waits for at least five minutes. He is living separately from time, each second stretching out infinitely. He wonders how long he waited with Doreen at Top Dollar. While one compartment of his brain starts to calculate, another stares into the blinding glare of the full white moon. Another voice, his but wiser, tells him that enough time has elapsed for a city to sleep inside its shell while a thick blanket of nothing carpets it. He finds this observation to be eloquent in its emptiness.

Phelps sees oncoming lights. As four points of light round the corner in front of him, they reveal themselves to be two more police department vehicles. An officer steps out of each. Both are strangers from stations in the far reaches of the city.

They introduce themselves as Officer Rafael Ortega and Commander Josephine Riddle. He drives over to assist Stephenson. She, a sternly short woman with spiky gray hair, stays with him and waits.

She mans the center lane, about ten feet to his right. She asks if he has heard about the massive fire in the section eight apartments, if he has heard about the officer who died in the inferno or resulting chaos.

Phelps says he hasn't. Josephine Riddle is incensed by the happenings of the night. Anger has cut the angle of her jaw, making bones protrude like misdirected nails. She has her standard-issue handgun poised in front of her, though no cars have passed by since her arrival.

A pickup riding high on huge tires appears and heads toward Officer Riddle near the center of the street. It stops short of her, and the passenger rolls down the window. She walks over, gun pointed, and starts a conversation he can't hear. After the passenger holds a piece of paper out to her, she drops the pistol and relaxes her posture. Her hip turns to the right, hand on it, as she points south along the interstate. She pats the side of the car door, making a surprised thunk, and the pickup leaves.

She reassumes her stance behind her squad car before explaining that the pickup had been carrying two National Guardsmen on their way to the nearby naval reserve base. "They had the actual military IDs plus photocopy," she says, apparently impressed.

Phelps notices that Stephenson has apprehended someone trying to cross from the west side. The man, not more than a boy really, looks subdued. He hangs his head and follows quickly. Stephenson has handcuffed him with thick plastic ties. No one speaks.

After another 15 minutes, Phelps sees another pair of headlights approaching. A yellow mustang, a decade-old model, drives straight toward him. Phelps waves at the driver, who slows down and opens his darkly tinted window.

Phelps sees that he is a Latino kid, still dressed in oily, garlic-reeking work clothes. "You coming home from work son?" Phelps asks him.

The young man says yes, he had to wait for the llave, the key, to close the shop.

Sounds plausible, Phelps thinks, and the poor guy looks terrified. His eyes dart in one direction then the next. He figures he already knows the answer, but he asks just to make sure. "Do you have a driver's license," he states with an apology in his voice.

"No," the young man looks down and says with a thick, crude Spanish accent. "No I.D." He spaces the I and the D with an onerous pause. "I work at Salvatore's. On Bellnap (which he says like beelnap)."

"What is your name, son?" Phelps asks. "Como se llama?"

"I am Javier Hidalgo," the driver answers.

Officer Phelps has never been in a more merciful mood in his life. He doesn't even consider detaining this poor Javier kid, who is probably exhausted and frightened. Just to be safe, he sticks his head in the open window frame and surveys the inside of the Mustang. Clean as a whistle. "Go home Javier," he says.

Javier understands and smiles. His eyes brighten like they have just seen a miracle.

Phelps tells Javier to go straight home and adds a blessing he remembers from somewhere. "Vaya con dios," he tells him.

The Mustang drives off, taillights growing tinier and tinier. He can no longer see them when he turns to Officer Riddle. "A nurse," he says the first thing to pop in his mind. "He's on his way over to the hospital. Emergency call for everyone."

STAGE THREE

DELIBERATION

CHAPTER SIX

ENCHANTMENT

Javier Hidalgo muscles his bright, yellow Mustang westbound down Thorndale - a route he has followed several hundred times, but never quite in this state of mind. His heart is aflutter, beating so quickly its rhythms are compounding upon one another. He feels his spiritual center fly away and reins it back in. He fingers the Virgen de Guadalupe talisman hanging from his rearview mirror and utters a gracias. Had the police officer not taken mercy on him, the night could have turned catastrophic.

The street is empty. His is the only car on the road, and the hour is late - later than he has ever been out driving around his adopted town. The sirens that have been starring in the night for the last two hours suddenly whir to a close, as if exhausted by their efforts. Now that the air's noise has returned to summer stillness, he imagines that the events of the day have not transpired. He knows he is lying to himself; he believes that forever after will be wiped off the map, but he wants to live in his fantasies for a little while longer.

Javier's car smells of grease, as usual. Although he fudged

the timeline, he *had* been at Salvatore's for most of the night. Only a pair of customers came in to eat the linguinis and scallopines he had mastered, so the head chef, that alcoholic tyrant Mark, had ordered Javier and the two other guys in the kitchen to scour the crevasses. While the guys grabbed steel wool sponges and assiduously massaged the grime out of the hard-to-reach places, they listened to the unfolding catastrophe on the Spanish broadcast radio station. News reports mixed in with happy ranchero dance tunes. This struck the cocineros as incongruous.

Rather than bristle at the fact that he was still working as the outside world crumbled, Javier used the cleaning as a meditative opportunity to evaluate his time in the United States.

Immediately upon his arrival, he thoroughly hated it here. The bright lights, fast food places, rude drivers and careless attitudes offended him to the very core. Since he couldn't yet comprehend any English, he thought that all the Americans were Godless people. He imagined them all to be wine-swilling Nazis who had no appreciation for the rest of the world.

At home, he could surround himself in Hidalgo-land, where the mores and conversations were gentle on his spirit. Salvatore's, however, was a cauldron of wickedness. He rued the day he walked in and applied for the job. He started out washing dishes. Every bit of grime he scrubbed, every chunk of ignored food he discarded into the trashcan stoked a quiet fire he had been tending in his heart for most of his life. Unlike the other Hidalgos, though, Javier never revealed his disdain for all things America.

Chef Mark would get drunk, literally every night he worked, and come back to the kitchen in a terror, taking his own broken life out on the kitchen staff that couldn't understand him. Javier would swallow his frustration at the situation and smile and nod at the regular tongue-lashings. After a few years, and thanks to a bilingual waiter, he had learned the real meanings of the words Mark hurled at him. He never indicated his understanding. He would hold his head down and do what he had been ordered to do. After all, life in the United States had been precarious for every single minute, just as Javier had always expected. His blending into the background of the country's capitalist workings was essential. The very last thing he could do was draw attention to himself, so he swallowed one injustice after another.

As he drives, he looks down at the checkered white and black polyester kitchen pants he is wearing. They are stained with my anger, he laughs. All his life, Javier knew that cataclysmic events would eventually happen, but he never expected to be wearing these ugly pants, to be sweating the gluttonous appetites of others through every pore in his body. The fact that he has been feeding the same people he had hoped to destroy is utterly ironic to him at this point. He laughs out loud, though no one can hear.

His body warms beyond the natural temperature of the night – an efflorescent heat that extends in all directions from the core of his belly. He says her name aloud, to no one. "Karma. Karma," the word is orgasmic; it melts over his tongue as he lets all that she entails slip from his throat. Javier, for the first time in his life, feels giddy. Though he would never make love to a woman before he sanctified their union in front of a higher power, he had held this lovely little being in his arms for both of the previous two nights. While she had slept deeply against his freshly showered chest, he had moved strands of hair as they fell over her face.

He still found it odd that Americans allow pet cats live in their houses and sleep in their beds, but her kitty (Tango?) was part of the family, so he accepted the cat's presence. Javier petted the little guy on its bumpy head. Both enjoyed the resulting purr. Javier, for the first time in his life, felt overjoyed. He didn't understand the mechanics, but he knew that a neurochemical change was rewriting his life's plan as he drifted in and out of a light sleep in Karma's bed.

Javier snaps back to reality as Thorndale Street runs straight into a place called State Flower Circle. His heart swells because he is only a few blocks away from washing all the hate and work off of his tired body and climbing once again into the warm and fuzzy closeness of his newfound love. He accelerates.

Proximity to Karma, though, means having to deal with the Hidalgos. For the brief time he had been in that half of the house last night, he hadn't wanted to be. Crazy Flor had taken Carlos' car and done something to cause the police to chase her. Their oldest sister, Maria, had picked up Lalo and returned him to the house. When Javier arrived, a tearful pandemonium had greeted him. The entire family, sans sleeping baby Nicolas, was gathered around the kitchen table, heads in hands, fretting that the police would be at the door any minute, threatening to send them all back to Mexico right then and there. Carlos had one of his crying boys in each arm. He kept telling them how sorry he was. Javier wondered if he had meant it. The two had never been particularly close.

Javier knows that the cops have different problems tonight and will not be turning up at the duplex. He hopes that everyone is asleep so that he can use the bathroom and slip next door, thus avoiding the circus that usually defines Hidalgo life. He feels genuine melancholy for Flor and her fate, but he does not dwell on it. He has a few other things reigning supreme in his mind. As he drives up the long driveway and parks behind Adolfo's clunky old Pathfinder, he knows that the time has come to break ties with la familia.

Javier does not know what to expect as he stands on his front porch, taking in the offending light of the bursting moon. The inside of Karma's house looks completely dark, but he can see lights on in the Hidalgo half. He wishes them all asleep before he turns the key and opens the door as quietly as he can.

No such luck. Carlos sits at the dining room table, his head buried in his hands. Little Lalo lies on the couch bed, his eyes wide awake with terror. Javier notices that, for the first time since they have lived there, the house is ice-cold.

He also notices a few items missing from the walls and a small row of suitcases lining the wall next to the door. Javier imagines that with about ten more minutes of effort, the house could be forever wiped clean of their presence. Neither Carlos nor Lalo greets him, so he nods and walks straight to the bathroom.

Once inside, Javier notices that the bathroom has been picked clean, too. Only his towel and toothbrush remain. The only other thing in the room is an extra roll of toilet paper sitting on the edge of the bathtub. He showers quickly in an attempt to clean reality and responsibility away. Covered in the towel, he makes his way to the storage area in the hallway where he keeps his small selection of Wal-Mart and thrift store clothing. He dresses in khaki pants and a clean red polo.

When he walks back out to the main room, he sees that Carlos has not moved an inch, though Lalo has closed his eyes. As he walks by, Carlos stirs and motions for Javier to sit down next to him. Javier sees the red sting of tears all over his brother-in-law's corpulent face.

"We're going back," Carlos says without waiting for any sort of response. He explains that earlier in the afternoon, the entire family packed what they needed and loaded the back of Adolfo's SUV. They had been minutes away from climbing in and moving toward the hills of Jalisco when the sirens started. Carlos explains that there hadn't been room for the television, so they turned it on, adjusted the digital antenna, and watched the noticias about the unfolding international crisis and subsequent lockdown of the streets in north Texas.

The house does look like it is in a state of purgatory. Javier mentions the low temperature and Carlos says, without humor, that they don't plan on paying this electric bill; settling up on utilities is the last of his concerns.

His brother-in-law looks broken but relieved; he is adjusting to the two-ton weight he will now be carrying. Javier asks if anyone has talked to Flor.

"No," Carlos says, looking especially pained by this admission. He tells him that their oldest sister Maria is still trying to get word. The police administrators had released Lalo into her care without asking too many questions, as Maria had documented permission to be in the States thanks to a now-defunct work exchange program. Carlos explains how she has been calling all day but cannot get a word of explanation about Flor's whereabouts. Apparently the jailers stopped answering the phones sometime during the mad events of the afternoon.

Javier notices that little Lalo has sat up on the couch and is listening intently. The boy's dark hair sticks up and out at random angles. If his mother were here, Javier thinks, he would be sleeping soundly in bed, hair straight.

Carlos continues; his beefy arms are bowed as if he wants to pray.

"We know we're going to get deported, sent back like animals, so we need to take control," he says in hushed Spanish. "I don't want to do that to my boys, to give them the memory of being hunted down, exterminated from their home. I've always wanted to go back, you know, to raise Miguel and Lalo on the farm. We may be poor, but we won't have to live like criminals. And now they won't have their mother. I don't know what else to do."

Javier can taste the guilt that Carlos has harvested. He

knows that his brother-and-law has been beating his sister since they got married. Javier never necessarily agreed, but neither did he feel the need to intervene. To him, relations between men and women were private affairs, even when those relations involved Flor, who had tried to teach him the meaning of kindness.

Carlos continues to outline the plan. As soon as the roads are safe, he says, they will be on their way. Esmeralda has made peanut butter sandwiches, so after they stop to fill the gas tank, they hope to make it all the way to the Mexican border without stopping. They even have a bucket for dirty diapers and other human excrement. Once they get going, the faster, the better, Carlos explains.

Javier asks what they will do about Flor.

"We'll wait for her in Jalisco," Carlos answers. "If the world doesn't end, and they let her out of prison one day, she will know where to find us." He whispers these sentences in a vain attempt to hide the awful truth from his son. "There's nothing else we can do."

The air conditioner rattles rudely in the ensuing quiet. Carlos, deep in thought, eventually sighs and vocalizes how happy he is to be leaving the United States. He is tired of working so hard and being treated like a dog. "And what a good time to go," he says. "This country is finally stewing in its juices. Mexico may be poor and filled with corrupt police, but it's way better than this shithole. I don't expect anyone to start bombing my farmhouse."

Carlos expresses regret that Flor has relegated his car to permanent impound, but he doesn't sound particularly angry when he laments that the Saturn would have been useful back in Jalisco. "Oh well," he says and sighs again. He looks over at Lalo, who is battling sleep so as not to fall back into his nightmares. His eyelids are obviously cumbersome.

Javier looks at his own pillow and blanket, currently being

used by Lalo. He wonders why no one has bothered to pack any of his stuff. He mentally pictures Adolfo's Pathfinder, tries to envision any way for his presence in it on a return trip to Mexico. He stretches his imagination but can't find his place in this picture. He can't see himself back in Mexico. Ever.

"What about me?" Javier asks Carlos.

His brother-in-law sighs one more time. "We all knew this day was coming, Javi," he says, not looking up. "The Hidalgos have given you a home for a long time, but you're not really family. Flor will be upset when she finds out, but Adolfo, Esmeralda and I all agree that we need to part ways. There just isn't room for you. I'm sorry."

Javier realizes that his time as a Hidalgo just ran out, and he feels unlinked from one part of his past, free to be the person he was born to be.

Without discussing Carlos' revelation, Javier gets up, takes an empty duffel bag from the floor beside the couch, walks down the hall, and pushes all of his clean clothes inside with one fell swoop. He enters the bathroom and puts his toothbrush, toothpaste, razor, soap and deodorant directly into the bag's side pocket. He is leaving several possessions behind, but he wants to make this break as clean and as symbolic as he possibly can. Since the day he showed up at the Hidalgo's doorstep eight long years ago, he had been careful not to acquire too many possessions. He always saw himself as a transient and knew that his time would be limited, which severed his attachments to the outside world.

The Hidalgos, especially Flor, had been so very kind to him. He was a tall, lanky boy when he appeared at their house, soaked to the bone in the middle of a rainstorm. He was wearing a woven cotton cover and answered their indecipherable questions with the few words of Nahuatl he could speak. The Hidalgos were pious people, and they were not going to let the itinerant orphan, so they believed, wander alone through the mountains of Jalisco. He was a passer-by without a past and a child, so they, without openly discussing it, enveloped him into their large family.

Flor had never been comfortable with her role as the baby of eleven children. She eagerly embraced his presence, fussing over him and teaching him Spanish. After about six months, he had learned enough words to piece together a story about how his parents had died in a calamitous Oaxacan mudslide, so he had walked alone, hoping to have a brighter future in the United States. Flor cried when he told her, her pubescent chest heaving and sobbing. Poor thing always had a soft heart. From that moment, they had been bonded.

Javier, always the quiet one, had learned general farm tasks and diligently helped grow agave for the next few years. He grew in girth and strength as he bided his time until he could more confidently enter the United States.

He found the Hidalgo family to be much like his own - God-fearing, traditional, tight-knit. They didn't have much to eat, but Javier found comfort in the endless plates of beans and eggs. He joined in the celebrations, held every other month or so in honor of everything from harvest to the constant marriages and funerals. The women of the village were especially kind, but he did not understand their insistence on being seen and heard. Where he came from, the men made the decisions while the women subserviently and anonymously took care of household matters.

After spending enough time around Jaliscoan women, especially Flor, with whom he had a deep, fraternal affinity, he grew to appreciate their forthrightness. The women's ideas were often as solid as the men's. After two years on the farm, Javier started in on his plan to convince Flor to accompany him to the

United States. Things would be easier as part of a family, he reckoned.

She bought into his fantastic descriptions of wealth and abundance that waited for them on the other side of the Rio Grande. His plan became hers. They waited a few years longer than they had expected after Flor met, fell for, and married Carlos, and when the group started off on the journey, Javier truly felt as if he were part of the family. As they rode north in the bed of a neighbor's pickup truck, he felt a tinge of sadness as the village vanished. He had enjoyed his time in Jalisco. He had almost become attached to the land and to the culture.

Back in the present, Javier lets the whole vision of that past disappear. He nods farewell to Carlos, who does not respond. He kisses Lalo on the head. The boy looks up at him as if he is a stranger. "Cuidate," he tells the little boy to take care of himself. Javier walks out the door and shuts it behind him. Just like that, he is no longer a Hidalgo.

He turns ninety degrees to his left and raps three times on Karma's darkened door. She doesn't answer. His face flushes in anticipation of seeing her, and he knocks three more times, trying to be louder but still enticing with a flick of the wrist.

He sees a light go on inside, and a red-eyed Karma, dressed in velvety, worn cotton pajamas, answers the door. She looks sad but not scared, he thinks. He knows that she, like everyone else, must be traumatized by the events of the day. Without saying a word, he holds her in a gentle hug.

He pulls back, holding her around her upper arms. She looks up at him, and her eyes are a mess. She seems to have arisen from some insufferably tragic stupor. Her wavy hair falls at her shoulders with effortless nighttime grace, and he thinks she is beautiful. This is the only thing in the world of which he is currently certain.

He hugs her one more time, and she sobs soundlessly. After a few minutes in this posture, she reaches her arms around him and hugs him back. Her Spanish is fair, slightly better than his skills at English, but the translation efforts are too much for a night like tonight, so instead of talking, the two embrace. He has pressing concerns on his mind - major decisions to make about his immediate future - but for the moment, he wants to inhale every filament of this incandescent love.

She stabs at phrases in an attempt to verbalize in a foreign language how she feels. She is grateful he is here again. After such a terrible day, she doesn't want to be alone.

"It's horrible," she says, letting her tears make noises this time. She feels heartbroken for all the people who are suffering. She is acutely worried about what is happening to the people in her life.

She says his name, "Christian," and Javier slumps. He thought they were over. After she tries to say it a few different ways, he understands that he has been injured somehow, and she has not been able to reach him on the telephone.

"Everything is wrong. Malo," she says. "I don't want to live in such a cruel world. I wasn't made for this."

He comforts her, wishing this Christian character dead. Karma is his now, he thinks. He had such a boyish crush for months, and his fantasies are now close to coming to fruition. He wants to ask her to marry him. The two of them, together, could disappear from the problems of the world, he thinks. He doesn't know where they could go, but he has seen enough of the earth to know that they could find a place to hide.

The night is slipping away. Light announces its nearness before making its presence manifest. He knows that the time is soon. He needs to sit and think. His thoughts and emotions are feuding on every front. His fledgling love for Karma is his only anchor.

She says that she needs to go to sleep. He holds her hand and follows her as she walks down the hall. Tank the cat meows sleepily from his warm spot on the foot of the bed, and she gingerly climbs under the covers, alone. He watches her briefly from the doorway to her bedroom. He needs to think.

After Karma is motionless, Javier goes to the trunk of his Mustang. The sky overhead has turned a promising shade of purple, and a lone bird chirps in the bushes separating his house from the similar one next door. A metal suitcase lies on its side in his gray-carpeted trunk. He grabs it and rattles the contents gently. He hears the chime-like ringing of loose metal pieces and takes a deep breath.

Javier looks down the street but sees no signs of life. He carries the suitcase into Karma's house and sets it in the middle of the floor in her dining room, which has been converted to a sparse office with nothing but a computer desk against one wall. He sits directly on the orange wood floor. One slat of wood buckles slightly under his weight. These floors are older than anyone living in the house, he thinks. He is happy to be alone in the predawn quiet.

The suitcase has crisp metal locks, and he undoes each one, trying to be as silent as he possibly can. He opens the lid and stares down into the mess of wires, tubes and screws. He has practiced this so many times, he doesn't have to think too hard as he starts connecting the loose ends of wires to their rightful partners. The repetitive motion, so portentous but also innocuous, allows him a still few minutes to think.

He has been preparing for this day since his boyhood in Iraq. He lived with his mother, father and brother on the outskirts of Baghdad during the fairly tranquil days of his youth. In retrospect, Iraqi life may not have been as faultless as he remembers, but his childhood remains an idyllic memory of laughter and family. His hands perform intricate tasks with wires and an electronic clock as he thinks about his father.

When the man now known as Javier was 12, the United States military appeared in the sky overhead. His dad, Sharif, had always been a faithful Muslim man. He believed in the sanctity of religion and followed each of the traditions. He allowed Javier and his brother the freedom of being children, but he never let them sleep on the fact that they had been called to the earth to do Allah's will. As soon as he could understand the spoken word, Javier knew that his mission in life was to expose the truth to others, no matter what that may believe. His mother, Allah rest her soul, had always been a quiet woman. Men from the neighborhood would gather weekly at the family's modest home while she stayed in the back room, masked by a veil over her face. Javier would listen as they discussed matters of tremendous importance. The men always looked so serious, he remembers.

One tall and haunted looking man, Nasib, spoke to Javier kindly. It was he, not the boy's father, who eventually invited him into the discussion. We are building communities inside Western nations, the men explained. We will become part of these civilizations, and they will not notice our growing presence. We will establish meeting centers, where we will come together to plot and pray, and when the time is right, we will atone for all the suffering they have caused our righteous people.

The tall man explained that children were the best infiltrators. Another part of the world would become home to the man now known as Javier. He was to make a place called Mexico his base and eventually enter into America, where he would need to get to Texas and find a like-minded group.

His father and Nasib fought. His father did not believe his sons needed to turn their lives over to the cause. Someone else could fight the battles. Javier agreed. He tried to comfort his mother as she wept at the thought of her dear son leaving home. He wanted to be neither spy nor murderer.

His peaceful attitude changed on the day that the American bombers accidentally ended the lives of the rest of his family. When he ran home from the uncle's house where he had been visiting, his house was splinters and memories. Though he could already recite most of the Koran, that the boy had carried his sacred text on that painful afternoon was certainly a sign from Allah. All that the boy had in the world was his Koran, and soon after, his plane ticket to Mexico City. His instructions were straightforward: to merge into Mexican life then eventually make his way to Texas. Once there, he could re-establish communication.

He wonders what is left for him in his homeland, knowing he will never make it back there. He has stayed tacitly true to his calling for many revolutions around the sun. He has done as asked. But now, on this very night, he feels that Allah is perhaps leading him in another direction altogether. He thinks of Karma, her name so soft in his ears, and of the strong feelings he carries for her.

Inspiration such as this does not happen randomly, he thinks. This may be Allah's way of talking to me. Euphoria rises within him as he imagines making love to her. His attraction, however, transcends the physical. He cannot understand many words she says, and he has much to learn about her, but he has found a real, Godly love for his life. Of this, he is certain.

He returns to the bedroom. A soft light from the hall illuminates the covers over her body. She does not move a millimeter. He gets closer and checks to see that she is still breathing. She is. He melts a little. His face is warm.

He returns to the room with the computer and stands over the open suitcase. He still needs to connect a few more components, but it is almost functional. He is torn between his heart and mind. The analytical and romantic sides of him are locked in battle.

He kneels, faces east, puts his forehead on the ground and prays. To the Virgen of Guadalupe. A woman should be the one listening to me right now, he thinks, daring the apostasy. His hard, vengeful nature is disappearing before him. He does not know in which direction he should turn.

As he prays fervently, the window starts to display the hazy covenant of morning light. He unfolds layer after layer of emotion until he feels again like a small child. He rocks with the tears of his family's untimely death. He feels love for them, and for Karma, even for Flor. If they would all listen to Allah, is the answer he receives, the world would be better for everyone. He feels okay with blending the two faiths. The light of his love for Karma causes a revolution in his entire belief system. Hormones add to the confusion.

After much consideration, he concludes that Allah and Maria have both spoken to him and are telling him the same thing: to complete what he has been waiting to do his whole life. The decision causes his ribs to contract. With regret, he finishes connecting the last loose wires that will turn electricity into suffering. He is immersed in what he is doing; he does not hear the front door open behind him. He doesn't hear the footsteps.

When he does hear, "What the fuck?" his heart sinks. He turns his head around, ready to spring on the intruder. He sees a tall, pale woman whose makeup has run down her face. The woman looks like a wild animal that has been attacked.

Marian Smythe looks at him then puts her hands on her tall knees. Her purse falls down over her shoulder as she cries hysterically. She cannot speak coherently. She is dressed up for a fancy party, but she is not wearing any shoes. Her feet are filthy, as if she has walked a long way. She sniffles obsessively, like in addition to whatever trauma she is experiencing, she has the flu.

She does not seem to notice anything except for the fact that she is in the presence of another person, somewhere she feels safe. Javier, as absently as possible, shuts the top of his suitcase and fastens the latches. The snaps they make are inaudible amidst the roar of this woman's emotions. Karma does not appear.

She repeats a word as if she is regurgitating rancid food. It emerges in two syllables: "over" and "dose." He doesn't understand what she is saying, so he just looks at her, helpless against whatever force has hold of her.

Springing, she moves from the computer room to the back of the house in what sounds like two long leaps. He follows her to the bedroom, where this woman is shaking Karma, who is trying to resist a return to consciousness. The woman yells at her, so loudly the Hidalgos likely are now awake. "Get up. Get up," she demands.

Karma finally holds her head atop her neck and brings some focus to her eyes. "Marian, what are you doing here? What time is it?" she asks. "Has something else happened?"

Marian has flipped on the overhead light switch and bathed the room in the color of anytime. Outside, the sun has simultaneously peeked over the horizon. Miraculously, the sky will be clear for another day.

Javier sits on the lower corner of the bed. It is so close to the floor that his knees sit above his thighs.

Marian asks Karma something about "pot," he hears. Karma gets up out of bed, stretches, twists her spine to flex her back, and heads to the corner of the room where a chest of drawers stands innocently against the yellow wall. She opens the top drawer, makes ruffling noises, then turns around with a glass object and a cigarette lighter. Marian takes the thing, lights it from above, and exhales a large, dense column of smoke.

Javier is stunned. What could this possibly be? It doesn't smell like tobacco. Something heavy sits at the pit of his stomach, and he does not like the sensation. His skin turns cold.

On one hand, he had always been under the impression most Americans did drugs. On the other hand, he never suspected her. Not his Karma. Had he been wrong about his belief in her inherent goodness? He now recognizes the nature of the strange incense he has smelled through the walls for the last few years. This must be marijuana, though he has never seen anyone ingesting it before. As Karma takes her turn with the pipe, his heart hardens. He takes this development as a pure signal from Allah. That some are past redemption, and the only just thing to do would be to destroy this entire wasted way of life.

He doesn't leave, though. He feels as if he has walked off the compass and into a parallel dimension. He wants to sit and observe a clearer reality of the American subculture. He wants to be sure. He needs to be. Satan can be exceedingly cunning, he thinks. Temptation, in the form of a woman, must be overcome.

After a minute, Marian visibly calms. Her tears subside into a whimper. She turns her long neck toward the ceiling then lets it droop. She turns to Karma.

"Look at all this. I just can't take it anymore," she says, tears returning to her voice.

"What do you mean?" Karma asks.

"It's just that I don't have any faith in anything," she says while rotating her face left and right. "I hear about a nuclear bomb, and my first thought is that this better be the end of the world. I know I just can't go on like this."

"Wow, I'm sorry," is Karma's response. Javier is picking up

a frustrated vibe and a few words here and there, but he is struggling with every ounce of his linguistic memory to understand.

"It's just that I don't even give a fuck about people, you know. Everything is out of control, and worse, it's all my fault," Marian starts crying again.

"Everything seems to empty and meaningless. None of my dreams will ever come true." She is in full meltdown mode again, the heat of the summer finally collapsing the integrity of another gravity-bound human. "I mean, what is life really about?"

Javier understands that last phrase. On a night like tonight, he can certainly relate to it.

Neither Karma nor Marian answer out loud. Both look as though they have realized something valuable and are simply searing it into their memories so that they do not forget. Javier doesn't want to chime in, doesn't want to participate in this conversation at all. He stares at a rough spot high on the wall, painted the same desert yellow as the wall behind it. He feels drawn to the area. It becomes larger than life, fills the space between the people in this room, who are all wandering in separate, insular worlds at the moment.

Javier looks over at the pillows, and Karma has relaxed nearly to the point of a return to sleep. Her head hangs down halfway to her right shoulder. She opens her eyes and makes an attempt to hold herself up. Finally, she gets up, grabs some clothes from her closet then goes to the bathroom and changes. She hasn't said a word to him during any of this, and he attributes her absence to the sadness she cannot disguise. He imagines that she must feel such shame at her evil ways.

She sits back down next to Marian, who asks about Christian. "Is he okay?" she says. "Have you talked to him?"

Karma hangs her head and shakes it no. A glaze of liquid covers her eyes as she explains that she can't get him to answer his phone. She doesn't know if he is okay or just mad or what. The two women hug. Javier feels even further away from the situation.

Marian cries some more; she holds her palms wide over her face. The base of her hand is on her chin; her fingers run almost to the top of her head. Her hands are freakishly large, Javier notices.

"I got raped," Marian says, too softly for anyone to hear at first.

She says it again, then again. Javier has learned this word, which the waiter at Salvatore's has been kind enough to teach him. The fence around his heart lowers just a bit. He is no advocate of cruelty.

Karma hugs Marian again, says she is so sorry. Asks if she wants to talk about it.

Marian shakes her head no but indicates that she would like to be taken to the hospital. "There's something seriously not right with me. I've never felt like this," she says.

The two women take a few minutes to straighten up and brush their teeth. Karma keeps extra toiletries in her bathroom. Javier finds it kind that Karma has agreed to accompany this woman to the hospital. Karma has also loaned her a thick purple t-shirt. If she had loaned her some pants or a skirt, the clothing wouldn't have fit, as one woman towers many inches over the other. Nothing can be done about the filthy feet.

While he has a minute to slip out, Javier takes both his duffel bag and suitcase and puts them in the trunk of his car, which still traps in Adolfo's Pathfinder. In the early morning light, Javier can clearly see the blankets, paper towels and diapers piled high against the window.

When he goes back into the house, Karma is sitting at her computer. She asks him if he will drive to the hospital. She is "out of it," whatever this means. She explains that, according to the Internet, no more attacks have happened anywhere else in the world. She makes a quick phone call to double-check that the hospital is accepting patients. They are busy, but the answer is yes. Now that the sun is up, the populace is allowed to venture back onto the streets.

Once everyone is ready, they walk down the driveway and get in the yellow Mustang. Without having to discuss or direct, Karma sits in the front passenger seat while Marian waits for Javier, to whom she still hasn't introduced herself, to move his seat forward so that she can climb into the back. The street is so calm, and the early morning so pretty, the city almost appears welcoming.

He backs out of the driveway after checking that no cars are coming in either direction. After his close-miss last night (a few hours ago, really), he wonders how functional the town currently is. He sees the bright red open sign of the donut shop down the street. On an impulse, he pulls in. He is the only customer, and the small Asian woman behind the glass counter greets him warmly. He has never eaten doughnuts in his life, so he points to the chocolate-covered ones. They look appetizing and cheerful, he thinks. She asks him how many, and he holds out five fingers on each hand. He pays cash, and the woman says goodbye. The coin-operated newspaper machine outside has already been filled. All the machine's window displays are the words "WORLD TERROR," all in capital letters. He takes a snapshot with his mind. He marvels that, even with the roads closed over the night, the commerce of the city marches on.

Back in the car, Karma grabs a doughnut and thanks him. He holds the box back to Marian, but she refuses. In his absence, Karma has changed the radio station to a news channel in English. He revs up the engine, and they make their way to the hospital, which is near Salvatore's in the center of town.

A few cars are out and about. The radio urges people to go about their business as normal but to be extra alert. Authorities believe that the explosions in New York and San Francisco may have been copycat bombings, and there is no reason to fear a multi-pronged Al-Qaeda attack in American cities. All National Guardsmen and women have been called up, though, and all major cities instituted a curfew during the night. Javier can't understand most of what the commentator is saying but recognizes both fatigue and relief in his voice.

The reports break to bad economic news coming out of Europe. Emergency measures are being taken to stabilize both the pound and the euro. Markets will be closed next week. Karma listens while Marian sits in an upright fetal position in the back seat, her legs up on the vinyl and pulled tightly into her chest. She continues to sniffle incessantly.

As they sit at a red light a few blocks from the hospital, Javier turns to look at Karma's profile. He is highly confused about the way her natural beauty intermingles with the horrible way she has chosen to live. He alternates between love and contempt - a dichotomy he can feel deep down in his bones. She turns to look at him. She almost seems frail, and semi-conscious. Her mood is the same level sadness that it always seems to be. Despite everything that has happened, an air of tranquility rules the car.

They see the traffic near the hospital as they turn onto a major intersection. Cars are backed up a block and a half. A security guard walks by and tells them that this is the line for the emergency room. Drop off and go, he says. The parking garages are needed for all hospital personnel, he explains. Karma gives him a rough translation into Spanish. She asks if he has to work this morning, and he nods his head yes.

They inch forward, car-by-car, for at least half an hour. The radio repeats the news stories, which have not changed while they listened.

Neither Karma nor Marian has said a word. Karma offers to walk Marian into the hospital so that Javier can get on with things. He feels relief, as the next step has now been decided for him. She and Marian both exit from the passenger side. Karma walks around the hood and gives Javier a kiss on the cheek. She looks right into his eyes, thanks him and says goodbye.

She looked dead serious, like she would never see me again, Javier admits to himself. Perhaps she knows, he thinks. Perhaps she saw me with the suitcase. He doesn't care; at least this is what the loud voice in his head is saying.

He waits for the car in front of him to inch forward so that he can make a U-turn in the narrow street. He is morphing in between his identities as Javier and his birth name, Hafiz Al-Assad. Half of him is a hard warrior, the other half a confused child. His thoughts, running by him in a constant stream, are conflicting one another. He cannot shake the image of his ruined, bombed-out boyhood home. He alternates between peace war, and the latter triumphs.

Earlier in the day, he had seriously contemplated dumping the suitcase in the dry, evaporated riverbed, but the hardness in his heart and the certainty of his life's mission convince him to go meet Faril at the mosque as planned. For years, he lied to the Hidalgos about his day job at Submarino's. He brought home Italian food from Salvatore's, and they never knew the difference. In reality, he spent six mornings a week at The Texas Muslim Men's Association, cementing relationships and communicating with the master planners on the sly.

Hafiz finally has enough room to turn and doesn't notice any cars. He jerks his wheel, hits the accelerator as he turns around and hears a light thud.

"God damn you," a black woman screams at him as she pounds her fist on the hood. Two other women -- one white and one black -- and two children stand behind her in disbelief.

"You could have killed me, you asshole. I already got shot. Damn you, damn you," she continues to pound.

The younger black woman grabs her around the shoulders and leads her into the grass. The older woman continues to shake. Hafiz gives a little wave and continues his turn toward violentville.

CHAPTER SEVEN

TEMPTATION

"That motherfucker could've killed me," Doreen Rucker says, emphasizing that last pungent e, to her daughter Lynn, who is leading her toward the emergency room of Hawthorne Hospital. Doreen neglected to put on proper undergarments before her little late-night jaunt, so her large breasts, which have been moving downwards for upwards of 30 years, are swaying improperly underneath her loose black t-shirt. Doreen is not normally self-conscious about her appearance, but she is wondering if her lack of restraint is the reason Lynn's friend has been holding her two children a few feet behind her. Under her breath, so quietly that even Lynn can't hear, Doreen swears, "Damn things fed two children. Woman should understand."

Doreen's right hip has been giving out for too many months at this point, and after as far as they have walked, every other step has turned into a challenge. The arthritic pain doesn't bother her, though. Doreen has become masterful at avoiding feeling anything. She can hardly feel her upper arm, which is missing a large groove of flesh. The white cloth wrapped loosely around the place the bullet grazed is now leaking thick brown blood. The other fluids that escaped from her wound earlier have migrated onto the rest of her clothes. The black of her oversized shirt is hiding a lot of it, but her white polyester-blend short pants are dotted with a creek-like ruddy color, redolent of iron and pain.

Doreen, Lynn, Mercy and her two children have been walking for nearly two hours. While Doreen waited patiently for her daughter in the ruined shell of Top Dollar Electronix, Lynn and her new girlfriend had been walking over two miles from a bar-and-grill on the other side of town. All are obviously exhausted by now, and the boy, the smallest one, has started to whimper about wanting to go home. The mother, whose name Doreen still hasn't asked, quietly tells the child she is sorry and that they will be going home soon.

The incessant bad turns of the evening, Lynn has explained, started with the appearance of sirens. The waitress at the grill, who couldn't have been older than 16, took almost 30 minutes to get them their check. When Doreen called pleading for a ride to the hospital, Mercy (Doreen has a name for the face) immediately offered to help. Her car, last night of all nights, would not start. That this woman would walk with her kids to the bad side of town on a potentially violent night strikes Doreen as strange. She says so to Lynn, who explains that the children's father is a policeman, and Mercy expected he would come get them. She has been calling all night and all morning but can't get ahold of him. She and her children are in an obvious panic.

The conversation detracts Lynn from the tired muscles all over her body that just want to be at a resting destination. The hospital is now 50 feet in front of them. The long line of cars waits patiently to earn a space in the circular drive-though in which people in scrubs look to be managing things. Doreen is momentarily glad that her entourage is on foot and doesn't have to wait any longer, but any gratefulness about this is erased when she sees a line of pedestrian stragglers wrapped all the way around the building.

As they walk closer, they see just how large the throng of injured people is. When they reach a small group of hospital workers attempting to control the chaos, a tall male nurse asks what the emergency is. Doreen tells him that she has been shot. He looks her up and down, focusing for a few seconds on the large spot of blood on the t-shirt bandage. He apologizes and directs them to get in the back of the line.

"We are working as fast as we can," he promises.

The little boy makes an audible gasp and pleads with his mother, as though she can fix this situation.

All five walk around the corner of the building to the somewhat brown lawn and its line of people. Doreen can hear agitated voices but no sounds or sights suggesting tragedy. The people waiting in front of them, a middle-aged white couple, ask if they have heard about the police officer that was shot. Both children cry out, and Mercy bends over to calm them. The couple looks energized by this reaction, as if catastrophes make them feel especially alive. Doreen does not ask what brings them to the hospital.

A father and his awkward teenage son extend the line behind them a few minutes later. Doreen hears Mercy inquire as to why they needed to be at Hawthorne, and the father answers that the boy has a high fever and has been vomiting all night. Doreen moves as far away as she can. She is handling everything negative happening in and around her body, and she doesn't want some ugly pathogen.

Doreen knows that she is an extraordinarily lucky woman to have such small problems in light of everything else. She thought long and hard about suggesting they go home to her two-bedroom apartment, but she would never pass up an opportunity to get prescribed narcotics. She tries to look a little more respectable by adjusting the white bandana over her shiny black hair. It's no use, she thinks, but I haven't been here in a long while. Maybe they won't recognize me.

Doreen thinks back to five years ago, when she was employed as an orderly at this very hospital. She worked in the medical field, doing degrading cleaning tasks, for 20 years when her girls were younger. These days, she tries to hit the other hospitals in town and avoid Hawthorne, partly because she doesn't want to relive the past. She also does not want to be recognized by any old associates in the field. Today, considering the nature of the walk they just completed, finding the closest E.R. was the smartest plan.

Mercy asks to borrow Lynn's cell phone. Her frequent attempts to contact her husband the cop have totally drained her cell battery. As Doreen gets lost in memories about working in this very building, Mercy finally gets her husband on the line. Both children heave in relief that their father is not the injured officer. Mercy's conversation is short, but he has apparently agreed to come get his family. The mother and her two kids hug and cry, relieved that he is okay. The father of the teenage boy comes closer and pats the little girl on her head.

Mercy explains that she and the kids will wait a few blocks away from all the hospital traffic. She and Lynn hug warmly. When they leave, Lynn doesn't look particularly thrilled about the development. Doreen has too much going on, too much pain to wish away, to pay her daughter's strange mood much attention. If she knows her daughter, she knows that Lynn can handle whatever is happening.

The line moves fairly quickly, and in no time, they round the corner and approach the same intake person who had sent them away an hour ago. He asks her basic questions about blood loss, fainting, and if she has any diseases, then directs them inside the building.

Doreen doesn't recognize the faces of any of the harried nurses who are running in every direction in the large emergency room waiting area. Voices are raised to a higher pitch in here, and people seem more frantic. She surveys the scene and does find a familiar face. "How strange," she says to no one in particular. "It's that girl Kamren. Or Korma. Or is her name Kamara? Whatever."

Their eyes meet as Karma walks off down the far hallway. Karma's eyes brighten as she gives a little wave.

The inside of the waiting area is full of people. Two dozen are gathered around a small television mounted on a column in the middle of the room. People in various states of disrepair look up at the bad news with glazed, zombie-like eyes. Some have been crying, as evidenced by the caked belts of tears on their faces. Others seem angry, jaws grinding into snarls. The majority, like Lynn and Doreen, are just tired and resigned.

Lynn spots two empty chairs on the far wall near the two vending machines. They go sit in a spot as far as possible away from the thin-sounding television, whose black metal mount is larger than it is. The fact that two anti-theft chains disappear into the ceiling bothers Doreen. People should be trusted, she thinks. Her hypocrisy strikes her but does not abate her indignant mood. Mother and daughter fall into the plastic orange bucket chairs, the gaudy color clashing angrily with the sea foam paint on the upper part of the walls.

A clock is on a column in the line of Doreen's sight. After looking twice, she makes out that the hour is almost ten. She shakes her head and exhales so loudly that a few faces turn to look. She is at the end of her rope. Doreen Rucker is tapped out like the stalling summer breeze, which promptly nudges her to sleep.

Doreen has strange, rapidly changing dreams. In one minute, she would be talking with her bookie, Chico. The next, she would be on a train with a cousin she hasn't seen in ten years. Nothing makes sense, but even her dreaming self is too tired to pay attention.

Lynn shakes her gently, waking her mother from some sort of supernatural chase dream. "They're paging your name," she says.

The two follow a nervous, bald man in scrubs to a large area partitioned into little rooms by plastic sea foam curtains. He points them into a vinyl cubicle, which is open at the bottom, closes them in via the curtains then promptly disappears.

The room is only large enough to hold a hospital bed, whose back is propped up, and a rolling metal tray whose contents are covered with a white towel. Doreen climbs up on the bed then turns around to face Lynn, who stands awkwardly in the corner, left with nowhere to sit. Lynn looks away and massages the back of her neck. She stretches her back, but the movement looks unnatural to Doreen.

The mother retreats in her memory to a time when she would have been responsible for keeping an area like this immaculate and germ-free. She notices that the little white tiles sprawled into hexagons across the floor still have not been replaced. Daily and nightly scrubbings have gradually eroded the brownish grout between the tiles, so a maze of grooves covers the floor.

"My, the things I saw here," Doreen says to Lynn. "Mmm, if these ceilings could talk."

Lynn doesn't want to discuss the hospital so tries to end the conversation by averting her eyes. Doreen doesn't want to talk about why she got fired -- another nurse raised her suspicion about misplaced narcotics, and Doreen failed a resultant drug test. She didn't want to talk about welfare, either. About food stamps, or about the many unpaid loans she still owes her daughter. This part she leaves unsaid but concludes the memory with an audible, "Whatever."

Lynn says nothing in reply. She folds her arms tightly across her chest, and she stares intently at something in the monotonous surface of the curtain.

Without warning, a flash of light enters the room in the form of a bubbly young nurse with tight blond curls falling over her face. Given the circumstances, Doreen finds her chipper mood odd. Both say hello, and the nurse, Suzie, speaks to Doreen as if she is a child. She makes cooing, supposedly comforting sounds as she unwraps the t-shirt. She looks at the wound, says a high-pitched, "Well, that's not too bad, is it?" and goes for a bottle of antiseptic which is on the lower level of the rolling table.

As Suzie cleans and disinfects her bullet wound -- her freaking bullet wound -- Doreen listens to the noise surrounding her. She can hear little cries of pain and nervous voices back here. She jerks her arm as the solution stings deep inside her muscular tissue. She winces too dramatically. She makes a theatrical display of drawing her wounded arm into her, whimpering with unconvincing force, even pretending to cry.

"Oh, you poor thing. Are you in just so much pain?" Suzie asks her.

Doreen nods quickly, still counting on the ruse of tears. It does hurt, but this is a sensation she can handle without pills.

Suzie goes on about how she will note that on her chart, which she is ostensibly populating as a tall, graying doctor with afro-like curls enters the mix. Lynn has to back up into the far reaches of the corner so that everyone can fit. The man introduces himself as Dr. Carter. Doreen recognizes neither him nor Suzie, so she speculates that they must be new. She doesn't offer any inclination that she had once been a member of the Hawthorne emergency team.

Dr. Carter is very matter-of-fact. A barely detectable veneer of sweat starts to glisten on his thick forehead. He reaches up absently, pulls a white handkerchief from the breast pocket of his lab coat and wipes it off. He takes a quick look at Suzie's notes, an even quicker look at Doreen's bullet wound, and concludes that everything will be fine. He turns to leave, orders Suzie to dress the wound.

Doreen moans. Very loudly. Almost howls, really.

Dr. Carter turns again, cocks his head and orders a morphine drip. "It's gonna hurt later, sir," she says. "I'm just not good with pain."

He doesn't answer but does scribble something on the chart Suzie has started. He leaves in a hurry, doesn't even bother to say goodbye.

Suzie apologizes for his behavior, how stressed he must be. She reveals that 13 different critical gunshot victims have been brought in overnight. They have lost a few, and a few more are in tenuous shape. The nurse leaves Doreen and Lynn to silence then promptly returns with a morphine drip.

She sets it up and administers the tubes to Doreen's unhurt arm. Doreen normally avoids pain medications -- she has battled this particular addiction in the past – but, after last night and today, she is happy to have it. The familiar rush of happy sleepiness overtakes her instantly. She drifts into a pleasant memory of a long-ago fantasy involving the girls' father. She sighs, smiles. She looks at Lynn and tells her that she loves her.

"I love you too, Mama," Lynn answers. She still holds herself at an uncomfortable angle but softens with the break in their communication barrier.

The waves of chemicals hit Doreen like jelly cannonballs.

She drifts further into the metal bed. She is happy to be staring at the ceiling. She massages her neck. It hurts from all the walking, she thinks. Doreen is swimming in a delightful, warm pool of I don't give a fuck. She couldn't be happier.

Doreen hardly registers when Suzie returns and tells her that the doctor has prescribed rest and oxycontin for the pain. He thinks the wound will heal without surgery. Suzie talks about getting the paperwork in order, and Doreen is too drugged to respond properly. She mutters something about Frankie Beverly.

Lynn offers that her mother is on Medicaid.

"Oh, okay. Does she have her card?" Suzie asks.

Lynn doesn't answer but grabs her mother's wallet from the front pocket of her pants. She gives the whole thick thing to Suzie. Doreen doesn't indicate that she has noticed.

Doreen and Lynn are now alone in the tiny hospital cubicle. The mother floats between regular consciousness and the thick white blanket of an opiate haze. She cannot distinguish the fantasies she is creating in her head from the reality of the crowded hospital. The insistent public address system has been working overtime since the minute she stepped into Hawthorne Hospital. Earlier, she hardly noticed. Now, Doreen hears the calls for personnel and indecipherable emergency codes in her dream state. She is in a grassy valley, and the trees are paging Dr. Robbins. The noise bristles at Lynn, but Doreen currently finds the sounds mellifluous.

Doreen relaxes into the metal hospital bed as if it were a plush mattress. Lynn, arms still crossed, looks at her mother as repulsion appears in the form of a bitter taste in her mouth. Doreen does not notice the way her daughter regards her but does hear the frustration in Lynn's little gasp.

To Lynn, the unfocused quietude in her mother's eyes, even given the atypical circumstances, is a sign of a greater problem, one that needs to be addressed. She starts compiling a mental checklist of offenses and begins to pace the two steps between curtains, back and forth, back and forth. She picks her phone out of the top of her purse and makes a call. She does not speak into the phone, apparently neither getting an answer nor leaving a message. Her frustration rises through her tense abdomen into the different lobes of her brain.

When the venom of her accusations reaches her mouth, the animosity surprises Doreen and briefly distracts her from the coma she is so enjoying.

"The way you are living makes me sick," Lynn says with a little-girl like hysteria in her voice. "Welfare? What kind of person stays on welfare? Isn't there something you could be doing besides trying to take as much as possible from hardworking people? Huh?"

She looks down at Doreen, whose hurt arm rests peacefully at her side. Her mother does not flinch or respond.

"Do you enjoy waiting in line for food stamps, Mom? How often to you have to go back and reapply? Do you not feel any shame at all? Do you get embarrassed paying for your food with government money? Do you look the cashier right in the eyes?"

She doesn't wait for answers to her litany of questions. Lynn bites her upper lip with her lower front teeth then tenses her neck, trying to exorcise her own embarrassment.

"This is so beneath you, Mom. So beneath our family. Why can't you just go get a job like everybody else?"

Doreen says her daughter's name aloud in hopes of providing a sufficient answer without extending this conversation. "Lynn," she purrs as maternally as possible. The PA system continues to chirp, its demands reflecting off the tiles on the floors and walls.

"Lynn," she continues. "You know that people are not hiring, especially a washed-up old lady like me. Do you know how many applications I've turned in?" The last part is a lie, but Lynn has no way to verify either way.

"I worked at that chicken place a few months ago, remember? It was terrible, really awful. I had to wear this stupid paper hat. Some kid with bad skin on his face yelled at me for being slow. Yelled at me all the time. Now *that* is beneath our family. When I came home from that place, my hip hurt so bad I couldn't move, and my clothes, my hair, stunk like chicken grease. I would scrub and scrub, and it wouldn't come off. I just can't do it."

Doreen would have risen and wagged her finger in an attempt to intimidate had she been capable, but from her prostrate position, the explanation seems pathetic to Lynn, who considers that her mother might actually be too old to contribute to society.

Her disappointment needs to be vocalized, though. "Are you ever going to pay me back, Mom?" she pleads, again reverting to her 13-year-old emotional self. This is the first time Lynn has ever brought up the maternal debt. "You've borrowed over thirty thousand dollars and never repaid a cent! Thirty thousand dollars!" Lynn works herself into a fit. She cannot pace as quickly as she would like, so she is currently turning herself in spirals of futility, led by her iron-straight crossed arms.

Doreen raises her hand off the bed as if to explain, but Lynn does not pause her tirade. "Did you ever stop to think of the problems this kind of money might cause in MY marriage? I mean, I love you, but you may be the main reason John and I are getting a divorce."

Doreen can feel enough to recognize her heart's growing heavy. The part of her that is awake feels guilty. She had no idea that Lynn's marriage had problems and that these problems might be related to her. She shifts back into mother mode, wishing she had the juice to stroke her daughter's straightened hair. She doesn't, so, in a soft, reassuring voice, she apologizes. "I'm sorry sweetheart," she says. "Do you want to talk about it?"

Lynn stares coldly at her mother, but like always, her eyes bear forgiveness. Lynn has always been a loyal daughter - she remembers how much her mother struggled to raise her and her sister, Tanniqua. The thought of her crackhead sister rekindles her ire. She is madder now than she was before. She imagines ripping one of the curtains off its hook and throwing the bundled mess at her mother. Lynn doesn't notice that mad tears are falling from her eyes.

"You gave that money to Tanniqua, didn't you?" she demands. "You know she spends that money on crack. You're stealing from me to kill her, dammit." The pitch of Lynn's voice has risen to the volume of the PA speakers. Lynn knows that people in surrounding spaces are now hearing her family drama, and she is usually a reserved person, but right now, she is too frustrated to care. Too stressed to restrain herself.

Still going, Lynn lets a decade of frustration flow from her mouth. "And what do you do at night? Do you know how crappy it is for me not to be able to reach my mother after five P.M.? I have to rearrange my day just to talk to you. What the fuck do you do at night? Tell me the truth, Mother."

Doreen is past the point of fighting. She might as well come clean; after all, she has survived being shot. "Honey," she admits. "I started drinking. And gambling. I lost a lot of money. I'm lonely and depressed. I'm not living right, I know. I could use some help." She shakes her head somberly, slowly from side to side.

The revelation placates Lynn, whose tears of fury melt into genuine sadness and empathy. She takes her mother's hand and holds it while Doreen's eyes close again. Doreen moans to make another show of her incredible pain, which in reality, she cannot feel in the slightest.

"We'll get through this. We're family," Lynn tells her. As a response, Doreen lightly squeezes her hand.

At that moment, nurse Suzie returns with an official-looking man in pressed khaki pants. Both have furrowed brows.

The man speaks. "We've had a problem with the paperwork, Ms. ..." his voice says before trailing off. His words carry both suspicion and derision. He starts to ask if Doreen will come with them, but he takes one look at her semi-conscious state and directs them both to wait right there.

Lynn and Doreen wait for whatever the problem is to be resolved. Lynn, assuming the hospital is experiencing paperwork issues after such a chaotic night, makes another phone call. Also unanswered. Doreen, on the other hand, intuits that she might be in trouble. Perhaps not, she thinks, so she retains her silence. Her happy floating state has been ruined by fear and a racing heart filled with premonition.

The man, who does not introduce himself or his role at Hawthorne, comes back in, alone this time, with a stack of papers. He doesn't notice Lynn behind him as he starts in on Doreen.

"We noticed, Ms. Rucker, is it?" he starts, "That your wallet contained several different Medicaid identification cards. At first, I thought you might be carrying some for family members, but I checked the different accounts just to be sure. Ma'am, are these all yours?" he asks as he fans out a display of photocopied papers, all displaying Doreen's face.

He has played his hand, but his opponent in this chess match is floored by the morphine and doesn't have any idea how to handle the situation. She looks up at him blankly, not wanting to admit anything.

He doesn't get the confirmation he would have liked but continues, "Ma'am, this sort of abuse is a very serious offense. I noticed four different prescriptions for narcotics on these accounts during the last month alone. This is a violation of federal laws, and one that we take very seriously. I'm afraid you won't be able to leave the hospital today."

Doreen finally speaks. "But I got shot," she says with dramatically slurred disbelief. "Please, sir."

He eyes her coldly, unaffected by her plea or her flesh wound. "You know, it's people like you who are making health care so difficult for everyone else. I'm afraid there will be no leniency."

He picks up the papers, stacks them into order on the metal rolling table, which makes a plaintive thunk. He tells her to wait there while he summons a medical professional to sign her into police custody. "Please, do not move," he says.

After he parts the curtains and disappears into the outside maze, Lynn reappears over her mother's worried face. She is no longer angry but genuinely horrified. She puts her hand over her proud mouth and just shakes her disapproval. She doesn't say a single word as she calmly puts her phone back in her purse, turns, and leaves Doreen alone to whatever fate might befall her.

Doreen is consoled by the fact that she is in legitimate pain. Even if they take me to jail, she thinks, they will give me medication. I have been shot.

Sated by the morphine, she is not overly concerned with the possibility of spending several years in prison. Doreen always knew that the other shoe would eventually fall, and the fact that this is happening now gives her a modicum of relief. Life has been so difficult lately; she dwells on this thought.

She remembers the pinnacle of her generally unhappy life. Both her daughters had reached adulthood, and she had a job, and a steady stream of the pills to which she was addicted, right here at Hawthorne. She had managed to keep her affairs in tight order, even put some money aside, when she lost both the job and the pills. Instead of becoming a junkie, Doreen struggled and fought against the dependence that had insidiously overtaken her. Fighting her addiction had been a full-time effort, so she didn't feel ashamed about the unemployment. The hospital could never prove that she had been taking patients' medications, so she was able to file for assistance. When it ran out, she got on welfare, for which she had no remorse.

After her so-called recovery, other parts of her life, one-by-one, started to unravel, Doreen found strength in the fact that she hadn't touched a pain pill. She drank heavily to numb things, yes, but Doreen found alcohol way less controlling.

Now, after more than five years, she is right back into the pill haze. Feels like the comfort of home. If she could be in jail feeling like this, she rationalizes that her fate wouldn't be such a miserable one.

She relaxes back into the metal bed, not noticing the hard resistance of its surface. Doreen is determined to make the most of her euphoria. It ends, she remembers.

After awhile, an older nurse, whose curly black hair is striped with gray, comes in with a clipboard. The nurse is named Ann. Doreen used to work with her. A kind woman, she remembers.

"Doreen Rucker," she says. "How the hell are ya?"

Doreen grunts and waves her hand a little in an attempt at a greeting.

"I was hoping this wasn't you here on my board," Annie says while tapping the hard surface with her long fingernails. "Now, what are we going to do about this?" Her eyes twinkle as she speaks.

Doreen moans again, trying to play the hurt card for all it is worth. "I got shot out there last night, Annie," she says. "Can you believe it?"

Annie makes noises of sympathy then sits down on the end

of the hospital bed. She puts the clipboard on the rolling table, gives it a gentle push, and massages her temples with her long-nailed fingertips.

"This has been the worst night of my career," she says. "You would not believe the shit that keeps rolling through the doorway. I'm starting to wonder if it will ever end." Her exhaustion fills the air. "Who shot you?"

"I don't even know," Doreen answers. "I got hit by a stray bullet. Hurts like hell."

"Well, you're lucky," Annie says. She, too, was once an orderly. She, like Doreen, was a single mom, but Annie, unlike Doreen, took nursing classes at night. She worked hard to become a high-ranking nurse in Hawthorne's system, but she never forgot her career roots. She rubs Doreen's exposed ankle to comfort her.

"I saw more gunshot victims last night than I did last year," she says. "People are crazy. You give them an inch, and they'll take a mile." She slumps a little, her fatigued spine showing through her clothes. Being in here with Doreen has given Annie an opportunity to relax. Even given the task she is supposed to complete, Annie is glad to see her old co-worker, with whom she used to commiserate often.

Annie still hasn't mentioned the fraud and the doctor shopping. She picks the clipboard back up and rifles through the pages. After a minute of distracting herself, she says softly, "You need to get your shit together, Doreen. Now, go on and get out of here."

The hospital suddenly smells of sweat, vomit and chloroform to Doreen, who is happy to heed her friend's advice, were it not for one little thing.

"But my arm," she says. "I just need one more prescription," she says. "It's killing me."

Annie looks down at the clipboard. "By the looks of this, you should have plenty," she says.

"I gave them to my daughter," Doreen says, pleading with her arms, her voice, and her gaze.

"Fine, I'll call it into the pharmacy downstairs," she says. "Doreen Rucker, you could cause me to lose my job over this. If last night hadn't been such a clusterfuck, I wouldn't even consider letting you go. Now go on, get out of here. I don't want to see you around here again."

"Thank you, thank you," Doreen sighs with relief. Annie's kindness has altered the course of her life, she knows. She sees this development as a miracle and plans to make the most of it.

Doreen, somewhat revived, sits up and pushes herself erect by applying pressure to the small of her back. She doesn't want to dally in this exam room in case the stern-looking man comes back. She wills herself onto the floor and gingerly walks out through the curtains. In her hazy vision, sea foam green is everywhere. At one time she probably knew up from down in this area, but she is going to have to guess right now. She takes a right and soon finds herself at an abrupt green wall. Doreen hears voices on her left and thinks she might be near the waiting room and exit. She pulls the curtain back just an inch. Inside, a grimacing young man's arm is being plastered in a cast. Not that way.

Doreen turns around and heads back in the direction she came. Her heart stops when a figure, outlined in dark white, walks toward her. If it's that man, she thinks, I will try to run. There are too many people in this damn hospital to get a cop to chase after me.

False alarm. A square-faced woman with a mouse-brown ponytail walks past her in a hurry. She does not indicate that she has noticed Doreen, who wishes again that she could remember the way out of this place. In a trance, she continues, finally coming across a curtain-framed aisle leading to an area where she can see activity.

As she walks down the new corridor, Doreen hears voices growing louder. The sounds arrive in wah-like waves. She stops and tries to make out shapes and faces, decides that the man is not among them, and steps out onto the large, half-moon nurses' station, then into the large waiting room beyond it.

Doreen wants to be anonymous, so she pulls her bandana low over her eyes. One nurse looks up at her quizzically then goes back to whatever she is doing. Despite the noise, Doreen can clearly hear every thought that crosses her mind.

The waiting room is twice as full as it had previously been. Doreen wonders how this is possible. A large crowd is pressed together, straining to see and hear the small television. Doreen sees Kamren's (or is it Korma's) profile and, saying please and thank you, makes her way through the mass of people so she can say hello. When she reaches a spot a short foot behind Karma, a TV broadcast distracts Doreen.

A handsome, All-American man is smiling, doling out relief to the viewers.

"Everything is at a standstill," the announcer explains in his strong, nasal-y voice. "No organization has claimed responsibility for any of the bombings. Police and National Guardsmen are protecting monuments and offices but have found no new indicators of trouble."

The screen cuts to a woman standing in front of the Washington monument (or is it a plastic backdrop of the monument?), and she recommends that people keep going about business as usual. "If we let these people disrupt our way of life," she says. "The terrorists win." She mentions that college football games are still being held today then makes a dumb joke about nothing standing in the way of football.

The male broadcaster comes back on screen and describes two bombings that have happened at Western mosques -- one in London and another in Florida. A convenience store owner, who was from India, was gunned down in Philadelphia. The anchor looks directly into the camera and urges that Americans not jump to conclusions. "Again," he says. "No one has claimed responsibility for the bombings."

Doreen chooses this moment to reach over and tap Karma, who is unmistakable by her eternal bed-head hairstyle.

Karma seems happy to see her. "Doreen," she says, looking at the bound and taped area on her arm. "Oh my gosh. How are you? What happened?"

Karma's eyes express more genuine concern than anyone else's have, at least this is how Doreen interprets them. Karma wants to know how she is feeling, if she needs to find a seat.

Doreen answers no, tells her that she will be leaving in a minute, but Karma asks again about the arm.

Doreen explains that she got shot but doesn't know by whom. When Karma asks where this happened, Doreen admits that she got caught up in mob mentality and joined a bunch of looters at an electronics store. Karma wants to know if she got anything, and Doreen tells her that, when she left the store, she forgot to take her booty with her.

Karma laughs. The two stand in easy companionship. Us two are on the same page, Doreen thinks.

Neither is particularly concerned with carrying on a proper conversation, but both are happy to be in each other's presence nonetheless.

I've always liked this Kamren person, Doreen thinks. Her bookie, Chico, had introduced them a few years back. How Kamren and Chico are associated, Doreen has never bothered to ask. The two women started making black market trades for painkillers, which is always a risky relationship, but the young white woman has generally been kind, so she has gradually earned Doreen's trust. Kamren is always so mellow, Doreen thinks.

As Karma looks back up toward the TV, Doreen weighs her options. She is enjoying the blankness of the morphine, but she has been down this road with these pills before. Should she get one last prescription and ride it out until her arm heals? Even though the addition of another intoxicant will probably make her queasy, Doreen is craving a tall bottle of cold beer. She hasn't had a drink since last night and is way overdue. She has no money on her, though, and is running out of cash back at the apartment. She also doesn't know how she is getting home and doesn't want to be out on the streets without a penny in her pocket.

Doreen makes up her mind, tells Karma about the prescription she is about to fill, then asks her if she would like to purchase it.

Karma's eyes light up. "Absolutely," she says.

Doreen inquires if she has any cash on her and Karma answers: "Of course. I always do."

Doreen instructs Karma to follow her to the basement, where she remembers the in-house pharmacy to be. As they wait for the elevator, Doreen half-heartedly looks around for the man who wants her in jail. He is nowhere that she can see, much to her relief.

They arrive at the green-tiled, cold pharmacy room, and to the surprise of both, the line is short. In five minutes, Doreen has talked with the pharmacist about filling her prescription. He tells her to wait by the wall, which she nervously does. The morphine is wearing off just a little, enough to make Doreen flinch every time the elevator opens. She still half expects to get arrested.

Nothing happens however, and before she knows it, the

pharmacist is calling out her name. Doreen thanks him and motions for Karma to follow her into the women's restroom on the right wall. The room is empty but in need of a quick clean. A few spots of water drip from the linoleum counter onto the floor, which has the same ugly tile as upstairs.

Doreen rips open the paper bag, which has been carefully stapled shut. She pulls out an orange bottle and reads the label, which identifies the contents as 60 tablets of oxycontin. She tells Karma, whose eyes light up perceptibly.

They settle on $200 for the bottle, and Karma pulls a stack of ordered, neatly folded twenty-dollar-bills out of her pocket, which she then exchanges for the bottle. Karma puts the whole thing in the front right pocket of her baggy shorts.

Skinny little thing, Doreen thinks. She can put a whole bottle of pills on her hip and still look like a rail. Without explaining why, she smiles and shakes her head.

Karma and Doreen shake hands, and Doreen pats the smaller woman on the back. Their encounters are always short.

Doreen leaves the bathroom and looks both ways before exiting into the larger pharmacy, which is still quiet and uncrowded. She presses the call button for the elevator, pulls her bandana lower down her face, and waits with her back turned to the room's few occupants. Doing illegal things has always made her uncomfortable and jumpy, and she makes a serious effort not to appear nervous.

The elevator arrives, and both its presence and the ten twenties in her pocket buoy her mood. "Almost free," she says to the elevator walls.

Doreen's new and redeemed life is going to have to wait a minute, though. She peeks her head around the corner of the little elevator hallway and sees the man from whom she is running standing up behind the nurses' desk.

He is engaged in quick conversation with two of them, one being Suzie, and Doreen wants to disappear but knows the only exit is directly in front of her.

A horde of people is in the waiting room now. The number keeps expanding, and to compensate for the additional voices, each and every person raises his or hers a decibel. The roar is an affront to Doreen's ears. She waits for at least 20 minutes. Several people use the lone elevator, but none give Doreen any recognition.

While she waits, Doreen tries to envision the rest of her life. "Jesus," she says in a hushed tone. "Please, forgive me and know that I mean it when I say I'm going to get my ass in gear. No more of this shit. I know what I need to do, and I'm going to start doing it. I could use your help now, though. Please."

Silently, Doreen swears to give up alcohol. Cigarettes. Red meat. She promises to have more patience, never even consider stealing again, quit gambling, and be kinder to her friends, family and neighbors. She looks at the ceiling and says to no one, "I deserved to get shot." Doreen, this whole time, had been aware of her problems, but up until this very moment, she had felt powerless to control them.

As her liver begins to flush the morphine out of her bloodstream, Doreen emerges into a clearer state of wakefulness. She peeks around again, and the man and Suzie are gone. To be on the safe side, she heads directly through the thickest part of the waiting room crowd. As she smiles and excuses herself through people, she decides that she needs to go first to the grocery store then straight home, where she will stay for as many days as she can.

With every step, she grows sleepier and sleepier. She wants to curl up right there and take a nap, but reason convinces that this is a terrible idea. She visualizes herself in front of her little television on its particleboard shelf, sitting on the old green couch and just being.

She finally makes her way to the other side of the throng and walks directly out through the glass doors and into the oppressive heat. It hits her, stops her in her tracks. Instead of wincing or complaining, Doreen registers the shocking increase of temperature on her skin and breathes for a minute before setting off.

Doreen looks to her left and sees Lynn, who sits in the pathetic shade of a desiccated tree, sobbing. Her daughter's head heaves, but she tries to conceal her misery by wrapping her body, head down, into a tight ball. The leather sandals look out of place on her feet, Doreen thinks. She is surprised that her daughter has waited. Lynn is the most distraught person she has seen all day, Doreen thinks.

"If I didn't know better, I'd a thought she was here with someone who died," Doreen whispers to no one. "Look at her, carrying on like that."

She walks over and gingerly throws both arms around Lynn, careful to hold the wounded area away from Lynn's shaking flesh. Lynn reaches up, grabs Doreen, and sobs even harder. Something is eviscerating her from the inside out, and Doreen feels terrible.

"I'm so happy you're not in jail," Lynn gets out between sobs.

"It's okay, baby," Doreen tells her. The maternal order has been restored, and for the first time in a long time, mother is taking care of daughter. She rocks her as she did when Lynn was a girl. Lynn's head is against her chest. She cries a little as she tells her mother that she has left her husband.

This revelation shocks Doreen. She continues to rock Lynn while wondering how she could have missed the signs. Had she been so involved in her sins that she didn't even recognize her daughter's failing marriage? All those times she went over there to borrow money, could she not have asked? Not even once?

An armed officer casually walks around the entryway to Hawthorne Hospital. He wears dark sunglasses though it is a cloudy day. Overcast, but as hot as Doreen can remember. She doesn't want to ask Lynn about phoning her husband for a ride, so she comes out and asks her, "How are we going to get home?"

This reality kick starts the crying again. Lynn's head now rests on her bosom. "I love you Mom," she cries. "I'm so sorry our lives are turning out like this. We deserve to be happy, you know. I wish you'd told me that things were going to be this hard."

Doreen goes through the motions, still comforting her daughter, but her mind focuses on the food she will buy when she gets to the store. She sees a basketful of lettuce, carrots, red radishes, apples, bananas and seeds. She sees water, several jugs of water. This memory will sustain her on the long, hot walk she is about to undertake. The possibility of one more beer comes into her field of imagination, but she shoos it away.

She wants to get going before the drugs totally wear off, so she tells Lynn to get up and walk.

After the two women take several steps, a commotion erupts behind them. They look back, and the armed guard has a tall woman in pajamas in a bear hug. Several frantic nurses try to calm the woman down, but she is consumed by a violent attack of hysterics. Doreen and Lynn both shake their heads in sadness. No one knew it was going to be this hard.

STAGE FOUR

TRANSIT

CHAPTER EIGHT

SALVATION

Marian Smythe struggles fiercely with the officer whose arms are wrapped tightly around her. She did not see his face when she ran by, barefoot in her hospital-issued pajamas, but she did hear the pleas of the two nurses chasing after her as she ran out of the building. "Stop her. Stop her," they panted in unison.

Marian met both nurses after she had been admitted to the psych ward on the seventh floor of Hawthorne Hospital. During her initial evaluation, Marian had admitted that yes, she did want to hurt herself. She had wanted to do deleterious things to herself for as long as she could remember. Now, she just wants to leave the hospital. After issuing her a private room and letting her change into white flannel pajamas, which are strictly starched and several sizes too large, a broadly built male nurse had injected her with something (he didn't say what) using a large hollow needle. She can still feel the sting of the intrusive metal in her upper arm.

While Marian may have wanted to hurt herself, she had also grown physically sick from all the awful things others had done to her. The needle was the last straw. She didn't come to the hospital to continue suffering and decided quickly after the shot that she needed to flee. She never got around to mentioning the prick that raped her, but she figures that no one in this hospital actually cares. Check that, no one anywhere actually cares.

Marian has been pouring her heart out in late-night drug and drinking sessions for years. She has cried about her problems over the phone to her mother, who is always exasperated. No one ever understands Marian, and she sees that today will not be any different.

The officer, who holds Marian so tightly that she can't flail her arms, certainly wouldn't understand. For all she knows, he is the same guy who sent her over this final ledge of sanity. She strains her neck down in a vain attempt to bite him, but his hands are too low on her body for her teeth to reach.

The large male nurse grabs one of her arms, and the security guard (who, turns out, is not the same guy) takes the other. They pull her back into the hospital. Once inside, panic starts to well up within her. She already felt like the walls were slowly closing in, and each of the frequent bursts on the public address system is a personal accusation against her. In the brief time she escaped into the sweltering afternoon air, someone must have turned up the volume, she thinks. The voice relentlessly paging others is screaming directly into her ears, at least this is the way it seems.

Marian looks around at the people surrounding her and barks, snarls at them. Strangers give a wide berth as the two men lead her to the elevator and back to her room upstairs. She struggles a bit but realizes this is no use.

"Why is everyone out to get me?" She screams into the artificially cooled air. The nurse mumbles something about being here to help her, but she knows he is lying. Everyone always lies to her.

An electronic box with numbers like a telephone sits on the wall next to the door to her room. The nurse presses in a code, and Marian hears a click as it opens. She hasn't noticed the security lock feature until now. The officer nods to the nurse but ignores Marian. The nurse leads her into the small room, with a bed draped in blue, thick windows and small television. He pushes a button on the wall and starts speaking into a metal grill.

Marian doesn't listen closely to the man, who still has his fingers curled around her arm, but she hears him say things like "sedate," and "thorazine." She laughs because this man is under the illusion that he can control her. He tries to utter soothing words, but they approach Marian's ears as indistinct syllables of threat. She knows she cannot trust him and is ready to fight again. Both of her fists are curled into tight squares, and her long fingernails cut into her palms, drawing little rivulets of blood.

Another nurse, a short woman with black spiked hair, joins them in the room. She holds a small paper cup and a handful of pills. The male nurse restrains her while the woman force-feeds the pills into Marian's mouth then massages her long throat until she has no choice but to swallow.

After a minute, the man releases his grip and excuses himself. The woman does not speak to Marian, who sits on the bed in defeat. The woman stands with her back to the door and fidgets as if she is waiting for something. If she expects me to fall over because of those damn pills, she is going to be here awhile, Marian thinks.

Marian's tolerance to all things chemical is astronomical. She has mixed many prescriptions with black market goodies; she is the ninth wonder of the world for still being alive. If she can handle a mound of cocaine in conjunction with five bars of benzos, she can handle the puny pills with which this nurse is trying to attack her. At least twenty minutes have passed, and the clock hands stand upright at the perfect symmetry of noon. Marian doesn't feel any different. The grooves in her palms have grown deeper, and the blood continues to trickle, leaving paisley marks on the blue cloth serving as a blanket for the bed.

Marian takes stock of all the drugs she has ever done. She started smoking pot in high school, when she was a seemingly normal teen who made mediocre grades and stayed out of major trouble. Her mom found the first sack of weed she ever purchased (in a flattened sandwich bag that smelled like gasoline) and promptly threw her out of the house. At first, Marian saw this as an excellent opportunity. She fought often with her mother and hadn't seen her father much (at all) since their divorce when she was ten. She hardly knew her little stepsisters; moving in with them would be a good opportunity to repair relationships.

Her plan unraveled as soon as she stepped foot in her father's house. His new wife hated her, talked down to her every chance she got. The wife didn't even want Marian eating dinner with the rest of the family -- told her that she might be a bad influence on the little girls. So Marian ate alone in the office they had hastily thrown a dusty bed into for her sleeping needs. After a mere eleven days (and no apparent fighting), her father came in and kicked her out of his house. Said it just wasn't going to work out. Marian hasn't spoken to him since.

Two months removed from her living with mother, Marian was sleeping on a couch in an apartment belonging to the older brother of one of her high school friends. She quit going to school and started smoking methamphetamine with him and his friends. She discovered the excesses of alcohol and starting working as a hostess in a restaurant to support her new habits. She doesn't remember much of that time, but as far as she knew, life was going great.

She didn't speak to her mom for nine months but did show up at the house for Christmas, expecting a happy reunion. Instead, her mother nagged her about being so skinny and strung-out. She accused her daughter of having aged ten years in the span of one. Said she was disgusted. Marian left, and later that night, injected cocaine for the first time. From the first moments after it entered her bloodstream, Marian, for the first time, felt okay and at home in the world.

The female nurse mistakes Marian's silent memories for sedation and punches a code to allow her to leave the room. Marian breaks back down into tears. "I'm all alone again," she cries. She gets up and looks out the window, sees families waiting on the lawn.

Her situation demands attention inside of her. Her outrage has taken the form of a snake that rises up through her windpipe. "Alone, alone," she says to the people seven floors below, but they don't hear her. Just like always, Marian thinks, the rest of humanity has betrayed me. She thinks of David, the latest in her long line of lovers, about how he wouldn't answer her phone calls. She thought he might give her some comfort after the rape at the Fallout Lounge, but no.

She thinks of her fat boss and his cruelty. The memory leads her to shake. She trembles in every extremity. She wills herself to shake harder, trying to exorcise the snake out of her innards. It doesn't budge. She is shaking so hard, she doesn't hear anyone re-enter the room, so the "Hey, are you okay," totally surprises her.

Karma stands inside the room with the female nurse. Marian can't trust either. She can't trust anyone at all.

Karma and the nurse continue to speak to Marian in a futile attempt to calm her down; in her ears, their words are distorted and nonsensical. She can see motion in their lower facial areas, but the sound pouring out is a low and murky hum. Back up against the windowpane, Marian tries to hold them off with her swollen eyes. Both Karma's and the spiky-haired nurse's faces are full of menace. She knows they have come to hurt her even more. Everyone on this planet wants to hurt her.

Karma makes a slow but sudden move toward the window, and Marian reacts by raising her long arms over her head, a wild animal on the verge of an attack. Karma stops in her tracks and resumes the low humming noise. Marian starts chirping loudly. To the other two in the room, her shrill threats suggest something sinister and dinosaur-ish, like they had wandered into the wrong scene of *Jurassic Park*. Marian continues to shriek while the other two women back up slightly toward the door. The situation is becoming highly unpredictable. Marian's new medications are producing undesirable results, which can happen in psychiatric emergencies.

Marian registers that she feels as she did during her erstwhile LSD trips. The surrounding noises are ominous, and she feels queasy as her stomach adjusts to the chemical intruders and a shifted reality. Colors all around her are highly pronounced, and something threatening is just at the edge of her field of vision, no matter which way she turns. Something horrible lurks, but she can't yet identify it. Not a pleasant trip at all.

Because Karma and the nurse are blocking the door, Marian considers flying out the window. She spins on the ball of her foot and presses her forehead against the thick glass. Several dozen people are milling around on a sea of dead golden hay on the ground far below her. They look like cockroaches, she thinks, but I can fit in with rodents. Marian wants to be down there with them, not in here where the threats are so heavy, calling out to her through a voice in the ceiling.

Marian starts to beat her fists against the thick, double-paned glass. She calls out for the cockroaches to notice her, to scale the walls and come rescue her from this prison. No one looks up in her direction. She stops banging, sensing the pointlessness, and demonic whispers swirl in the atmosphere surrounding her head. She can't decipher what it is that these whispers are saying, so she strains to listen. Uneasiness like nothing she has ever experienced weighs her down. The PA continues to accuse her of wrongdoings. She hears the accusations from the faceless announcer. He describes in detail how everyone at the hospital is planning to dismember her, limb by limb.

A cool breeze appears to her right, and when she looks, a tiny, fat man is standing next to her against the window. He can't be more than four-and-a-half feet tall. He wears thick bifocal glasses and has a peculiar haircut - longer on the top but shaved on the sides. She is certain she has never seen this man before. In a brightly colored Hawaiian shirt and clashing plaid shorts, he looks out of place at the hospital.

"Hi," he says. "I'm Atticus."

Marian allows her muscles to relax a bit in his presence. He, unlike the others, speaks as clear as the night sky. She can make out every pockmarked little scar on his face, and he has an air of having suffered, just like she has. Marian knows immediately that Atticus is her ally.

"You know they want to kill you, right?" Atticus says as he points toward Karma and the nurse, who are still looking blankly at Marian.

"In fact, they are going to pump you so full of shit that you can't move, and then they are going to burn you alive. If you don't believe me, I'll show you the furnace in the basement."

Marian just stares at him, saying nothing.

"Also," he continues. "See that thing up in the ceiling." He points to what looks like an air vent. "That thing is recording all of your thoughts. You would not believe the kinds of technology these people use. Their plan to get you in here was so elaborate, you know.

"You should probably think about protecting yourself before it's too late," he says this last part in a loud whisper.

Karma and the nurse are talking, too, but unlike Atticus, who projects clarity, their voices are transformed by a wave-like wah-wah-wah.

Atticus smiles. He seems to be enjoying playing the role of informant for Marian. He repeats everything he just told her, in case she didn't get his messages the first time around.

After he has gone over his information, verbatim, he points to the telephone on a plastic tray that swings over the unoccupied bed. "They also tapped the phone," he says. "Look at that thing. You have no idea what it's capable of recording. If they knew what you were going to say, they would burn you even longer. They know all about you. Tsk, tsk, tsk. These technologies they have – it's a crazy hegemony. Crazy, I tell ya."

Marian lunges forward, knocks the receiver off the large phone base and takes the connecting cord into both hands. The unit is the old-fashioned kind that joins to the wall via another cord. The face of the phone has white buttons, grayed by use, and the handset cord is off-white and curly. Marian hasn't seen a phone like this in years. She figures that they would use something anachronistic like this to trap her.

She takes the cord and pulls it apart with a surprising burst of force. Karma and the nurse back up all the way to the door with surprise and worry painting their brows.

Marian only straightens out the cord; it does not break. She doesn't relent for a second. The wires rub marks across her already-sore hands, but the pain only incites her more. She has to destroy this phone before they trap her. Atticus eggs her on.

169

Marian suddenly screams at the other two people in the room. "I know what you're doing," she yells rabidly. The plastic coating of the cord breaks, and she continues pulling until several of the inside wires have unraveled and severed. She picks up the receiver, yells a resounding "fuck you" into it then throws the light piece of plastic at the opposite wall. She strains so hard, the ligaments on both sides of her neck protrude to unhealthy distances.

Marian's body now tingles all over, like every ounce of her has been asleep in some terribly uncomfortable position. Atticus is behind her; she hears him congratulate her on destroying the phone. "I knew you could do it," his little, tiny voice repeats over and over. "Hey, do you smell the roses," he demands out of the blue.

She does indeed smell the roses. The scent is so overpowering, the thought that someone made a perfume out of a rose garden in bloom crosses her mind. The flowery stickiness crowds her nostrils. The smell is so strong it nearly chokes her.

"Will you believe that?" Atticus says.

Marian, suffocating, screams again. Karma and the nurse hurry out of the room saying something she can't understand.

Marian needs to find the source of the sickly sweet odor. She thinks that they may have put the flowers in every hidden space just to trick her. She hops over the bed, goes into the adjoining small bathroom and pulls the shower curtain back, but she doesn't find any roses. She tries to lift the porcelain top of the toilet tank, but it is screwed onto the body. She goes back out in the room, crouches and looks under the bed. No roses. Incredible.

After looking behind every surface and in the pillowcases, Marian is spent; she gasps for air. The oxygen infusion in her alveoli settles her a tad, but she is still on the verge of paranoid anaphylaxis. She concludes that someone sent the person in the next room a gazillion roses. Bastards.

The smell is too much. Atticus holds his nose in protest. He has been following her through her search, pretending to help but actually only observing her. Atticus gasps and chokes like he is perishing from smoke inhalation. Marian feels she is perishing from the roses. She lies on her back on the bed, trying to breathe. She pounds her chest in an attempt to jumpstart her lungs. She starts thinking about how no one would ever send her a single rose - much less several thousand. Tears re-form in the outer corners of her eyes.

She remembers Atticus, certain that he would send her roses. She lifts her head to ask him, but the little man is gone. She calls out. No response. Marian has never felt so hopelessly alone in her entire life. The weight of the rose odor presses down heavily on her.

She sobs gently for what seems like an eternity. Out of nowhere, Atticus calls out to her from the other side of the door. "Hurry," he says in a hushed but pungent tone. "Come on. It's not locked."

Atticus is correct. In her haste to leave the room with a potentially violent Marian, the nurse has neglected to reset the code. Even after four years of working in the emergency psychiatric ward, animalistic fury knocks this particular nurse off kilter.

Marian gets up off of the bed and goes to look at her face in the bathroom mirror. She can't hold her gaze on her eyes - they are ringed with a brownish purple ugliness. The irises are devoid of life. Her hair hasn't been washed for days; strands have congealed together into thick, oily gangs. Her bangs hang to the right side, but the rest of her hair is short and spiked. She runs her hands up and down the back of her head then sighs. She can't go anywhere looking like this, dressed in these ginormous pajamas.

Atticus calls out again from the hallway. "Hey," he yells a little louder, "Aren't you coming? All clear out here."

Marian, feeling she has no choice in the matter, tries the metal door handle and, sure enough, it opens. Atticus is right there underneath her, smiling and waving. "Welcome to the world," he says.

An orderly with a mop bucket walks by but doesn't say anything. When he is many feet behind them, Atticus tells Marian to run. "Quietly," he reminds her.

Marian's bare feet make gelatinous thumps on the tile but do not seem to be attracting any attention. When they approach the nurses' desk, which is manned by a lone, unrecognizable woman, Atticus tells her to start crawling and not stop until she gets to the elevators.

She does as told, and the hallway is preternaturally quiet. She makes it to the edge of the elevator hall then disappears inside, sits against the wall, and pulls her knees to her chest.

She can hear Atticus before she seems him, skidding to a halt and cursing. "Dammit. Dammit," he says with a trace of nervous energy. He is pacing with his short little steps.

"We're found out. They always find out. It was that telephone, I bet." He continues pacing, mumbles something about "technologies."

Marian expects to see that menacing spiky-haired nurse. Whoever appears will grab her and force her to return to that rose-smelling prison, she thinks. The smell lingers in the elevator hallway, but here, it is not as overwhelming.

Instead of a nurse, Marian sees a tall, pale woman in thin white robes standing between her and the light fixture in the ceiling of the hallway. Marian assumes she is another patient.

Atticus raises his fists as if he would like to fight, but the woman's presence comforts Marian.

Inexplicably, the tall woman calls her name, "Marian." The timbre of her voice is warm and velvet-y. She folds her hands and tells Marian to "atone and reinvigorate." She forgoes the hard t, so it sounds like she is saying 'a-tun." Her voice is like the perfect cooling of the breeze.

The woman draws Marian into a trance. She can't take her eyes off the stranger's face, though her position relative to the light prevents a clear picture from emerging.

She has forgotten all about Atticus, who starts yelling directly in her ear to snap her out of this spell. "She is one of them," he explains with urgency. "She's going to hurt you, too, if you don't watch what you say. Keep your mind blank, or she'll use your thoughts against you. There are microphones everywhere. Even in your head," he says. "This woman is a spy. S - P - Y. She absolutely cannot be trusted."

The woman hears every word but does not react to the insults. She offers no explanation or defense but begins to cry. The layers of sadness peel off her and mist the floor. She does not move; two enormous tears appear right under her eyes. Both take an agonizingly long slide down her cheekbones toward her nose, over her lips, then off her chin. Both teardrops land on the floor. Marian raises her hands so that her face won't get splashed.

The same orderly with the mop bucket walks by and looks at Marian. He purses his mouth but continues on his way. Marian doesn't know whom to trust, so after an acceptable amount of time, she looks into the main hall, sees that it is empty, and scampers to the windowed wall at the near end of the wing. A smaller corridor, with only a few doors on each side, opens up to her left. A sign announces her arrival in the "Philip Cannifer Wing."

The woman is suddenly in front of her, holding out her pale hands. Marian notices that the woman's fingernails are painted a bright scarlet red. The woman motions for Marian to follow her then disappears behind a closed door to the left.

Atticus looks defeated. "We can't outrun her," he tells Marian. "She always finds us." He leans roughly back on his heels in a show of frustration. He disappears through the same door. Marian follows.

Atticus, the crying, quiet woman and Marian crowd into a supply closet that has also accidentally been left unlocked. Shelves line three walls from floor to ceiling. A four-by-six-foot space is the empty center of the room. An energy-efficient, low wattage light bulb illuminates the scene.

Marian surveys the contents of the shelves. On the left are the rubber items - gloves, mats and bags. Directly in front of her are upright, open little boxes with odd labels. She doesn't know what Ethilon, Plain Gut, Silk, and Ethilon Excel are, and she doesn't feel the need to find out.

To her right is a soft fabric collection: a folded pile of white linens that Marian unravels and finds to be straightjackets. A plastic tray with a peel-off lid sits haphazardly in between those and a pile of pillowcases. Atticus urges her to pick it up, and the woman continues to cry.

Marian lifts the tub off the shelf above her and peels the translucent lid back. Inside is a collection of two-inch razor blades. Marian takes one of the cold metal pieces in her hand, letting the rest of the box fall to the floor. Razor blades now litter the clean concrete floor, but none of the room's occupants seem to notice.

Marian carefully turns the blade in her hand onto its other side. Perfect symmetry, she notices. The smell of roses has returned, temporarily distracting her from her new possession.

The scent, more concentrated this time, seems to emanate from every object in the room, culminating in a roar of olfactory trauma in Marian's head. She can't take it but is too tired to run.

The vision of the metal blade, in its splendor of hard angles, expands as she regards it. It calls out to her, asks her to play with the possibilities. She maneuvers it with her fingernails until the broad, dull edge is between her thumb and index finger. She strengthens her grip, straining the team of minute muscles in her index finger. Fascination overtakes her anxiety. For the first time in months (years, really), Marian feels empowered, in control of her destiny.

Atticus and the white woman, who sobs without sound or tears, say nothing. Marian holds the blade, long and vertical, on her outstretched arm. Very gently and slowly, she applies light pressure and drags the edge down to her wrist. She doesn't draw blood. The sensation tickles, gives her goose bumps.

The closet has no ceiling vent, but the air is so cold Marian can see her breath. Normally, during this part of a Texas summer, the heat would penetrate even the most expensive electricity bills. It is inescapable, except for in here, where an igloo might survive.

She lifts the blade, positions it exactly where it had been before and repeats the motion. This time, she presses a little harder. She draws a scant trail of blood, and the laceration hurts a tad, but the pain is utterly intoxicating, better than she has ever experienced.

Atticus breathes in, audibly savoring the moment. The woman, immobile, sears through Marian with an overwhelming sadness. The overblown rose aroma multiplies, but Marian is too drunk with control to notice. She considers her options.

"My life has been a complete shithole," she tells her audience. "I have no real friends. My family hates me. Dangerous

175

fucking pigs think they own me. My drug problem is honestly out of control, and I can't stop."

Atticus nods, in total agreement. The woman might as well be a statue except for the wordless plea she projects at Marian, who feels the force. The room brightens, casting suspicious shadows on the blade. Marian can almost hear a breeze and the far-off tweet of a bird. The noxious PA announcer is a distant memory.

Marian has been trying to escape her entire life. If she had ever truly wanted anything, she wanted to evade her usual self. She had come pretty darn close, and one more step, she could permanently reach her goal.

So much has been on her mind lately, and the crap has piled into insurmountable heaps. So tall they are, she can't see over all of her issues, and she realizes that, in her hands, she holds the escape hatch.

Panic. Abort mission. She surveys her life and finds nothingness. No reason for anything.

She makes her decision but wants to do one last thing. Just in case, you know. Her estranged father had dragged her to church before he quit the family unit, so an idea of "something else" calls out from her childhood.

Going back in time, she can see the purple floral pattern on her rough, uncomfortable Sunday school dress. She remembers coloring scenes from Noah's Ark. Through her adult journeys, Marian has dabbled in her fair share of yoga, reincarnation discussions, and abundant nihilism (though she couldn't always articulate her beliefs in this manner), so she, like all rationalists, expects to fade to black. She figures that one little plea for pardon can't hurt. Just in case.

She frames the words differently than she remembers, something she heard that guy who drove Karma and her here saying.

"Dear Mary," she starts. "I know I haven't always been the best person. I know I've made horrible mistakes and even treated others unkindly. I've spread so much gossip. I've slept with people I shouldn't have even been looking at. Married men. Women. So many times I don't even remember.

"I meant well, though. I really did. I wanted to ask you for one more thing: that, if possible, you will keep a helpful eye on me in the other side. Not that you did here, but if you will, I would appreciate it anyway."

With the blade still between her fingers, Marian folds her hands into namaste and bows her head.

Suddenly, she hears several muffled shouts of shock from somewhere far down the hallway. She hears frustration, futility and outrage, and she can relate completely. She hears some faint swear words from the hospital room across the hall. Something is happening, but it isn't happening right here, she thinks.

With a sense of urgency, she places the blade back near the crease of her elbow. She presses it down in the path it cut a few minutes ago. More blood. The pain actually hurts her now.

Without warning, the door to the closet opens. The nurse with the spiky hair stands there and takes in the situation. Marian lifts the blade so it isn't cutting her and makes a defensive stance as far in the corner as she can maneuver. "What!" she demands.

"Ms. Smythe," the nurse answers with sadness and surety in her voice. "You're pregnant."

Marian drops the scalpel onto the floor. The sound rings like a bell, a signal of comprehension. She turns to gauge Atticus' reaction, but neither he nor the tall woman is anywhere to be found.

Marian crumples to the floor. She is somewhat pleased but otherwise drained of all emotion. She reaches down to her stomach, which is imperceptibly rounded, and wonders who the father might be. She dismisses the possibility of the pig and admits to herself that the options are numerous.

She had totally quit caring about her fate somewhere down the line, and this bastard would be the consequence. Things could be much worse, she thinks in a dreamlike haze.

The nurse, who looks soft in her dark blue scrubs, kneels down to rest on the balls of her feet. She reaches over, straightens Marian's unruly hair, then unobtrusively picks up several of the blades littering the floor. Marian is dazed, just staring at the shelf with the plastic items. The nurse can't tell how she is responding to the news they discovered on her intake blood work, and she attributes the lack of emotional affect to the cocktail of anti-psychotic drugs swimming through Marian's blood.

Without pausing for a reaction, the nurse launches into a calming explanation of the next steps. "While you're here, Ms. Smythe," she says. "We will need to do some psychiatric tests and figure out what's going on up there. No matter what the problem may be, though, there are treatment options. We see cases like this all the time, and mother and child can go on to lead normal lives."

"I can't pay for all this. I don't have insurance," Marian tells her.

"Oh, don't worry about that," the nurse responds. "The office downstairs has plenty of options. This is America, and we take care of our people. They can help you find all kinds of assistance."

The answer satisfies Marian. She is even optimistic about the future, for once. She imagines that her mother will be pleased by the news. If anything can turn things around, a baby certainly can.

Marian can almost see and hear the mumbling, unfocused

fat face of her child, who will certainly have a better life than she had. She makes that little promise and truly feels like she can keep it.

"Now, you wanna get up and go back to your room? You need some rest." The nurse continues to speak in soft maternal tones, aware that this particular crisis hasn't ended. She knows that if she can get Marian back to a brighter space, safety might be tenable, at least for the short term. She stands up and lifts Marian, who does not resist, from underneath her arms.

The nurse puts one arm around Marian's waist and leads her out of the storage room, which she carefully locks before exiting. The hallways of the psych ward are more active than they previously had been. Several hospital staffers and patients crowd around the main nurses' desk. Or, more specifically, around the TV which has been placed on the uppermost part of the counter for everyone to see. People murmur in helplessness.

Marian pushes the nurse's arm off her waist and finds a spot where she has a clear view of the screen. Scenes of rubble. The sky keeps changing colors, but the overriding theme is a tapestry of jagged concrete. Reporters onsite are in a panic. People are running everywhere, and one live shot goes blank as the cameraman is pushed or falls. More of the same. Whatever these structures were, they have been ruined.

The nurse now stands behind Marian, equally entranced by the horror unfolding in real time. The patients and workers are unified in the camaraderie of shock. The television reveals the terrifying reality that non-nuclear bombs are currently exploding all over the United States.

Authorities urge people to go about their normal routines, but whoever planned these bombings has chosen pedestrian targets. The first happened in Boston's most crowded grocery store. A Wal-Mart in Little Rock, Arkansas has been decimated. Hundreds of cars remain in the parking lot. The traumatized reporter poses the awful question of whether the rightful owners of these cars will ever show up to return the vehicles to their rightful homes.

The anchor comes back on, looking shaken and disheveled. Off script, he expresses his thanks that today is a Saturday. "Our children are not in schools, and government offices are closed. So we can feel a little relief," he says.

In all, 21 bombings have been reported in the last two hours. These acts of terrorism have resulted in untold thousands of deaths. The extent of the tragedy is yet to be understood, but a calm certainty hovers over all of America. Things will never be the same. Even if the country makes it through the day.

The anchor comes back on, contradicts the government employee who spoke earlier and urges people to go home and avoid crowded places.

The patients and hospital staff survey each other. Hawthorne Hospital is a densely populated place. Thousands are inside at this precise moment.

One hospital worker in brightly colored scrubs says to no one, "I have children at home," and tries to leave via elevator, which will not come at her call. She runs down the hall to the emergency stairs and disappears through the heavy metal doorway. An orderly follows her.

For better or worse, everyone else stands together in the seventh-floor psychiatric wing of Hawthorne Hospital. A few shoulders slump, but no one makes any overt signs of distress. They can all smell the roses.

Live shots appear on the TV screen from Darrell K. Royal Stadium in Austin, Texas. Orange-clad fans run through the parking lots as a large cloud of dust follows them. The scene switches to a view from inside the stadium. The east side of the bowl empties quickly. People are jumping over one another in a panic to leave. The other side visibly crumbles as a live television audience watches.

A bomber has targeted one of the most crowded college football games happening in the country. The announcer feels compelled to add that, on the heels of the Mike Black scandal earlier in the week, the Longhorns were losing to the North Texas Mean Green by three touchdowns. All other football games have been called off, he tells viewers.

"Again," he concludes. "Please go to your home or to an uncrowded place and remain calm while authorities get a handle on the situation."

Marian has seen enough. The last few days have been insufferable, and she is not prepared to process any of these new developments, so she shakes everything loose from her mind, leaving a plain white screen. She can't remember where she is supposed to be going, only that she is a very lucky person, so she wanders down the hall. The ferocious sounds of televised bombs pour out of every hospital room, but she no longer notices. The hospital has turned into a cloud, and she wants to ride it to oblivion.

Marian wanders into a room occupied by a sleeping person in a bright yellow robe. The loud hum of the air conditioning unit does not cause this person to stir in the slightest. She feels that this is a place of refuge and that perhaps Atticus will find her in here, so she closes the door and sits on the faux wood and blue fabric chair. Alone with the person, whose broad back is to her, Marian starts to drone in a meditative voice. After making incoherent noises for a few minutes, she consciously strings some notes into "Mary had a Little Lamb." She makes a mental note to learn all sorts of lullabies. She will sing them to her baby as he or she develops in her belly.

When she initially changed into them, the thin flannel pajamas made her skin itch, but now they are fuzzy and comforting. She considers falling asleep right there in the chair but wants to wait for Atticus. Surely he must be wondering where I've gone, she thinks. He must have slipped out when that nurse opened the door.

After she tires of humming, Marian tries to do the breathing she learned in yoga. As she takes equal measures of air into then out of her lungs, pale warmth rises up through her.

She is finally in total peace. She has entirely forgotten about the terrible things happening outside in the world. The sounds of her breath and that of the sleeping person dominate her current reality. Somewhere in her mind, she notes the juxtaposition, even priding herself on the detachment.

Somewhere else inside of her, unheard, she feels truly happy to be alive. The evening sun, far outside the thick windows, suggests a calm autumn day. She imagines playing patty-cake with her little child. She can hear the sound of a bubbling brook. From the vantage point of this hospital chair, the world is a marvelous place.

A desire to console this sleeping person suddenly seizes Marian. She gets up, rests her hand on his shoulder and gently presses down on the muscle connecting his shoulder and neck. He stirs and looks up at her with glassy eyes. She sees that he is an older man (older than her, at least). He needs a haircut and a shave. He reaches up lazily and takes her hand off his shoulder, pulls the covers tight and promptly returns to his slumber.

Marian finds the movement sweet, so she chuckles happily. She imagines that many people inside this hospital need comfort and compassion. What better way to redeem my life than to start giving others the understanding they need, she thinks. She exits the room and floats back down the hallway. Most of the same crowd from earlier is still glued to the television with shock plastered between their ears. She catches a glimpse of the coverage. More of the same American rubble. She feels sadness at the images but doesn't register it as such.

Two nurses right in front of her are engaged in a worried "what if" conversation. Both shuffle their feet nervously. One admits to the other that she wants to go home. That Hawthorne is not necessarily a safe place to be right now. Marian interjects. "It's lovely here," she says. Both look at her with a mixture of amusement and worry. She can't relate to their negativity. "The world is what we make it," she tells them.

The spiky-haired nurse from earlier sees the conversation, walks over, and pulls Marian's hand toward the room she is supposed to be occupying. They get inside, and the nurse tells Marian that she will be just fine in here. By the happy complacency written all over Marian's face, the nurse knows that the desired drugs are in full effect.

Later, when conditions in the world and in Hawthorne start to normalize, they will figure out which exact chemicals the patient needs and which are conducive to pregnancy. For now, the narcotic semi-coma is a perfect state of being.

The nurse explains that she has two daughters and needs to return to her house to calm their nerves. "My husband shouldn't have turned on the TV in front of them. Kids pick up on anxiety, you know," she says.

She promises Marian that lots of competent staff members will remain at the hospital and that "All will return to normal" in the next few days. "For now, you need to get some rest," she says.

Marian climbs into bed, and for the second time in an unbelievably distracted day, the nurse forgets the digital code to lock the door behind her. Marian notices and feels miles away from sleeping. She is so happy and optimistic, she can't even dream of sleeping. After about a half hour of happy reverie,

Marian gets back up and re-enters the hall. She wants to continue her mission to spread cheer.

At least ten people are still glued to the TV, and no one notices Marian try the elevator button. No response - still on lockdown, she sees. Without breaking a sweat, she waits by the doors, willing them to open, half expecting to see Atticus come out of an ascending car. He doesn't, but eventually, the orderly, without mop bucket this time, does emerge from the steel doors.

Marian rushes inside and presses the close button. On a whim, she chooses floor four because of the rhyme. She twists it in her mouth a few times. "Floor four. Floor four," she says into the stale elevator air. The words smell like flowers.

The scene is similar on floor four. Many people are glued to a similarly small television, which continues to project screams and ruin. Marian keeps forgetting about all the bombings, but those things happen on TV, she thinks, not in my world.

She wants to be a volunteer at the hospital, like a candy stripe girl, but she has no candy. She strains her ears to listen for anyone calling for help, and she thinks she hears a plea down the hall to the left.

She follows the perceived cry to another hospital room -- a replica of hers minus the code box next to the door. An unmoving man, whose face is bandaged and swollen, lies under the covers. She sits down next to him and takes his hand softly in hers. He opens his eyes briefly, registers something then closes them again.

The man's forehead is stacked with white gauze, and thick stubble covers the lower half of his face, which has the residue of a bruise spread all over.

A nurse walks in the room and stops in her tracks when she sees Marian. "Oh," she says with her hand over her heart. "I thought you might know this man, but I see you're wearing a hospital bracelet. Just here to visit?"

"Yes, I'm a volunteer," Marian answers.

The woman nods without making a fuss over the obviously incorrect answer then adjusts a drip bag running into the man's veins.

After she is done with her duties, the nurse, whose body is clenched with worry, tells the story. "Poor guy," she starts. "Police found him on the side of the road with a massive head wound a few nights ago. With all the trouble out there, we haven't been able to find out who he is. He lost so much blood, and his heart was real erratic at first. We didn't know if he was going to make it. He did, but still hasn't woken up."

She looks at the sleeping man sadly then concludes, "Probably a good time to be sleeping."

For a split second, both women look elsewhere. Christian Cantrell chooses this moment to lift his eyelids and survey the situation. He doesn't like his surroundings or his company, so he promptly closes them.

CHAPTER NINE

TWO WORLDS

Christian Cantrell opens his eyes for the first time in several days and sees Marian Smythe -- the last person he wants in his field of vision -- so he promptly shuts them closed. His next thought is conscious recognition of the throbbing pain in his head. The sensation's edges are dull, and he ascertains that chemicals are preventing him from feeling the full force of what is happening to his body. He is massively disoriented, doesn't know where he is or how he got here. To begin assembling the puzzle, he re-opens his eyes just a millimeter so that he can take in his surroundings.

His gaze immediately rests on metal machinery; he also notes the firm starchiness underneath his prostrate body. A hospital bed. Dammit. Christian's initial thought about the past is the memory that Marian is trying to get him arrested.

He moves each arm just enough to find that he is not handcuffed to the bed. Thank God. He strains his mind momentarily, trying to piece together the course of events that led him here to this room, but the effort is overwhelming. He sinks back into sleep.

When Christian wakes again, he thinks about his precarious situation before opening his eyes. His hatred of Marian burns as badly as whatever is eating at his skull.

He wills her away from this place then opens his eyes a sliver. He is alone in the room - definitely a hospital room. His vision is hazy, but he can make out the form of his feet underneath a thick blanket. He moves both legs to ensure he is not paralyzed.

He isn't. As far as he can tell, his head is the principal problem. He can feel the swollen skin extending down his face. He reaches up to find a mass of bandages covering his scalp. He moves his head slowly from left to right on the pillow.

Christian wanders back through his memories and finds his prior self at the Dragon's Lair with Karma. He remembers being angry and relives the emotion.

He does not know why he was angry, but recalling the fact that he *was* makes him clench his fist. The movement leads him to earlier that same day. He recalls a fight with his mother, Gladys. She had lit into him about "his lack of direction in life" and told him to find another place to live. He can hear the resounding "kink" of the slap he applied to her face. The bitch! He never could count on anyone.

Gladys and his father, a faceless memory named Mike, are responsible for every little thing that has ever gone wrong in Christian's life. Even with the chemical dulling of his rage, he hates them. He hates that they gave him everything he ever wanted. How was he supposed to learn about life under those coddled circumstances? He can picture the new Ford Explorer waiting in his driveway on his 16th birthday. He doesn't remember even thanking them for it.

187

He pictures piles of presents under the Christmas tree -- an expectation, not a gift, for this only child. He can remember preparing to feel shame as a high school student when he drunkenly stumbled into the house at dawn. He recalls Gladys and faceless Mike laughing, forgiving him in advance for any little thing he might do or say.

The anger boils through him. He is angry that neither Gladys nor Karma is here with him in this damn hospital room. They said they were "there for him," but where are these people now?

He feels as alone as he ever has, as unsatisfied as humanly possible. He wants to yell but doesn't want that bitch Marian to come near him again. He collects quick and troubled intakes of air and tries again to figure out why he landed in this uncomfortable hospital bed.

He closes his eyes to marinate in the mad confusion then hears soft, squeaky footsteps approaching him. He can hear this person fiddling with something -- he doesn't know what -- then another pair of footsteps.

Two female voices start to speak back and forth, but he doesn't think either belongs to Marian. One woman's voice is low and stained with worry. She keeps repeating the word "horrible," which adds to Christian's anxiety. He feigns unconsciousness while trying to derive meaning from the conversation he is hearing.

He catches something about possible airlifts from Austin and disbelief about something happening at a football game. The other voice chimes in, discussing how mad she is that so many others are leaving.

"Who is supposed to take care of everyone?" the high-pitched voice asks.

"We are," the other answers. "Yet another reward for being single and childless."

Christian hears the bitterness in her words. The two delve into conversation about how they just don't understand how the world could have come to this. They touch on religion and its underlying message of love. They speculate about the near future, and when this will all end. Because he cannot understand what they are talking about, Christian is even angrier. He has always been the type of person to be in control of everything, and he has never felt so confused and helpless in his entire life.

The women's talk makes him sick to his stomach, which is empty and unsettled. He wants to escape his body, which is in certain pain, and he also doesn't want to alert these women to the fact that he hears them. Based on the timbre in their voices, he doesn't believe either to be a trustworthy human being. Certainly they will leave him alone soon so that he can make his break.

Flexing his muscles imperceptibly, he scans over his body to make sure it is in working order. As soon as quiet descends over his room again, he plans to flee. Christian still doesn't know why he is here, but he figures the best place to finish putting that story together is elsewhere.

He thinks about his phone and makes a mental note to check the drawers and closet. He is going to need to call someone for a ride, but no name immediately pops in his mind. The women keep talking, now about Jerusalem of all places, and he hates them.

Without warning, Christian feels a hand on his head. Next, he feels hairs tearing out of his scalp and the cacophony of peeling tape. The pain, which had previously been blunted, reaches a fever pitch. Something horrible plagues the skin of his head, and this person is making the sensation worse. He hears her grossed-out vocalizations as she peels another layer. The word "yuck" hits him where it hurts.

The pain is too much, and he can't keep up the ruse.

Christian's anger spills over as he opens his eyes and grabs the woman's forearm. His vision is still blurred, but he registers the wide-eyed shock in the faces of two women dressed in hospital scrubs.

A split second passes before the woman whose arm he is gripping jerks backwards. Christian's grasp does not waver, and the force of the nurse's movement pulls him sideways out of the hospital bed.

The time between when he sees the floor and when he hits it drags on for what seems like minutes. His field of vision darkens as he approaches the tile face-first.

The impact is unforgiving. He hears a loud crack, and all he can see is red. The pain is worse than anything he has ever imagined. For the first time ever, he feels real terror. The consequences of his choices have now become irrevocably severe. He screams. So do both nurses.

An insistent beeping noise rings out through the room. Christian can clearly see the tubes still protruding from his arms. Blood is everywhere - in a pool on the floor, splattering the pants of both nurses, even dotting the wall and the side of the bed.

He has never seen so much blood. The sight brings the incident in the bathroom at the Dragon's Lair back into his conscious mind, and he starts to put two and two together. He watches while one nurse spins and runs full throttle out of the hospital room. The other stands there in shock, her arm pointlessly stretched out to him.

That the pain is no longer with him doesn't immediately register with Christian. He watches the whole thing, detached and majorly confused.

The other nurse returns to the room, running in as quickly as she left and hurriedly tells the other nurse to help her pick him up and that a doctor is on her way. Both are in an obvious panic as, from an upper corner of the room, he watches them lift his motionless body back onto the bed.

Both women are now covered in the crimson of his spilling life. Neither makes any indication of noticing that her hands and arms are covered in red. Christian amusedly thinks that the splattering of red on white looks like modern artwork. His rage is gone, and he feels the easy lift of appreciative laughter.

The volume of the machinery's importunate beeping increases. Christian can read the fatter nurse's mind. He knows that she is bothered by the sound, that she can't focus on anything else because it is so loud.

The thoughts of the other nurse totally surprise him. He senses that she doesn't want to lose him, too, after such a horrific turn of worldwide events. He sees her visions of falling buildings, triage camps and explosions. None of this makes sense to him, but the confusion is no longer a burden. He intuits that this is the end, the apocalypse, and the verdict almost calms him. He is at once in the room and entirely out of it.

The heavier nurse sighs loudly in despair. He knows that she feels guilty for pulling him off the bed (she keeps replaying the vision) and helpless to stop anything. He hears her echo the sad thought that she just wanted to help heal the world.

She moves to re-cover the wound on his head, which continues to bleed through everything she applies to stem the flow. The other nurse yells out into the hallway for a Dr. Martin. She yells the name three times, raising her voice each time in an attempt to best the loud beep of the machinery.

A stern older woman wearing a lab coat over her scrubs enters the room. Without an introduction, Christian knows that this woman is Dr. Philadelphia Martin and that she has arrived to help him.

"What in the world happened here?" Dr. Martin asks in disbelief.

The bigger nurse explains that it was an accident. That he grabbed her with murder in his eyes and he fell off the bed onto his head. Dr. Martin gently pushes her aside and wraps a piece of plastic around his arm to take his blood pressure. She stares at the wound as she drops her head.

"Code blue," she pronounces. She grabs the stethoscope from around her neck and listens to his heart. "Not good," she murmurs as much to herself as to anyone else. She gives an order that Christian cannot decipher to one of the nurses, who quickly leaves the room again.

The nurse returns with a needle and a vial, and without making a fuss, Dr. Martin confidently fills the needle with a clear liquid then injects it into his heart. She listens again, and Christian senses that she is purposely willing away the annoying beep of the machine. Dr. Martin hangs her head one more time and asks for "the cart." Both nurses turn and leave this time. The whole scene perplexes Christian, as if he is watching a movie in a foreign language.

He can read Dr. Martin's mind. She is repeating to herself that she has to save him. Something about liability and waste. He sees her cycle through memories of dying young patients and picks up on her sadness and disappointment.

She absentmindedly puts the stethoscope back onto his chest and shakes her head. She turns to the open door of the hospital room, willing the nurses to return with the crash cart. He hears her ask herself why she chose this profession and whether she should just leave the hospital right now and go home to be with her husband. Speakers inside his mind project her thoughts.

Both nurses return pushing a crash cart. Dr. Martin charges two metal paddles, rubs them together, and places them squarely on his chest. She orders a nurse to press a button. The sound of the electric current is so loud Christian can feel it. He sees his body jump up several inches off the bed. The machine continues blaring its beeps. Dr. Martin repeats the action, then again. Blood is everywhere, dripping off the bed onto the floor.

When Dr. Martin says aloud, "Time of death: 4:43," Christian awakens into the reality of what has happened. Not until this moment has he found the distant, mind reading perspective odd in the slightest. He realizes that he has been dead for a few minutes and starts to panic.

Where is he now? And where is he supposed to go? Although he is weightless and formless in his current state, he still feels very much like Christian Cantrell.

He now has access to all of his memories. He can see himself stumbling out of the Dragon's Lair, bleeding from his head. He watches as he walks several blocks into the neighborhood and collapses. He sees his body lying on the night-darkened sidewalk for what seems like an eternity until two stoned college kids discover him and call 911.

He thinks that someone needs to notify Mike and Gladys but remembers that the hospital doesn't know who he is. He can even remember leaving his wallet at home and his phone on the couch at the bar.

He watches as the bigger nurse, who is racked by guilt, takes the crash pads into her hands and reapplies them. He wants to tell her to quit trying; what's done is done. He even tries to speak to her, but no words escape his mouth. She tries again to no avail.

He feels disgust at the way these people have electrocuted and stabbed the chunk of meat that used to be his body. A sense of acceptance overtakes them as he resigns himself to his new order of being. He admits to himself that he had grown tired of his entitled, meaningless life. He doesn't know what to expect from death but concludes it will probably be an improvement. He has yet to experience any fear.

The scene in the hospital room grows distant. He is still observing Dr. Martin and the two nurses, but they grow smaller and smaller as his perspective is higher and higher. He can almost see the whole city, which is unnaturally quiet early on this hot evening. Then he can see the whole country, then the whole planet, but he is still himself.

The sound of loudly rushing water fills his ears. The noise is so overpowering, it is like his ears are submerged in a tumid springtime river.

Out of the blue of the sky, he feels whatever remains of him being sucked into a grey tunnel. The sides are viscous yet crinkly, and the speed of his free fall through the tunnel approaches quantum levels. He is flying away from everything he has ever known. Unlike the denseness of living in a body, he is weightless and without feeling.

After an eternal yet infinitesimally brief journey through the tunnel, Christian emerges in a warm white light. He assumes an ethereal body that closely matches the one he just left behind, but when he reaches up to touch the hole in his head, he feels no resistance. He exists as pure energy.

He explores the exciting sensation of buoyancy and feels empowered, like he could accomplish anything. Modulated energy courses in and out of him, fueled by the perfect shade of white-pink light that surrounds him in all directions. Christian is in a state of total bliss that eclipses any high he had ever achieved in life.

He notices the beautiful music singing to him from every direction. The sound surpasses anything he has ever heard. It is simultaneously familiar yet altogether foreign. A trillion perfectly clear chimes ring in harmony with one another.

This is the famed music of the spheres, he thinks. He has never heard anything so unearthly and breathtaking. Though the music is not accompanied by words, its depth and meaning overthrow him. The infinite tones are stationary while Christian's imaginary body wanders between them. He, not a beat, controls the way the sounds blend together, and every choice he makes results in a song even more beautiful than the last.

The light all around him is more stunning than any color in the rainbow. In contrast to the brutal heat of the Texas summer, its warmth is all encompassing and sensual.

Floating in the gentle heat and listening to the heavens sound off against one another, he is beyond serene -- even joyous about the fact that he is dead. Though he sees nothing but the light, Christian has never been in, nor imagined, a more beautiful place. The center of his being swells with bountiful happiness he never dreamed might exist.

Christian calls out a jubilant thank you to no one at all. He realizes that death is not something to be feared, but a transition to be embraced. He comprehends that the fearful way people on earth live is silly and simple minded.

If they only knew about this place, he thinks, they would never be scared or make foolish decisions. If they knew, though, they wouldn't want to be there, so maybe it's better that this place is a secret to the living. The juxtaposition of life and death is beautiful in its own right. He wishes he had died a long time ago but perceives that everything in the universe is in exactly the right place.

After he revels in the newfound joy, Christian sees dots of concentrated light moving toward him. As the points get closer, they take shapes he recognizes. Three of his four grandparents now stand before him.

His mother's mother June is still alive, but her former husband Frank is right here. He is not old as Christian remembers him, but a young, vibrant military man that Christian only ever saw in pictures. His father's parents Helen and Thomas stand to his right, both wearing giant smiles and plain country clothes.

Simultaneously, all three tell him how happy they are to see him. The words do not take auditory form but move through him like waves of delight. Grandpa Tom gives him reassurance, which Christian doesn't need, then expresses confusion about why his grandson is here so soon.

"We didn't think this was quite your time," Tom says. "But welcome nonetheless."

Christian feels as if he is looking at his grandfather for the very first time, though he got to spend the first 12 years of his life a few blocks away. Gone is the list of perceived insults and offenses. Gone, also, is the defensive stance Christian has developed toward everyone he ever knew. In place of those things is a boundless love that feels supremely natural.

Christian is so busy basking in the warmth of his family members that he does not notice the two additional beings that take shape next to him. His old friend Marshall literally moves through him to get his attention.

Marshall died in high school after an ugly drunk driving accident. Before his death, he had been cultivating the ragged, unhealthy stoner look, but here, he is hale and powerful. The two wordlessly exchange greetings. Another friend, Dale, is next to Marshall. Dale overdosed on heroin a few years ago, and Christian remembers the young man's mother being loudly devastated at the funeral. Dale picks up on Christian's memory and communicates that everything is okay, that eventually, every mother would understand the universal order of being.

All three grandparents and both friends tell Christian that they had been trying to convince him to make better decisions from this dimension, but that every transgression and cruelty had been immediately forgiven. Christian can't imagine making a wrong choice when every path leads to this wonderful place. Not a fiber of the universe's hair is out of place, he thinks. He is so connected to these people, he feels that he is as much them as he is Christian Cantrell. Every boundary that separates people on earth ceases to exist in the white-pink light, and the unity is beyond delectable.

Grandpa Frank doesn't seem to be in total agreement. Christian senses his concern before he articulates it. "I don't know that you should be here, young man," Grandfather Frank says with serious force. "I'm concerned that your death will be too much to handle for some extremely vulnerable people. You should go back to where you are needed."

Grandmother Helen agrees. "What about that lovely girl Karma?" she asks him. "I think she really needs you. You were meant for each other, you know."

Though Christian does not like what his grandparents are telling him, he feels blanketed by their love and acceptance. He fears that their focus on those he left behind might mean that he has to go back to his clunky body. He has only been here in the light for a brief amount of time, but he is already convinced that he never wants to leave.

He thinks about Karma and his mother Gladys, and he can feel how sad they will be when they learn of his death. The anguish brings a heavy sensation that would have made his body cry, but here, the depth of emotion is exhilarating.

He understands the complex interconnectedness of all things and people. How the way beings feel is what keeps them eternally tethered. Life, while he lived it, had never been so clear in its machinations. Emotions in his life had been a distraction, an inconvenience, but now he sees that feelings are the force behind everything that is.

The beings form a circle and hold out translucent hands. They cannot physically touch one another but consciously send energy through the circle. Grandpa Tom suggests that everyone join forces and pray for the people on earth in their hour of dire need. Although calmness is the undercurrent, everyone other than Christian takes on an air of seriousness.

The light around them brightens, eclipsing available divisions, as they begin to pray. Christian is happy and unencumbered; he does not understand that they are praying for him.

As the group continues to pray, Christian is transported back to the hospital. Though he doesn't physically seem to be in the room like he was when the adventure started, he can clearly see everything happening around his body.

Marian kneels behind Karma, who sobs uncontrollably with her head on the bloody hospital bed. Someone has pulled the hospital blanket over his body's head and removed the crash cart. Otherwise, the scene is exactly as he left it. Both Marian and Karma now stare at the collection of red substance that had once given Christian life.

Karma starts to command, "No! No! This can't be. He can't be dead." She repeats it several times in between pitiful sobs. Marian is silent but there with a firm hand of support on Karma's shoulder. Karma goes on an on and demands into the air that the doctor come back and try again.

Finally, Marian answers. "They did everything they could," she said. "It's over. The doctor has moved on to someone else. She's not coming back. I'm so sorry."

Karma will not accept the proclamation. She turns her head toward the open door and screams at the top of her lungs for someone to get in here and help him.

Christian has never seen Karma so sad and broken. He is honestly surprised that she would react so violently. He has long suspected that her "love" for him was some selfish, disingenuous act.

He tries to send her information but doesn't know how to get her to hear him. He wants her to understand that he is just fine, that in fact, she should be happy for him. He also wants her to stop screaming because the last thing he intends to see is someone else in that room trying to revive what used to be his body.

He continues to focus on Karma until she is the only thing in his vision. He forms words in his mind and tries to force them into her consciousness. He repeats, "Death is a gift. Do not be sad," like a mantra.

In his mind, he articulates every syllable, doing everything he can to get her to understand, but she keeps wailing. He almost pities her but remembers that the living cannot possibly understand the bliss of the dead. He feels no regret, only love for her. But this close to what used to be his own body, he feels a tinge of anger. His whole life, he was paranoid that others were trying to control him. He is bitter that, in death, they will not relent.

He begins to identify completely with the scene in the room and starts to panic when he realizes that his grandparents and old friends have disappeared, as have the sublime music and brilliant light. He doesn't want to be here and wills himself back to the place he had just been.

His efforts work, and he relaxes back into the approaching presence of the white-pink. He says a prayer of his own never to have to go back there, to earth, where suffering and misery are the norm. A voice calls out of nothingness, startling him. "An intelligent person does not need the promise of heaven to see the merit in good deeds," the voice says.

Christian looks around the interminable field of light until a man with long brown hair in a floor-length white robe appears.

He is immense and looks down at Christian like a parent would regard a disobedient child. The man holds a parchment notebook carefully while he waits for Christian to come back into a state of openness and peace.

Christian lets the light penetrate him. When he relaxes, the man, who does not introduce himself, says, "We need to go over a few things here. Don't worry, this is normal procedure."

The man instantaneously appears directly in front of Christian and holds open the notebook, which is alive in a way no piece of technology could ever be. The man points at the book, which then turns to a scene from Christian's childhood.

He and his mother are making Christmas cookies. The little boy is four and dressed in a large red sweater. Both are smiling and happy while they cut reindeer shapes out of the sheet of dough. Out of the blue, Christian turns toward his mother and sweetly says, "I love you Mommy."

Reviewing the scene from this perspective, Christian realizes just how powerful his proclamation was. The man conveys that those simple words carried Gladys through years of marital troubles and the death of her father. Those words from the little boy, by far the kindest he had ever spoken to his mother, gave her a reason to keep living and to show kindness to others.

The man flips the notebook again, and Christian recoils as the next scene begins. He recognizes the t-shirt he had worn a few days prior. He recognizes the intolerable fury he had become and feels utter shame when he watches himself slap his mother.

He can see that she was only worried about him and saying what she thought he needed to hear to get his life back on track. The notebook somehow makes him experience the depression and self-hatred he had inspired in his mother. The man continues to look at him seriously, and he doesn't need to verbalize anything to convey the prodigious mistake Christian had made in treating his mother this way.

The man flips the notebook again, showing an older but still childish Christian kicking his dog for chewing through a video game cord. He senses how bad the dog felt and ties the kick to the dog's untimely death a few months later. That one act had stolen the dog's will to live.

Again, Christian feels remorseful. The notebook shows more scenes he wishes he could take back: making fun of the nerdier kids in high school, leading women on in college just because the lies made him feel powerful, intimidating people as he drove. Christian begins to sense that this man is demonstrating all the ways he had wasted both his life and his inborn love.

The man turns the notebook one last time to a split-screen view. On the left, Christian opens his phone to the "I love you" message Karma had texted him. On the right, he sees himself laugh and immediately delete the message.

He witnesses Karma's shoulders sag, feels the brokenness of her spirit and realizes that he alone is responsible for his cruelty and the exponential effect with which it painted his surrounding world. The more he watches, the more he starts to feel like he caused all the problems, everywhere.

The man finally speaks to him. "You were put on earth to do one thing: to love," he says. "And you failed."

Christian blubbers his apologies. For the first time, he is truly sorry for his behavior. Previously, he didn't realize just how terrible he had been to others. "Why did I do all that?" he asks the man.

"It's not just you," the man answers. "The human way has descended into a path of hatred. Now they have really reached a crisis."

The white-pink light darkens, and the music ceases in a whir. For the first time since he died, Christian is terribly afraid. His religious upbringing floods back through him as he anticipates being sent to hell. The man's final words echo throughout the empty space. "I need you to remember," the baritone voice rings over and over again.

Christian feels a kick at his side. An unceremonious kick. He can feel it in what used to be his ribs as he tumbles back through the same tunnel. As he spins through the blackness, he starts to feel denser and denser. The pressure builds in his ears to the point of unbearability. He is confused and terrified. All he can hear are the words about remembering.

Without warning, he lands with a thud in his body in the hospital bed. The pain in his head is a hundred times worse than it had been before. The sensation of being back in that body is horrific. He screams as loudly as he can, praying a mistake has been made.

Back in his body, Christian attempts to cry out, but his mouth is frozen while a faint sound trickles through his teeth. He hurts like hell all over. In sharp contrast to the bliss he has just experienced, being back in this hospital bed is worse than hell could possibly be. His head is the worst part. It doesn't feel like it is *going* to explode; it feels like it is *incessantly* exploding. From the center of his brain to the outer edges of his skull, Christian's entire head feels like it has been possessed by Satan.

Even parts of his body that are ostensibly unscathed are practically bending under the pressure. His little toes feel like they are being incinerated. Each scant movement of his heart is a starved and impossible journey. The muscle seems to weigh a million pounds or more.

All of him is heavy and buckling under the gravity. The body seems the wrong size as well as crashed and burned. He tries to make his spirit escape. He can make his ethereal body move slightly left and up, but for all practical purposes, he is tethered to this throbbing chunk of flesh. This realization leaves him bitter and devastated. He wants to be anywhere else in all of existence except for right here. Something oppressive holds down his breath, and each intake feels like a thick cloud of smoke.

Christian can't believe that he is still alive. Not in this condition. Not when he knows that he doesn't have to be. He silently begs God, Jesus, Mother Mary and the universe to free him from the shackles of life.

He can see the five praying people in a circle, shortened by one link, and he knows they can hear his pleas. Why won't they help me, he wonders.

He can still hear the delicacy of those sublime melodies. He can remember the soft and velvety warmth of the spectacular light. He can remember how happy he felt, so he is deeply affected by the cruelty of his pain. He imagines it to be much worse than anyone has ever experienced, anywhere.

He tries to adjust to the reality of his suffering for a few minutes before he remembers the disastrous life review. While up there, he had felt remorseful for all he had done. Here, the poor decisions manifest as a broken, limping body. The memories intensify his pain a few additional degrees, which he didn't think could be possible. Since no praying people are answering, he tries to beg for Karma, who he thinks is still in the room.

He musters everything inside of him and tries to say her name. The word comes out in a barely audible croak. So quiet, his plea is like a speck of dust settling on the floor. For the purpose at hand, worthless.

She doesn't answer. No one can hear him through the thick blanket cloaking his face. The lack of response is another dagger. If he could do so, he would say how sorry he is for all the terrible things he has done. He wants Karma to help him now, when he needs it the most, but she is gone, which she should be.

He would do anything for the pain to stop, but it is everywhere -- inside his jawbones and in the marrow of his shins.

He tries again to call for anyone who might help. His breath is such a challenge, making noise a worthless endeavor. A hot presence blankets all the air he is exchanging with the room. He opens his eyes, but they are crusted, swollen shut with brown blood. He strains the muscles in his forehead. They scream in defiance but eventually relent, allowing a dark, muted light to filter in through the eyeballs. Christian is still stuck under the blanket, which is so thick it nearly suffocates him.

Christian takes on a depression ten times worse than his frequent bouts with being low. Being away from his ecstatic bliss is distressing enough, but the memory of the memories of all the pain he has caused is what really crushes him. As punishment for all the terrible things he did to it the first time around, Christian is being shoved back into the brokenness of humanity.

The insistent fire from his head and elsewhere is the culmination of all the wrongs he has ever caused. This realization is awful and somehow makes the pain even worse. His sides feel like they are rolling upward toward his armpits.

He believes that if he stays perfectly still, no one will ever find out that he isn't dead. As is, he feels like he is hovering between two worlds, and a repeat of the ending cannot be too far away.

He stays motionless, trying not to breathe until he hears the word "remember." The word flies around his body, hurting everywhere it lands but somehow healing him, too. The more the word makes its presence felt, the more Christian realizes that he needs to go on with whatever life this will be. He must do his best to change the ways of the world. The worst possible fate would be to have to relieve another failed life review. The memory of the shame compels him to make a movement.

Christian gingerly reaches up and pulls the blanket off his

face. The hot, polluted light burns the portion of exposed retina. In addition to the flames of pain singeing every nerve ending, the heat in his body is oppressive. He sweats out what little moisture remains. He feels the dryness in his mouth and tastes the scars of his blood where it pooled and dried inside his mouth. The bitterness of the iron disgusts him.

After a minute, he hears his heart assume some sort of slow regularity. Its rhythm is faint but undoubtedly there. In turn, he takes breaths that supersede shallow. Slowly, Christian comes back to life. He wills his eyes open a little more and sees his blood spattered on the walls.

Everywhere, really.

He cries out for help again. This time, he can hear that he makes a sound, even if the room is empty, and no one else can hear. Karma really isn't here with me, he decides.

As the outside light fades into the early evening, a man with a mop bucket makes his way into the room. The man, who is skinny and nervy-looking with wire-rimmed glasses, surveys the room and starts whistling "Zip-a-Dee-Doo-Dah." Christian tries to move his arms, to speak, but the man is focusing on the blood he has to clean. He doesn't even seem to notice the body in the middle of the room. He is probably used to these sights, Christian thinks. After all, he is in a hospital.

The man pulls out his mop and first attacks the lower tile portion of the wall. He continues to hum, "Zip-a-dee-day." He moves a little closer to the bed, and Christian exerts himself as much as possible, raising then lowering both hands.

The movement catches the man's attention. He watches for a second, so Christian does it again. The man's eyes grow wide, and he drops the mop. He holds out his palm as if to ward off the bloody, immobile man then turns and runs from the room.

After a handful of seconds, Dr. Philadelphia Martin, breathless, runs in the room to see with her own eyes. Christian is now sitting up in the bed, cradling his head in his hands. Bewilderment has been transcribed over her face and posture.

"I've never seen anything like it," she says out of the side of her mouth. She doesn't directly address Christian as she explains, "He had bled out. I checked three times, and there was no heartbeat. He was dead. As dead as I've witnessed."

Finally, she looks directly at him and proclaims, "This is a miracle." Dr. Martin is a perfectionist, and she can't help but blame herself for the near-catastrophe. She steps over the mop, which rests where it was dropped, shuffles to the bedside, maternally puts her hand on his leg, and apologizes profusely.

The orderly stands in the open doorway, his jaw wide open in shock.

The word sorry spills from the very depth of her soul. Christian is touched by her manner. He had watched, after all, as she tried her best to save him. He had even tried to prevent her from doing so.

"I almost made a terrible mistake," she tells him. "We thought we had lost you. It's been such a hard couple of days. I am so, so sorry."

"Understandable," he manages to mutter. She knows that this young man has awakened to a much different world than the one he fell unconscious in. She shudders as she thinks about his unintentionally prophetic word.

Christian doesn't move much (because doing so causes serious pain) as she peeks at his head wound through his hands and takes his blood pressure again. She shakes her head as she reads the measurements. She is still in disbelief. She asks him who he is and does he have family they can call. She says they have been waiting for him to wake up for a few days. That all the nurses felt so sad for him. Dr. Martin was not on the floor during Karma's meltdown earlier in the afternoon.

Christian croaks out the names of Michael and Gladys Cantrell. The orderly nods and rushes to tell someone.

Christian finds the fact that he can't remember their phone numbers funny. He is not sure if he actually does know them or if technology has driven that large a wedge through humanity. He would make a joke about it, but he is far too weary. He notices that Dr. Martin is sort of slipping over the blood that still covers most of the tile floor. He wonders how he is possibly alive.

The fatter nurse, who winces like she has been stung by a bee, enters the room with several IV bags on wheeled poles. He asks her about Karma, but the word comes out more like army. He asks again, but both Dr. Martin and the nurse wag their heads uncertainly.

"I don't know, honey," the nurse finally admits. "It's really been such a madhouse around here." She pauses then adds, "I'm glad you're back, sweetie."

Dr. Martin proclaims that he needs to rest.

"Lucy here will get you going and rehydrated. She'll also help out with the pain a bit. I really need you to get some sleep. We'll figure all this out later," she says. She then gently pushes his chest until his back is on the bed. She looks at him, takes a deep breath and slowly leaves.

Nurse Lucy giggles nervously as she attaches new IV tubes into his left hand. The blood and drugs being infused into his veins make Christian feel as if the parched earth has just met the rain. The opiates kick in immediately, and life once again feels bearable.

The pain is still there but much less sharp than it has been. He feels like he can think a little more clearly and tries to process what just happened to him. He remembers every inch of the experience and is rattled, but increasingly placated.

Lucy wipes his face with a wet cloth, and without the mask

of blood, Christian feels a bit like a human again. Sated, he drifts into a superficial sleep. He dreams of light and sound and drifting. The drugged sleep is a welcome and familiar relief, but he misses the white-pink perfection.

When he opens his eyes again, the room is lit only by the fading daylight. This is the certain time of the day in which the gloaming illuminates the dust particles. The feeble rays coming in through the window fall directly on Marian Smythe, who sits in a chair by the wall. She is staring straight into the evanescent light, lost in thoughts about the mystery of it all.

Christian breaks her reverie by inquiring about Karma. The sound of his voice startles her, and she shakes her long arms before sitting upright.

"Where is Karma? I need her," he repeats.

Marian almost looks scared, but at least she treats him like a kindred soul. "I cannot believe this shit," she tells him. "You are going to flip when you find out about everything that's happened. Oh man, it's bad, bad, bad."

He doesn't know what is so bad but sees how deeply it affects Marian, whose body lazily slumps back into the chair. He understands that she is suffering and immediately adopts her exact emotion. He consciously tries to share her burden, and as a result, she lifts and her face brightens. Because he feels compelled to do so, he apologizes for being "such an asshole" to her.

"Oh, it's fine," she says, dismissing his reparation. "With everything that's happening, none of that shit even matters."

Christian assumes she is talking about his encounter with the afterlife and wonders how she knows. Maybe she had the same experience, he thinks.

In her reality, Marian is talking about the series of bombings happening in cities all over the world. She doesn't want Christian to find out in his vulnerable state. His parents are on their way, and she decides to give them the privilege of imparting this information. Still, she does foreshadow with a few words. "Terrible," she mutters quietly. "Terrible world. I hope it's salvageable."

What does Marian know about salvation, he wonders. Although drugged and in pain, he is, at long last, thankful to be alive. He doesn't want to waste his second chance.

Marian gets up and goes over to the window. "There she is," Marian says while pointing down to the ground below.

"Who?" Christian asks.

"Karma," Marian says with a little hesitation in her voice. "She's leaving."

Marian does not mention that Karma is leaving in a bright yellow Mustang.

STAGE FIVE

VISIONS

CHAPTER TEN

ATTEMPTING REDEMPTION

Karma calls him Javier, an identity he has inwardly discarded. The mention of that name inspires a mental picture of his false family, probably on its way back to Mexico by now. He drives the yellow Mustang away from Hawthorne Hospital, and for all intents and purposes, away from life as he has known it.

He tries to ask her about that girl Marian, but Karma seems shaken, almost comatose. He uses the silence to pray again, which is what he has been doing all day. After he dropped them off at the hospital, he headed straight for the Muslim Men's Center, where he and a small group of men prayed all afternoon before telling each other a cursory goodbye, not looking one another squarely in the eye.

Hafiz, even as Javier, prays relentlessly. Remaining devoted while masquerading as a workingman has not been an easy task, but Hafiz would pray while piling pasta atop plates, while driving, while ruminating on the sinful American ways. No one ever figured out that he spent every morning at the men's center, where his prayers, in conjunction with his secret community, took on a whole new level of fervor.

Less than an hour ago, he was on his way to his target destination, letting incantations roll off his tongue as he turned the steering wheel, carefully avoiding disrupting the violent cargo in his trunk. He hadn't expected Karma to call his cell phone. He had mentally said goodbye to her for the last time, but her reappearance, like all developments in his life, must have been a sign. He has a few hours to spare, and traveling with an innocuous white woman would make him less suspicious. He looked past her Godlessness and decided to retrieve her from the hospital. Another curfew has been imposed on the city, but it doesn't take effect for another two hours.

He tries to ask her again about the hospital, but she is too morose to communicate. Her eyes are puffy, an odd mix of red and yellow. He doesn't know what sorts of things she might have witnessed at the hospital, and at this point, he doesn't see any reason for prying.

He focuses instead on the lavender dusk. The sky is calm and serene, which comforts him, shows him the presence of divinity in all things. He is so engrossed in trying to maintain his humble connection with Allah, he doesn't see her move to flip on his car radio.

The news channel they had listened to earlier returns to the speakers. He understands the English better than he lets on, not that she offers a word of translation. Unsurprisingly to him, the domestic bombings are intensifying.

Their Texas town is the largest place in the United States yet to experience any form of terror, although a shopping mall in nearby Dallas has been destroyed. Because of the chaotic nature of the day, the crowds were lighter than they could have been, but the casualties were enormous.

The radio announcer declares that no organization has taken responsibility for any of these horrific acts, but that counterterrorism officials believe this to be a coordinated attack by an international network of radicals.

Hafiz has listened to many reports on domestic terror; he does know much of the lingo. He chuckles inwardly as the whine of locusts intensifies in the air outside of the car. Bugs love the waning hours of light, but people go crazy, he thinks. He has long since written off the vagaries of this gaudy, unfamiliar world and feels no remorse for its impending demise. People and their sacrilegious ideas have gotten so far out of hand, and if humanity will flourish in the future, people like him are necessary mercenaries. Allah wants these dramatic changes - he has told Hafiz as much.

The word responsibility rings through his head. Responsibilidad in Spanish. Most use it to take the edge off of boring or difficult tasks, but the meaning is much more to Hafiz, who feels he has the responsibility not only to avenge the murder of his own family but also to help usher in an age of absolute obedience.

Karma finally turns to him to speak, asks if he understands what martial law means. He makes a vague nodding motion, leaving his answer inscrutable.

Of course he knows, he thinks to himself. After all, Hafiz Al-Assad has been planning this day for most of his life. He knows that martial law means nothing at this point. His piece in the puzzle is just that - the big picture will unfold with or without his involvement. Martial law does mean that this final mile of journey is that much more treacherous, but he has surpassed an avalanche of obstacles just to get to this point. The little clock inside the suitcase in his trunk is already clicking, so, barring a complete reversal of heart, his own fate has been sealed.

He pictures the bounty awaiting him in the afterlife while he listens to the locusts, which are currently roaring in warning - not that anyone is listening.

Karma is quiet again. She turns up the volume on the radio in perhaps an attempt to offset the noise of the locusts at the edges of her conscious ears. The announcer tells a story about widespread looting of grocery stores all over the country. The sound clips cut to a regional water expert who claims that tap water is still okay to drink, but to be on the safe side, people might want to consider boiling it. Hafiz has been taking residential streets as much as possible all day, so he can't affirm or deny claims of chaotic, mob-like behavior in this city. The announcer then repeats his words twice while urging people to remain calm.

Karma slumps back in the passenger seat of his Mustang, seemingly defeated. She is calm, very calm, he thinks. Her head hangs down in obvious depression, but he can't veer off track by delving into her own private world of hurt. He again dismisses his previous attraction to her as one final test from the devil. Though depositing her back at the house they used to share would mean a little extra risk, he carefully weighs this option. Keeping her around during the last minutes of his lifelong mission is probably more trouble than it is worth, he imagines.

Assuming he makes it past any military inspectors on the way to the house, he shouldn't have to worry about the Hidalgo clan. He wonders if they have made it back to Mexico by now. He doubts it but also doesn't concern himself with that little detail. He prays again for guidance, settling his running mind while searching inside and out for an answer to this final dilemma.

He doesn't receive an ostensible answer from God, so he literally puts Karma's fate into her own hands.

"Do you want me to take you home?" he asks her.

She slowly shakes her head no. "No puedo," she answers, meaning she cannot go there. On that, and without asking, she picks up a plastic water bottle he had grabbed from the men's center. She twists off the cap of what is now lukewarm water and takes a swig. She then pulls a little orange bottle from her pocket, drains it into her mouth, and finishes with another gulp.

She makes a gagging sound then shakes her head again and repeats her assertion that she cannot go home. She calls him Javier.

Hafiz gets his sign, and he will not argue.

As Hafiz weaves slowly through the empty residential streets, the air thickens with the blackness of night. He can see the glow of televisions through unshaded windows, but the actual people are all behind closed doors. He doesn't see a soul, not even police or army personnel, along his path. The locusts quiet their song, settling into the night.

Karma is still, like a ghost, right next to him. The radio continues to prattle, something about a hospital in Seattle. He looks out of the side of his field of vision to see if this news, or the mention of the word hospital, registers. Apparently not; she does not flinch.

When Hafiz had imagined the violent crumbling of Western civilization, he saw scores of people in bright clothes running around and waving their arms in panic. On the precipice of that very scenario, the city, as far as he can see, is tranquil. He wonders if everyone inside those houses is as dull and motionless as Karma currently is. He can't believe that residents are not conducting an exodus from the city en masse.

He mutters another prayer for this last little bit to go off as planned, even prays that no one will have to suffer too much. He asks God for special favor in the afterlife. After all, he, Hafiz, has traded his entire life to be in the service of his one true God.

He is in mid-prayer as the turn-in to a small parking area opens up to his right. The night has descended to the point of being almost too dark to see, but, as if ordained to do so, a yellow streetlight flips on just as he arrives. Hafiz pulls the Mustang into the empty lot and heads to a little turn-around to the right. Several large trees hide his chosen parking spot from the adjacent street. When the car reaches its final destination, he cuts the engine and plunges the vehicle into silence. Karma still doesn't move.

Hafiz uses the quiet to say a prayer out loud in his native Arabic tongue. He has been asking for guidance since he was a boy and has always believed that he received it in enigmatic signs. Now is not the time to succumb to doubt, he knows, but the presence of this little woman shakes his resolve.

In a language she cannot understand, he asks why she has been placed before him at this particular time. He humbly asks to be given an answer if God feels like blessing him with an explanation. Although many of his existential questions have remained mysteries, as is Allah's way, the act of constant prayer has buttressed his will when all else failed.

He receives a vision of himself explaining the situation to Karma, so he begins to do so. In a clumsy mix of English and Spanish, he tells her that his name is not really Javier. She doesn't ask for his real identity, so he doesn't offer it.

She does turn and look at him, blinking her eyes a bit, when he goes on to say that Flor and the other Hidalgos aren't actually his family. If this development shocks her, she shows no sign. He continues to say that his real parents had been killed in a horrible accident when he was young. She looks at him sadly but says nothing.

Flustered by her lack of response, he tries to explain his unique relationship with God. "I pray so much," he says. "I know what I do." He feels pangs of guilt, knowing what he is about to do, and he wants her forgiveness as much as he wants God's vengeance.

The lack of air conditioning begins to make the heat in the car insufferable, and her silence only exacerbates the sensation of suffocating. He has just spilled out the private details of his life for the first time, and his confidante doesn't seem to care.

She finally breaks her reverie and asks, in English, if he still speaks to them.

"To who?" he responds, quizzically.

"To your parents."

"No, they are dead."

"I know, but tal vez [maybe] you can still speak to them."

Her postulation takes him aback. He has never considered a direct line of communication with his deceased parents, though he fully expects to be reunited with them, and soon, in the afterlife.

For Hafiz, who lives in a mix of the physical and faithful worlds, her question is confusing. He has been praying so passionately, culminating with his pleas for guidance and understanding today, and he doesn't know if her words are a sign or her delusion.

He does miss his parents and thinks of them often. He has always assumed that his father, especially, is angry about the cruel manner of his death. He expects the man to congratulate him on a job well done when they meet on the other side of the veil. This certainty has propelled him through Mexico and right to this spot in between the trees and the dry creek bed in Texas. After all these years of praying, he has never once considered the possibility of asking his father directly for guidance.

He does not answer her while he tries to make heads or tails out of what she said. Karma again turns to look straight out the windshield, lost to everyone but herself in some quiet contemplation of the oncoming night.

He tries to imagine what she may be thinking. He wonders if she has any inclination of what he is planning, of the person he really is. His mind comes up with many explanations of what is going through her head, but he finally admits that, about this subject, he will not get clarity.

He starts to pray aloud again. His foreign tongue must be raising alarms inside her, but if so, she makes no inclination that she cares. He prays loudly, asking God what he should do with Karma. This time, he sees a vision of the two of them sitting side by side on a wooden pew, so he decides to take her with him.

He switches the electric lock on the driver's side door, and the resounding click echoes sullenly throughout the vinyl and plastic in the car. She moves to open her door first, going along with his plan without having to be asked. He assumes that she is part of God's gift for him. An unexpected development, yes, but she will be welcome in his heavenly paradise. There, her heathen habits and societal sins will be a thing of the past. He sighs, knowing he cannot blame her for the wicked ways of her homeland.

Though the night air is still hot, releasing the stagnancy inside the car provides a small reprieve. The moderate cooling relieves a bit of his anxiety as he pops the trunk with the lever next to his seat. He looks in the rearview mirror as it lifts behind him. The streetlight reflects brightly off the yellow metal.

He takes his phone and wallet out of his pocket as she gets out of the car. He places those items in the glove compartment as he utters yet another prayer. He feels certain about his mission, but his hands shake.

He gets out of the car and shuts and locks the doors. He stretches his back underneath the moon and the yellow streetlight. The air is immobile - they are the only things alive in the immediate environment. He constricts then relaxes his fists then asks Karma, "You want to pray?"

She nods diagonally, indicating neither yes nor no.

Hafiz walks slowly around the car and pulls the suitcase out of his trunk. Thick steel locks latch it shut, and a rubber seal prevents any air from entering or leaving the case. The aridity and temperature of the environment is vitally important for the teeming vials of virus inside. The little glass tubes rest perilously against steel bores that will puncture the glass at the electronically specified time, forever altering history.

Once opened, the virus will spread devastatingly and quickly -- a certainty that has ben tested and re-tested by groups similar to his in isolated, impoverished areas of the planet. Sharif, his biologist acquaintance from the center, imported this particular specimen on a fearful plane journey from Europe.

What is inside that suitcase is crucial for phase two of the master plan. If dissemination calculations are correct, anyone breathing outside air in a mile radius will be ill and infected within two hours or less. None of the test subjects, mostly Africans, had lived more than 36 hours. The test centers had been carefully insulated, as the fast-moving contagion would probably wipe out the entire planet in due time.

If the fact that he is carrying a suitcase is of any concern to Karma, she does not show it. They walk toward the adjacent street under the fake yellow light. No bugs surround it this evening -- they have apparently perished from the interminable heat. He feels a moment of compassion and tries to hold her hand. Casually and awkwardly, she pulls away from him and starts walking across the street.

Hafiz hears a car somewhere nearby and hesitates while Karma disappears into the shadows on the other side. He pauses quietly while the sound of the motor moves away from them. Otherwise, the night is eerily quiet.

While he waits, his eyes adjust to the darkness. He can make out her silhouette. She looks tiny compared to the towering church and its splendorous stained glass windows and spire. Above her, a multicolored glass portrait of the Virgin Mary weeps while cradling her child. The colors dancing in the window are brighter than the streetlight or the moon. The tan colored bricks are too dark to register, but he has driven by St. Stephen's church for many years. San Esteban, he would say to himself every time he passed.

After a minute, he tightens his grip on the case's handle and walks across the street. Karma is right there, waiting for him. He says a silent prayer of thanks for having been allowed to proceed this far.

Side by side, Karma and Hafiz slowly walk up the steep hill, which is covered in dead grass, toward the brick entryway. Avoiding the hot concrete walkway, they cut diagonally up the hill and head straight toward the mouth of the cathedral. The incline tires Karma, whose loud breathing Hafiz can hear clearly.

Two substantially solid wooden doors, tapered to meet at a point under a simple brick cornerstone, are closed in front of them, but the light from the lobby shines through two small, eye-level windows.

Hafiz pulls on one of the large iron handles. As he expects it to, the door opens confidently to welcome them to the church. Before entering, he silently prays that his local co-conspirators have found their target destinations so easily accessible. Karma walks in without being invited, and he follows, pausing until the door shuts all the way behind him.

During the long and intense deliberations, conducted over the Internet in code, Hafiz' group debated the pros and cons of attacking churches. One of the overriding factors leading to places of devotion being chosen for phase two was the belief that, even during the most extraordinary circumstances, churches would welcome those desiring to pray. St. Stephen's, which serves an intellectual middle class in the area around the university, welcomes Hafiz and Karma with cold conditioned air and bright lights in the lobby.

Hafiz walks in and takes in the details of the small entryway. Empty coat hooks adorn both walls. The left wall offers a bible in a protective display. He looks, and the pages have been left open to Ecclesiastes. He leans over to inspect and slowly reads the verses aloud, though he cannot comprehend the message:

"There is a time for everything
And a season for everything under the heavens
A time to be born and a time to die
A time to plant and a time to uproot
A time to kill and a time to heal
A time to tear down and a time to build
A time to weep and a time to laugh
A time to mourn and a time to dance
A time to scatter stones and a time to gather them."

Hafiz strains his mind to remember a similar verse in the Koran. In his book, the words are far more mellifluous.

Karma has turned to the opposite wall, writing something into the guestbook. While she is distracted, he places the suitcase in the corner of the rectangular room, under a small table topped with a donation box. Carefully, he angles it behind the furniture so that no one will be able to see it if not actively searching. Later, he will find a way to climb to the highest point in the church and activate the mechanism that will begin to scatter the sacrament, as he calls it, to the invisible current in the night air. Karma writes slowly and deliberately, never noticing his behavior.

He waits behind her until she finishes, then he motions her through a set of arched wooden doors into the main chapel.

*   *   *

The lights are on inside the great room as well, and Hafiz can see that they are not alone. A priest, dressed in the careful black and white of his robes, paces by a table of candles and makes esoteric motions with his hands. He seems to be entranced and takes no notice of the new entry.

A blond-haired man sitting halfway up front on the right side swivels around and takes a long look at Hafiz and Karma, who are both standing there taking in the ornate carvings of angels in the buttressed ceiling. Hafiz meets his gaze as a second, smaller head pops up to the man's right, then another. Hafiz respects the man, assumes he has brought his children to pray. He hopes they leave before he takes action. The priest's lightly rhythmic footsteps echo throughout the tall and carpeted room. He is offering something from his own tradition, but all Hafiz can hear are whispers.

He tries to retain his certainty, the knowingness he has about this plan, but the presence of children in the room starts to shake him. He can't help but compare his childhood gone awry to the effect he will have on these kids. He thinks about Lalo and the other boys, whom he truly loved. Even surrounded by the supernaturally cold air inside the church, beads of sweat start to collect at Hafiz' temples.

Karma makes her way to a pew, which is covered with a rich red cushion, and sits down. He joins her and prays with as much of his soul as he can possibly offer. He prays for continued guidance, for one undeniable sign that he should follow through to the end of this trajectory. He silences his mind, waits, and hears nothing. He remembers what Karma said in the car and asks God if he could speak to his father. His voice would be a balm to the panic rising from the pit of his entrails.

After waiting expectantly for an answer to his prayer, Hafiz gives

223

up and settles his mind into rest. He is exhausted, ready for the end. He hangs his chin down to the point where it nearly touches his chest and comes within millimeters of a light sleep when he hears a voice in his ear.

"Hafiz, my dear son," the voice calls out, warm and clear. Without opening his eyes, Hafiz can feel the corporeal presence of his father. The part of the young man that died when his parents did springs back to life, and for the first time since that horrible day so long ago, Hafiz feels whole. He breathes, and the thick scent of myrrh, of which his father was always so redolent, fills his nostrils. The smell reawakens his memory, and in his mind's eye, Hafiz can create a real picture of his father. In this vision, the man is radiant, as alive as he ever was. A certain joy spreads from Hafiz' heart and warms his body, which has been cooled by the church's air conditioner. The goose bumps on his forearms disappear.

"Hafiz, my boy," the voice repeats. "How I have longed to speak to you. Thank you son, for calling out to me."

Hafiz Al-Assad is incredulous. Nothing in his Islamic upbringing ever suggested that he would be able to communicate with the dead while ensconced in the mortal coil. The surprise has locked his tongue, frozen his mind. For a man so eternally focused, Hafiz is at a total loss about what to do. So he says two words, "Thank you."

The salutation energizes the voice. Hafiz opens his eyes and finds the room to be unchanged from the previous minute. His father is nowhere the naked eye can detect. Karma's head is tilted toward her left shoulder, and her eyes are closed.

"Thank you," he says softly in her direction, wanting to give her credit for suggesting that he attempt to find parental guidance. If Hafiz has ever needed a clear signal -- ever in his life -- he has picked a perfect time to ask for one.

He takes a deep breath and readies himself to launch into

the barrage of questions so long unanswered, but before he can formulate a single one, his father's voice offers direction.

"My son," it says. "Go. Go up to the altar and pray to Mother Mary. She is the repository of all slights and grievances. Talk to her and rest your weary back."

These words shock Hafiz. His father, a devout Muslim man, never would have muttered the name of an icon from another religion. In fact, he would have considered another's invocation of Mary's name entirely blasphemous. Now Hafiz is confused and wondering if dark forces are trying to destroy him. He vacillates for a minute but decides to trust the honest timbre in his father's voice.

He stands up straight from the pew and grabs the bench in front of him to steady himself. With his left hand gripping the back of the opposing bench, he slowly makes his way to the center aisle then turns and walks directly toward the ornate, ivory-colored altar. When he reaches the blunt side of the pulpit, he kneels carefully onto his right knee.

Before concentrating on prayer, he looks around. The priest is to his left, still lost in his private conjurations. No one else is moving or making any noise. Hafiz bows his head and draws his palms together. Before he closes his eyes, he stares at the golden cross so immobile in the middle of the altar.

As he clears himself of all things so that the spirit of Allah may enter, Hafiz hears his father's voice again, louder and more urgent this time. "Wake up, my son. Please wake up," it says.

Though Hafiz has never actually intended a Christian prayer until this very moment, he has uttered the words many times as a supposed member of the pious Hidalgo family. He asks the Lord to have mercy on him as he begins to tremble, unsure about the new direction this night has taken.

A new voice enters the mix -- this one soft and womanly. Her syllables are haunted, but the concern is tangible. She asks him to "consider love."

She repeats this axiomatic phrase several times, eventually searing it into his ears. At this point, the concept of Hafiz is identical to the advice to "consider love." He is no different from the voice desperately pleading with him, though he has yet to understand why.

As he loses himself, Hafiz' heart softens. Until this point, he had not realized that his vital muscle is perpetually folded in the manner of an angry fist. The relaxation is nearly liberating. Desultorily, the tension melts from his chest cavity, down through his liver then out of him through the lower reaches of his body.

The dissolution of the hatred buoys Hafiz, who had not realized the density of his vengeful persona. The warmth and ease transport Hafiz into an ecstatic state. Involuntarily, his head and eyes roll back. He falls from his knee over onto the carpet. He turns his head and looks up at the beautiful ceiling of the church. Two angels are reaching out to one another, touching only at one fingertip. The glass depiction of Mother Mary, while weeping, looks on at them approvingly. The confluence of colors and lights joins in his mind like a symphony. Hafiz is insensate, overwhelmed with joy.

When he can re-enter some sort of physical reality, Hafiz notices that the flesh on his arm has turned almost as red as the carpet underneath him. Pure energy courses through every vein in his body, and he feels like he will explode and be permanently embedded into the ceiling of this chapel. He welcomes the possible fate, now convinced that he is currently in the most perfect place on earth or in the heavens.

Without warning or explanation, Hafiz begins to cry loudly. The woman, who he can't see or even picture in his imagination, blankets him with her words. She sticks to her script, urging him to "remember love, remember love."

He doesn't fully understand what she is saying, but the air infusing her meaning brushes over his soul, bringing him closer to God than he has ever been.

His father wants to be heard again, as well. "Please remember, my son. Wake up," he says. But Hafiz, still curled on his side on the church floor, closes his eyes again.

This time, he sees a vision of Karma running through a lush and grassy field. Her hair is longer, her skin smoother. She is wearing an ethereal white gown, which is nothing like she would wear in daily life. A chain of daisies encircles her head. She is at peace, frolicking under the gentle sun. Hafiz tries to capture her attention as he wills her to look at him, but she is oblivious to all but her own pleasure.

Hafiz feels he could watch this scene forever, but suddenly, the ice-cold grip of reality grabs him at the nape of his neck. He sits up in a start. Suddenly, his bliss has been replaced by panic, and he remembers the suitcase. The intent of his father and Mother Mary's message washes over him, and he jumps up, determined to redirect the winds of fate.

Hafiz runs down the aisle at a full sprint, not even looking over at Karma, who is now fast asleep in the pew. He throws the doors to the foyer open so violently that he almost crushes a little boy into the wall. The kid's father, the stocky guy for whom sparks of recognition clamor, pulls the child into his chest, as he angrily demands, "Hey, watch where you're going."

Time moves at an alarmingly fast rate, and Hafiz cannot think clearly at all. He has trouble putting together sensible words, or a cohesive thought at all, so he shoves the man, whose arm is around a young girl, toward the exit door.

The man's eyes grow wide with surprise, but he does not

argue. As calmly as he can, the sturdy blond man assuredly guides the children out into the hot night, and though he is not sweating, Hafiz reaches up to wipe off his brow.

Alone now in the bright foyer, Hafiz carefully retrieves the suitcase from where he had left it earlier. He places it on top of the enclosed bible and starts to unlock the latches before he realizes that the key that will allow him to do so is in his wallet. In the glove compartment of the Mustang.

Though the timer isn't poised to set off the chain of events for a few more hours, Hafiz knows that he wants to take Karma and get as far away from the city as possible. He also wants to "consider love," so he wants no part of the suffering and sadness locked into vials inside this metal case.

Focused only on one thing and in a growing panic, Hafiz barrels through the middle of the double doors and runs so quickly down the hill that he slips and tumbles down, scratching his forearm on the rough earth in the process.

His eyes rove wildly from side to side, though he doesn't see anything, not even the man and his two children. Hafiz has already forgotten about them, though. He gets back up and quickly shakes the dead grass off of his pants before continuing back to the parking lot. Out of habit, he looks both ways before crossing the street, but he is alone.

The streetlight has flickered off at this hour, so the nearly full moon provides the light Hafiz needs to operate. His hands shake badly as he jerks the key ring out of his right pocket. His fingers are sweaty, and the moisture coupled with his violent motion causes the keys to fly from his hand and out into a patch of bushes leading down to the adjacent creekbed.

A panicked moan escapes his lips as Hafiz makes a fist and hits himself in the center of his forehead. He is usually excessively careful, taking pride in putting everything in its right place. Of all times to make a horrible mistake, he has chosen a particularly bad one.

He tries to keep the exponentially growing panic at bay. He tries not to make mental calculations of just how much time he is losing. He considers going to get Karma and just running away on foot but feels that by the dead hour, when suitcases like his will be releasing the bitter end all over town, they would not get very far.

Hafiz takes in a deep breath while trying to make sense of the shadowy patch of wild vegetation in which his only current hope of salvation lies. He has to find those keys, and now, but he doesn't see the moon's light reflecting metal anywhere in front of him.

Knocked so far off kilter, he doesn't even think to pray for help. Instead, he launches himself like a predator onto the dead and dying plants. He madly sticks his hands over every surface, coming up with nothing more than handfuls of dry grass and brittle twigs.

He moves deeper into the dark area, frantically looking for the keys. He spends at least twenty minutes blindly searching for them before heat and exhaustion force him to pause. He is now covered in sweat, which has dampened both his shirt and pants. He pulls the polo away from his chest in an attempt to cool his insistently pounding heart, but the fibers stick to his skin.

Hafiz winces his eyes, but no tears are forthcoming. He doesn't know what time it is but figures the mechanism won't release the virus for another two or maybe three hours. He reconsiders getting Karma and running but again knows it would be no use. He even considers strangling her so that she won't have to suffer, but he decides he could never do something so cruel and violent ... at least not with his bare hands. He knows he needs to find the keys at all costs and thinks to pray for assistance.

After his prayer, and when his breathing stabilizes, Hafiz explores the bushy area to the left of where he was previously looking. While his hands fumble through the bare limbs of a waist-high bush, his feet cause something to jingle against the ground. The noise is extremely faint, but he hears it. Without moving his feet, he bends over and blindly searches the area under the bush with his fingertips. In a moment, he pulls up the key ring, which feels cold to the touch.

He hurries back to the Mustang, taking care not to lose the keys again. Once inside the car, the air returns to his lungs. He takes several deep, thankful breaths. From his lungs' standpoint, his body has almost drowned in a lack of oxygen. He doesn't want to waste time but rests his head briefly on top of the hot plastic of his steering wheel.

A few tears escape his eyes. He can't believe anything about this current situation. The Hafiz from the past who decided to precipitate the end of the world seems like a hateful stranger. Right now, all he cares about is saving Karma. Her brought her here, after all.

He knows he could never look God in the eyes again if he doesn't disassemble that suitcase, so he maps out the steps to do so in his mind in an attempt to ward off any potential disaster. He can visualize the exact wires that need to be cut to prevent the metal bores from breaking the virus-filled glass.

He even considers taking out the vials and burying them somewhere near the creek before leaving. He figures he needs to be at least sixty miles outside of town by the time this thing starts. If possible, he will take Karma and head all the way to Mexico, where, to his knowledge, people will continue to live normally (whatever that means) until the virus reaches their communities. Perhaps several more weeks. Plenty of time to get lost in the mountains.

Hafiz opens the glove box and pulls out his wallet, where he finds the one-inch key that will unlock the suitcase. He puts it carefully at the bottom of his pocket, gets out of the car, and, out of habit, locks the doors. He walks purposely up the hill in big, confident strides. He is almost back to the doors when he hears a voice ordering him to "freeze."

Hafiz does not recognize the word but understands the intention behind the man's tone of voice. Officer Cody Phelps steps out from behind a large pecan tree and levels his pistol straight at Hafiz' chest. "What's going on here?" he demands.

Officer Cody Phelps and Hafiz Al-Assad look directly into one another's eyes. Phelps tries to find an explanation for this odd behavior, tries to convince himself that apprehending a man at a church is an acceptable extension of his duties. He figures that given the circumstances, he is better safe than sorry.

Hafiz, on the other hand, has gone blank, his eyes unfathomable. He weighs his available options: he could charge at the man, whom he has yet to recognize as the officer from the previous night; he could let the dust settle as it may, reconciling the opposition to be another bit of divine guidance; or, he could come clean, tell everything that he knows. The debate paralyzes him. The difficulty breathing in the thick night air causes his lips to turn faintly blue.

Phelps' eyes contain curiosity and a measure of confidence. He has the power in this transaction, and the man's frozen indecision intrigues, not worries, him. Holding the gun steady, he twists his head all the way around to the right. He sees the faces of both of his children, Emma Grace and Scotty, staring at him, teary-eyed, from the windshield of his cruiser. He had hoped to safeguard them from the scene, but they ended up at a clearly visible angle.

He'd rather his children be nowhere near this place, but Mercy had called in a panic, something about Lynn's mother, so he had changed into his backup blue jean outfit and picked the kids up in a hasty exchange. He was driving them home, police duty be damned, when he drove past the church. Cody had given up his Christian views a long time ago, but at that moment, he had felt prayer in Saint Stephen's would be a vital part of the evening, so they made a stop.

Phelps doesn't recognize Hafiz as the man from the Thorndale barricade the night before, but a familiarity strikes him. He tugs on his memories, getting lost in the process, when Hafiz breaks his silence.

"Mi novia," he says, pointing in the church. "Esta enferma," which means she is ill. Hafiz pulls his arms around his stomach and makes a vomiting gesture. He tries to make his eyes wide with pathetic misery.

Phelps does not buy it. The twitch at the corner of one eye and the hypervigilant, tensed stance suggest that the man is lying. He does remember seeing the guy in the church with a woman earlier, though, so he motions with his gun for Hafiz to walk inside. Once Hafiz is all the way through the doors, Phelps holds up one finger to his children to indicate that they hold still for just a minute. He then takes three deep belly breaths and creates a circle of white light around both the kids and himself, to protect.

Hafiz walks hurriedly toward the doors into the interior part of the church, but Phelps believes he is walking too deliberately because his neck does not move a millimeter; the overhead light reflecting off of his black hair doesn't waver a bit. "Parate," Phelps says with a convincing Spanish accent, and Hafiz stops, too suddenly, like he is afraid the officer was going to say that.

Phelps looks around the room - first at the ceiling - then at the corners. The obvious placement of the metal case on the bible shocks him when he sees it. The fact that the case is cold metal is odd enough, but the four locks, clearly visible, are excessive.

Phelps' Spanish is limited, so he asks in English. "Is this yours?"

Hafiz continues standing with his arms to his sides and his back to Phelps. He doesn't answer, so Phelps repeats the question, louder this time.

"Is this yours?" he asks with angry emphasis on the final syllable.

Hafiz raises his shoulders and says he doesn't know, "No se."

Phelps cautiously moves over to the case. While keeping his gun trained on Hafiz, who his kind heart wants to believe is innocent, he bends down to where the case is at eye level. He can see that the seal has been coated in clear polyurethane. Probably not good, but feasibly, his rational mind speaks, some terrified person might have left his or her life savings in the foyer of St. Stephen's. Many in the area are very wealthy, he thinks, and most of them surely have some serious atoning to do. Desperate times, you know.

Phelps genuinely wants to believe that this kid is in the church praying for the salvation of the world. He has already forgiven the love of his life, and the act was emancipating. He prefers the numb, optimistic side of his brain. Feelings are something to be transcended, he thinks.

He wants to believe this because right now he is hoping that this kid with the black, sweat-glazed hair is not a cold-hearted terrorist. He tries to talk himself out of the paranoia, but it is relentless. His heart starts to beat quickly and in perfect sync with the rattle of the air-conditioner. A vein underneath his left eye pops out and begins to throb in unison.

Hafiz raises his hands as if in surrender and, agonizingly

slowly, spins around so that he is facing officer Phelps, so serious in his civvies. They lock eyes, and Hafiz feels like no one, except for his parents, has ever looked so deeply into him in his life. He can visibly see the seething mixture of trust and mistrust, give and take. Hafiz feels vitally connected to this man, so he makes his decision.

"It is dangerous," he says in choppy English. "Sickness. Everywhere." He repeats the motion of grabbing his arms around his belly and pretend vomiting. "Everybody die."

Phelps stands up straight and pulls his cellphone out of his back pocket. He had turned the phone off when he went inside to pray. Now, the wait for it to jump back to life marks time by the invading current of ice in Phelps' veins. As he dials the number, he does his best not to panic, though the uncontrollable emotion approaches quickly.

The phone rings, but he gets no answer. Tries 911 again, gets the same. He can't believe that the chain has again broken to the point of not working. This is it, the thinks. The terror, a turgid river of panic, knocks his spirit right out of him.

Hafiz has dread written all over his face, and the depth of his sorrow strikes Phelps. He can't keep the worry at bay. All he can see are the crying faces of his children sitting in his patrol car. He feels like the police department, for which he had risked his life, is letting him down when he needs help the most.

He gets no answer on another call, so he follows the digital instructions and leaves a message about a bomb in St. Stephen's foyer. He nods at Hafiz, considers shooting him but decides he doesn't want to waste the bullet, then runs to his squad car, choosing to take care of his own over his duty to society.

Hafiz just wants to leave. He realizes that he will not be able to stop the locomotive of death, so he, too, just wants to escape with the only person in whose company he wants to be.

He bursts through the interior doors but doesn't see Karma. He sprints to where they were sitting and sees that she is asleep on the red cushion of the pew. Without pausing, he runs to her and shakes her leg forcefully, needing her to wake up quickly.

She doesn't stir; her body flexes awkwardly at his pushes. He keeps trying but gets no response. After a good minute of shaking her, his panic is out of control. He sees red and hears the gnawing of stray dogs. He can feel pain as if the dogs are real and are really sinking fangs into the flesh of his calves. He kneels and puts his fingers under the crook in Karma's chin, feeling for a pulse. He moves his fingers around until the fact is undeniable. Her heart is not functioning, at least not as far as he can tell.

CHAPTER ELEVEN

KARMA

Karma wakes up into an intimately comfortable scene - she is walking down the aisle on the west side of a football stadium. Her football stadium. She takes each step carefully as she heads down toward the field and her seat.

Each step is a deliverance from the world in which she'd rather not live, a step closer to peace and enjoyment. What should be no more than a hundred steps turns into a million. She walks down and down, but the field gets no closer. The odd spatial arrangement does not concern her, however; she knows the exact location of her destination and is in no particular hurry to arrive.

Because of a feeling, not a visual cue, she cuts to the left, toward her seat. The people on that row smile as they stand up and allow her and Christian, who walks right behind her, to pass. This friendly, welcoming attitude is pervasive throughout the stadium. As she traverses the crowded aisle, people get up and sit back down, doing a happy little wave.

The afternoon couldn't be more perfect. The sun, which

hangs low in the sky behind her, provides the perfect air temperature. Its light is warm; it appears to emanate from inside of her. The heat simultaneously leaks from the orb in the sky and the pit of her belly. It has the consistency of wet sand. Her body feels soft and gooey to the touch, like melting butter. The sensation lends to her increasingly tranquil state of being.

The announcer, in a voice reminiscent of the sound of diamonds, says that her team has scored. The humongous crowd filling the stadium erupts into confident joy. Their happy exclamations roll through her like waves of ecstasy. She couldn't possibly be happier. If she has to spend forever at this game, she will, gladly. Some things should never end.

Moving is a bit more of a challenge than usual. Her muscles are so complacent, she must exert extra effort to expand and contract them. She feels like her bones have been replaced by hot jelly. Her body will comply with her wishes, but the process of taking steps is slower than it should be. Walking has never been so pleasurable, so the odd sensation causes no alarm.

Karma can be a claustrophobic person, but her location in the midst of innumerable people now invokes serenity. Instead of feeling starved for space, she feels expansive. As she continues to walk, down what seems like another mile of aisle, people in the seats -- a colorful array of folks -- clap languidly. Several reach out and massage the normally tense area between her shoulders and her neck.

Each touch dissolves a lifetime of tension. Christian wordlessly guides her by holding his fingertips at the small of her back. She doesn't have to look back to communicate her thanks at the way he blankets her with pure love and acceptance.

She is so happy to be here, on this perfect day, in the middle of the most epic game. Happy to be with him. Their destinies are intertwined, she has always known; their fruitful bond her penultimate achievement in life.

At every step, a new sea of people opens up before her eyes. People of all shapes, colors, and sizes populate the rows around her seat. This sea is constantly expanding outwards, infinitely. She looks up and is mildly surprised at what looks like millions of people between her and the top of the bleachers. That many weren't there the last time she looked up, which is puzzling, but she makes some justification to herself that they must be adding on to the stadium.

While the depth between Karma and the sky continues to grow, the field remains comfortably where it should be -- about forty feet to her right. She keeps walking, getting no closer to the end zone, but she remains confident that she and Christian will soon arrive at their seats.

As far as they have walked down this row, they have not moved relative to the yard markers. They are at the exact position they were when they cut through from the vertical aisle -- twenty-five yards from the end zone and twenty-five yards from midfield. Karma does not notice that, for all intents and purposes, she is walking in place.

She stops for a quick rest, and the corpulent man whose view she now obscures genially squeezes into the space behind her so that everyone has a clear view of the unfolding play. Her team is at the middle of the field, aiming to move the ball closer to where she stands.

She can hear the chatter from the line of scrimmage as the quarterback adjusts the play call before taking the snap. She watches as the hapless defenders, in ugly silver pants and worse starred helmets, ineptly try to stop the progress that will inevitably lead to another score for her beloved team.

The on-field brilliance results in a first down, and the joy of the crowd causes her eyes to roll back into her head; it feels so good. Karma looks up at the scoreboard, which hovers over the end zone in front of her. The numbers are obscured and nonsensical, but she does not need numeric proof to know that her team, the eternal good guys, is winning.

Karma crosses her arms in front of her chest and feels the velvety-soft sleeves of her t-shirt. The fabric is green and broken-in with the familiar comfort of old pajamas. The fabric, soft as can be, shields her from anything unwanted. The shirt is a delicate, warm copacetic. Just feeling the way it adheres to her molten arms makes her sleepy. She briefly considers taking a nap but decides to press on for her seat so that she can settle into the game.

She has loved her team since she fell in love with Christian. He loves them because his father's best friend, Kyle Clifton, played with them for many seasons. Though Clifton has long since retired, Christian is still a fan because the loyalty has been written into his DNA. He could never consider cheering for another team, and by default, neither could she. Her passion for the squad is an extension of her unending love for him.

She marvels again about how lucky she is to be here, in the midst of this perfect fading afternoon, with the person she loves most in the world. Their team is on top, so balance has been restored in the universe. Everyone in the stadium enjoys winning in perpetuity.

After many more steps, with Christian's fingers still pressing against her lower spine, Karma comes upon their seats. Both are folded down, pristine in a fresh coat of green paint. Though the wooden slats look hard, she knows they will be comfortable. She feels like she could sit in hers forever. A large soda waits for her in the cup holder. After a lifetime of wandering, Karma is at long last home. She spins around to give Christian a kiss. Surely he must be as happy and as peaceful as she is.

But Christian isn't the one behind her. Not at all. She tries to scream, but no sound comes out. No one around her even seems to notice the faceless hooded creature that begins to suck her soul right out of the stadium. Her peace vaporizes into horror.

Though Karma has been motionless and without a pulse for over a minute, Hafiz will not give up. He sits down next to her and absently, but forcefully, shakes her leg, which feels stiffer than it should be. His mind has succumbed to the panic he feels, and he can't make any sense out of the situation.

His instincts are telling him to flee as fast as he can, to get away from this woman, this church, this city and this country. He continues shaking her as his options pugnaciously state their cases in his twirling mind.

Without realizing what he is doing, he starts angrily shouting at his father, who, minutes before had sounded so reassuring. In a guttural howl, Hafiz screams at his father for all the anger and hurt he has had to endure throughout his pitiful life.

That this night has become the culmination of a hateful struggle is too cruel for the young man to bear. Between yells, Hafiz lets out uncontrollable sobs. The ruckus breaks the priest from his spell of prayers, and the man rushes over to the pew to ascertain the cause of the commotion.

Judging by the girl's limp, bluing body and the young man's fury and desperation, the priest quickly comes to a conclusion about what is happening in his church, so he immediately sits down next to Hafiz, takes his hand, then bows his head in prayer.

As if in an immediate response, Karma jerks up, her upper leg flailing and connecting softly with Hafiz' ribs. He looks over at her with a jolt. She lifts her head an inch and turns it to him. He can see color returning to her thin lips and unnaturally pallid face. Though she struggles to do so, she makes several shallow expeditions for air.

Karma is confused by her surroundings and unable to paint a

clear picture of why she is in this room, with its harsh light and uncomfortable benches. She just wants someone to hand her a blanket so that she can curl up underneath it and return to her happy dream.

She recognizes Hafiz' face but cannot recall his name nor her relation to him. She is too exhausted to care and too physically spent to ask. Everything appears in a narrow haze due to the fact that she cannot open her eyes more than a few millimeters. Her eyelids are intolerably heavy. She has never been so tired.

Half of the entity that is Karma Hill still stands inside the stadium. Here in the church, the earthbound half continues to hear echoes of the crowd's gentle roar. Something nags at her mind. She is completely unable to remember why, but she still feels the residual dizziness of being shaken by something unexpected. A wordless feeling cautions her against descending back into that stadium, but her limbs are so heavy.

She decides to close her eyes again, so Hafiz roughly pinches her cheek. Karma opens her eyes wide, and she looks at him with derision. Whoever this guy is, she thinks, he has no right to touch me. What does he want?

A little voice inside her urges her to stay awake, not to go back to sleep. The priest's spoken words confirm this sentiment. He talks and waves his hands in an attempt to capture her attention. She tries to listen, but the pull of the spiritual gravity is far too thick to overcome.

She starts to succumb to the overbearing fatigue. The inviting warm sun over the stadium settles back over her. The voices outside her ears fade to memory as she resumes her trek back down the vertical aisle of the stadium, where she is most at home.

Karma's body becomes unresponsive again, so both men shake

her. Hafiz puts his hand squarely on her elbow, and the priest stands up, squeezes past, and places his palms on her knees, which he moves from side to side, trying to encourage her back to wakefulness.

She lets out a tiny groan, as thin and as delicate as a spider web. Both continue to shake her, but she gives no further response. After another minute of efforts to wake her up, the priest abruptly places his hand on her chest to feel for a heartbeat.

His motion startles Hafiz, whose bile leaps up from his intestines. In his worldview, strangers do not touch women in inappropriate places. No, strangers do not touch women at all.

That the man is a fully clothed priest is of no consequence to Hafiz. The unfolding situation takes a darker turn, and Hafiz feels his emotions sliding over the edge of his sanity. Karma's arms are unnaturally limp beside her, but she halfheartedly lifts one in a wasted effort to fend off the intrusion.

Hafiz is now wild with panic. His fight-or-flight response kicks into full gear, and the differing options are at full-blown war inside of him.

He can picture himself running back down the hill and driving off for good, but he cannot continue living if he lets this man do what he will with Karma, whatever the rest of her fate may be. He is too honorable. The chaos of the midnight hour strikes him with force. He has been planning this evening for years, and never in any scenario did something like this arise. He has tried to map out every motion, to have a contingency plan for any development, but this, this is far beyond what he is capable of dealing with right now. He is frozen but also quite literally out of control.

The lights from above him, the lights from the lit candles, the lights reflecting off the stained glass windows strike him as surreal. Intensely surreal.

He imagines he can see every ray of light; each one is a missile aimed straight at his eyeballs. His temples begin to throb. The invisible sound is deafening. He has no experience with how to react to what he is going through, so by default, he begins to laugh.

His deep cackles intermingled with dry sobs echo throughout the mostly empty room. The priest looks up and immediately dismisses the reaction as a product of shock.

The priest pushes his fingers deeper into Karma's chest, hoping against hope that he will find a pulse over her heart. Her dying on his pew on this of all nights is an ominous omen, and he wants to do anything he can to prevent that from happening. Though thousands, if not more, of lives have been lost around the world in the previous dozen hours, he can only focus on this one in front of him right now. To the priest, her fate is symbolic of the next step for humanity. She is his only hope for salvation.

The priest fills his lungs with God's spirit and the cool air. He then bends directly over Karma's face and attaches his lips to hers.

Hafiz jumps up and yells at the ceiling in an explosion of rage. The priest ignores him and continues to try the CPR.

Hafiz can only see red; everything seems to drip with blood. He stands in a pool of it. His teeth press so firmly against one another that his jaw begins to ache, joining the insistent pain overtaking his head. Much of the awful sensation collects at the crown of his head. He tries to hold it there, inside of him, but the emotion is too much to contain.

He makes balls with his fists. The priest doesn't even see the punch coming before it lands squarely on the side of his head. He looks up in shock, and Hafiz hits him again, harder this time, right between the eyes. Hafiz knocks him unconscious, and the priest's body slumps gradually onto the floor.

*   *   *

Hafiz kicks the priest aside so that he can maneuver himself to scoop Karma into his arms. He puts one arm underneath her back and another under her neck, gently lifting her so that the bulk of her body rests against his chest.

She is even lighter than he would have guessed. Her head hangs at an oddly obtuse angle, a pose devoid of muscular effort. Looking at the floor the entire time, he swiftly carries her straight to the doors to the foyer. Hafiz' heart is in his throat; its rhythm is an impediment to his ability to breathe normally.

The physical distraction of the pulse prevents him from solving the riddle into which this night has morphed. He can only function by considering one thing at a time. Right now, he needs to escape the suffocating atmosphere inside this cursed cathedral. He has trapped his breath at the top of the sternum and will not consider taking in additional air until he can have the hot, natural variety rusting underneath the moonlight.

He kicks the hinged doors outward and barrels straight through the foyer, forgetting all about the suitcase still resting on top of the bible. He has to transfer Karma's weight onto a shoulder and a knee in order to free his other hand so that he can pull the outside door toward them. He props the open door with a foot and spins a half moon until they are both in the dark night. They are alone.

Hafiz needs a minute to think, to settle back into some semblance of order. To his right, he spots a wide area behind the bushes obscuring the corner of the church. He rests her against the wall, but as soon as he lets go, she slumps onto the dirt. He wonders if somehow she got exposed to the virus; he has never seen anyone crumble out of life like this. He remembers the suitcase and gasps at the thought that thousands, millions will be going through a similar experience in a matter of hours.

With shame in his eyes, he looks over at Karma, who has at least managed to move a hand underneath her face. He believes that if he can absolve all the hate he has harbored, he can save her.

He gathers all of the vulnerability of his being into his lungs and tries to exchange the words of his prayer with the dust in the stale air. He begs God for forgiveness and pleads that he save her life. Hafiz offers anything in exchange. He offers to dismantle the suitcase and bury the deadly vials. He offers a lifetime of service to those less fortunate. He promises never to hate again. He even offers to trade his own life for hers.

When he finishes, he reaches over and brushes his fingers against her luminescent cheek. Her skin is clammy and plastic. He leans over her to listen for a breath. He hears a slight wheeze and takes it as a definite sign of encouragement.

He straightens up and rests his back against the wall, which transfers heat to his spine through his shirt. He tries to make mathematics out of his breath in an attempt to return to rationality. Never has he been thrown so far outside of himself. Not even when he witnessed his childhood home in bombed-out shambles.

He has never felt so alive, but the intensity of the awakening is overwhelming. The thought that he has taken on her emotions, in addition to his, crosses his mind. The ability to register a new idea means that the tornadic storm of mental activity is subsiding.

The memory of the man with the gun jumps back to the forefront and tenses Hafiz' muscles into action. The man could still be here or could be returning with friends for all he knows. Staying here is not safe for Karma. In a quick revival, he launches to his feet and sprints toward the door to the church and the suitcase, which he cannot leave here.

Hafiz is only certain about one thing after maneuvering through the furious chain of the night's events - that he must inactivate the virus before it destroys everything around him. He has felt the abrupt and incisive pain of loss one time in his life, and he thought that by being proactive, he would never have to experience it again. This second occurrence, though it came like a left hook into his life, is cruel, and he does not wish to inflict this deep sadness on any other creature. He has no right. Not even to that lecherous priest.

His duty takes center stage as he briefly collects himself before entering the church for the third time. He summarily brushes the dirt off the seat of his pants. He must be careful, or he will not be able to undo what he had initially planned. If he works quickly and efficiently, and if they can drive past the road blockades out of town, they still have time. He has faith that God will bring Karma back to life.

Karma, having already forgotten about the football game, is floating through a thick, dark and empty cloud. Nothing surrounds her. She is nothing except for a tiny little spark of recognition that contains the concept of an identity. In this depleted vapor, she has no need to think. Sensations of meaningless pleasure wash through her, so intoxicating that they would cause her to lose balance were she not a phase of a formless, shapeless being.

She can still hear, but the sounds are muted, like whale calls or underwater human conversation. The noise is distant, soporific. When she commands herself to, she can conjure languid visions. Somewhere, a thunderous sound knocks little pieces of spirit against one another, stirring Karma briefly into cohesion. When she retreats into total disassociation, she finds her energetic being floating in a gelatinous substance.

She intuitively knows that she can survive forever in here. That this viscous world will give her nutrients and keep her warm while she sleeps for as long as she would like. To some, the emptiness and loneliness might get to be too much, but

Karma is perfectly willing to be ensconced into such a gentle fate.

Her thoughts fade in an out. She is alternately walking in a field with tall grass, where she can feel flowers in her hair, and reliving an actual memory. She witnesses her eighth birthday party at the bowling alley. She remembers the bright rainbow painted on the otherwise blue wall. Every inner experience is a happy one. From this point of view, everything under the sun is equally calm and brilliant.

She drifts away, and when she comes back, she is flying over a forest in the shadow of an ice-capped mountain. She can feel the chill in the cold, thin air. She can see long white birds flying alongside her. The excursion requires no ostensible effort, her entire being an effortless smile. She is grateful to be so far away from the ground, which she associates with messiness. She is pristine from this high above. She flies and flies, over rivers, hills, then oceans. She could keep going forever, but in the distance, the sky abruptly changes into a teeming horde of thunderclouds. She tries to stop, but she is unable to do so.

Hafiz grabs the suitcase's handle firmly with his right hand then pauses momentarily before lifting it from the bible. The faint scent of roses emanates from the quiet interior of the church, but he is too distracted to identify the name of the smell. He stands frozen, unable to move, until an electrical impulse travels from his heart to his arm, which replies by contracting and hoisting the case before lowering it innocuously to his side.

Before indecision can creep back into his actions, he jerks open the outside door and runs blindly down the hill, almost taking another tumble in his haste. When he reaches the Mustang, he is so harried that he accidentally drags the key along the exterior of the trunk in a clumsy attempt to unlock it. He can see the scar of his carelessness in the dim moonlight. Normally fastidious about appearances, this mark doesn't concern him. He places the case on its side against the partition separating the trunk from the car's interior, then picks it back up to ensure the seal around the edge remains unbroken. Given the urgency of the circumstances, he can afford no more mistakes.

Certain that the contents of the vials will not spill into his air for at least an hour, he checks to see that the keys are in his pocket before slamming the trunk closed. The echo of his action reverberates in the eerily silent dark.

Hafiz runs back up the hill, pausing briefly on the incline to collect his breath and wipe a few beads of sweat from his forehead. He can feel the dampness from his armpits leaking through the fabric of his shirt.

When he reaches Karma, he sees that she has not moved at all from her previous position. Gently, he puts two fingers underneath her chin and can detect vague activity in her veins. That she is still alive calms him. He feels his heart slacken as he surveys the lawn to make sure they are alone. They are.

He picks her up, carefully bearing her weight with his legs, a lesson inculcated in all children of the earth. For some reason, Karma is more cumbersome this time. Her arms protrude at odd angles; one pokes at his stomach. He tries unsuccessfully to reposition her before ignoring the discomfort and starting back down the hill for the last time.

With the unwieldy load, the incline seems steeper, and he steps slowly so that he won't fall and injure both of them. He tries to keep her head from bending too far backwards, but it rolls in a sickening direction, exposing the cartilage of her throat.

He never sees nor hears another person on the trip back to the car. He tries to arrange her in a sitting position, back to the car, as he unlocks the door, managing not to scrape the paint this time. He takes his eyes off of her for only a split second, but when he turns back, he sees her head hit the gravel before he hears the soft thud. She does not awaken on impact.

Hafiz briefly considers placing her under the belt in the front seat but decides he is better off laying her across the back. He picks her up and tries not to bang any part of her against the car frame. Her skin feels colder to the touch, though the cauldron that is the night air heats him adamantly.

Back in the driver's seat, Hafiz stops to consider that he had planned never to return to his car. He marvels at how the program of prayer does not always unfold in the manner one intends.

By habit, Hafiz utters a plea for a safe journey. He needs to get out of town and get rid of the suitcase in a rural area immediately. The code of murder by which he lived for most of his life has fled from his heart. To do no further harm at this point, he needs to escape, as far away from the city as possible, and the martial law surrounding him will ensure this to be no easy task.

He turns the key, conscious of how the thick rubber casing rubs against his thumb, and the engine springs to life, breaking the silence of these forgotten hours. He reaches to flip on his headlights but decides against it. As he backs out of his parking space, he formulates a mental map that will hopefully lead him to the interstate with the least amount of interference possible. Because Karma is catatonic, he will use her to answer any questions about why he is on the road when it is supposed to be empty.

Straining his forehead skin in thought, he practices the English aloud, "Yes, officer," he says, trying to drive the fear from his voice. "My seestah, she very sick. We must go to Mexico. My mother, she a..."

He looks in the rearview mirror as he turns onto the street, searching for the English translation for curandera. He can't find it, so he decides to stick with the Spanish word.

Hafiz is somewhat familiar with the surrounding neighborhood, having driven through it a few times in his years in this city. Three-bedroom brick houses are buffered from the road by large lawns whose thirst the darkness conceals. Lights dot windows here and there, but, as far as he can tell, everyone is asleep. He heads east a few blocks, crossing the intersections quickly while trying to scout Thorndale, which runs parallel, in the process.

At the third intersection, he sees activity and what he believes to be army vehicles in the middle of the main street. Instead of adding to his panic, the affirmation that life still exists calms him somewhat. He can see the end of the street up the hill in a few blocks and tries to modify his route to avoid the military.

When he reaches the cross street, which normally runs one direction toward Thorndale, he hooks to his left in hopes of continuing east along the next side street. He holds his breath as he slowly drives the wrong way down the street but doesn't see another headlight. After about 200 yards, he turns up the hill back onto a side street.

He can go no further, though. Two men with low-hung caps and sand-colored camouflage outfits lift up automatic weapons, pointing them at his windshield.

Hafiz reminds himself that he expected a similar development and forbids himself from panicking. The center of his body and soul, usually consumed with a mix of faith and hatred, is strangely empty. He understands that a higher power will determine his fate, so as the men take slow steps to approach the driver's side door, he holds up his hands.

Two more army men emerge from a similarly camouflaged

truck that is parked sideways, blocking the road. They stand and watch as the first two circle the Mustang, guns drawn. One lowers his weapon and shines a flashlight through the car's windows, appraising the contents.

Hafiz tries to take slow breaths and rehearses his explanation a few more times in his head. The one with the flashlight opens the door, and the first thing Hafiz notices is fear in his eyes. He is roughly Hafiz' age and size, and Hafiz sees him more as kin than adversary. With his hands still raised in the air, he has enough time to marvel at how this night has shifted his perception about everything.

"Sir," the soldier says. "No one's supposed to be on the road. Why are you out right now?"

Hafiz opens his mouth to speak, but Karma beats him to it.

In a slurred, sleepy voice, she asks, "What's going on?"

Karma's ears are ringing as if channeling a fierce electric current. Every few seconds, a sharp, bee-like noise cuts through her consciousness. Her eyelids droop heavily, but she can see enough to make out the shock on Javier's face, which is swiveled around on his neck from the front seat of the car.

She has a vague recollection of some strange story he recounted, but she can't, for her life, figure out where she is or why she is here. She sits, slumped against the side window and devoid of all emotion, waiting for an answer to the question she posed.

A man, whose sand-colored hat she can make out in the light of an approaching dawn, leans in through the open front window and assesses her with his eyes. Mildly self-conscious, her eyes wander down and notice how wrinkled her clothes are. She can also smell the slightly sweaty odor of her unwashed skin.

"Ma'am," the man begins. "I am U.S. Army. There's a city-wide curfew, and you guys aren't supposed to be out right now."

Javier's head is frozen 180 degrees from his body. His eyelids do not move. Karma's head feels heavy, and she doesn't know what to make of any of this, but she is also unconcerned. The soldier looks from one to the other, waiting for some sort of explanation.

Finally, Hafiz offers palatable words: "She very sick," he says, trying too hard to appear frightened. "We are going to the hospital."

Karma recoils, bumping her head lightly against the window. She feels sleepy, not sick at all, but she has no solution and doesn't want to sit here in confusion until the morning sun returns. The man nods his head and orders them to wait there. Karma turns her head and watches as the man goes to confer with a few other soldiers, who are also heavily armed. A bit of drool makes its way down the side of her mouth before she notices. She wipes it off and wonders if she is genuinely sick.

While she waits, she remembers about Marian in the hospital. She backtracks and remembers that Christian is dead. Her memory takes a few more steps into the past until she can picture Doreen in those same green halls. She sees herself in the bathroom in the pharmacy, and her stomach drops. Her head rolls to the side, and with considerable effort, she reaches for the mostly empty bottle of pills in her pocket.

"Oh Jesus," she slurs aloud. Her sorrow reverberates throughout the car. Javier does not react. She grasps for bits of mental pictures and pieces together the interior of the church. In one moment of horrific clarity, she knows that she unsuccessfully tried to kill herself.

Now she wants to go to the hospital. Her mind wakes up, and she knows that she probably should have her stomach pumped. She wonders how Javier came to the same conclusion. Without explanation, she thanks him. He is very brave to venture out in the middle of this crisis to try to save her life. If successful, she will be forever indebted to him.

The visible dawn begins to break, and Karma starts to sob silently. Life hasn't been perfect, but she didn't honestly want to die.

A suggestion of reddish sky directs her eyes upward, and she does not notice that the soldier has walked back over to the car. She tries to make out what he is saying, but the heavy weight of her eyelids pulls her back into oblivion.

Karma's dream now takes on a dark, metallic hue. A veil of bulky black air complicates her vision. She wears a thick gray fabric that runs all the way to the mist covering the ground. In her right hand, she holds a long sword. Her fingers are wrapped tightly around the brass hilt, redolent of fear. Voices discuss something indiscernible in the fog, and a pale grey sun hovers directly in front of her. Her body tenses, not with obvious muscular effort, but in anticipation of the looming battle with the unknown.

The voices continue to exchange words in her surroundings while the floor underneath her feet begins to lurch. As she is propelled toward the unnatural orb in the sky, another figure, equally armed and similarly dressed, emerges in the opposite fog. Her competitor is taller and broader than she will ever be, and she feels both hands tremble, culminating in a sense of total paralysis.

The hooded figure approaches cautiously, one foot after the other. A bright glint of light reflects off of his sword, blinding her as she waits, immobile. The tone of the voices rises into shouts of warning, and the ground trembles underneath her like an earthquake. She almost loses her balance as the floor jerks up to her right, but she manages to steady herself.

The sudden movement has confused the approaching warrior, causing his sword to fly off into the mist. She hears it clank, making the sound of stricken metal.

An unfamiliar voice, unseen, calls out her name. She cannot think, cannot move. Karma intuits that her fate rests on the outcome of her battle with this hooded figure, but the fight has evaporated from her heart. She is broken. She drops her sword as the ground tilts in front of her, sending the weapon flying to her competitor's feet. He bends, inch by agonizing inch, picks it up and regards it carefully.

Pure terror has seized Hafiz as he attempts to escape the pursuing military vehicle. "A la madre," he curses in Spanish, replaying the insistent orders from the soldier. That dumb guy wanted to take Karma to the hospital in another vehicle and detain Hafiz right there next to his car. Certain death. He had to flee; he had to, he repeats inside his panicked mind.

His initial U-turn lands the front right area of his hood right into the army vehicle. A piece of metal audibly bends backwards and is now impeding his ability to drive and steer, but he does everything he can to stay on the straight and narrow. He has to get away from here. If he can lose the two city police cars now chasing him, he can grab Karma and hide. If she survives the next day in hiding, perhaps they can escape the virus. This is their only hope at redemption.

The fog has risen to Karma's mid-section. She is ready to meet her destiny, so she removes the rough hood from her head. She chokes on a breath of the thick grey air and gags at its putridity. She kneels onto the ground, and only her unmasked head rises out of the fog. Her assailant walks right up to her and bends down, scanning her eyes from behind the impenetrable veil. She bows her head.

With the sword securely in his right hand, the man lifts his left arm and removes the hood. He is Christian, with black pits as eyes. Karma shudders at the hideous sight. Tacitly, he raises the long sword above his head and prepares to drive it into her. As he begins the final motion, the entire world tumbles upside down several times to a cacophonous crunch of metal. When she regains equilibrium, Karma stands up; the fog is gone, and she sees Christian, impaled and limp upon her sword.

Karma awakens to the terror of her screams and a sharp pain in her head. Just like in her dream, the physical world around her has been robbed of its equilibrium. Up is down, and she can't make sense of her surroundings. She reaches her one free hand up toward her head and finds it next to a broken piece of glass, bleeding. She struggles to remember things about this world and determines that she is in a car that is on its side. A pale purple light streams in from above her. A barely discernible whimpering sound comes from someone directly in front of her.

She shivers violently on the inside, but as she leads her hand down her face, her skin is hot to the touch. She can make out a deployed airbag and a limp arm from the area in front of her, but the overriding and terrible vision coursing through her mind is that of Christian on her sword. Although she isn't sure which is which, both life and death seem to offer only crushing defeat.

Sirens and loud conversation filter in through the gaps where sheer glass used to separate the car from the hot air, but Karma is too exhausted to attempt to restore mental order to the commotion. The nightmare of the sword through Christian's abdomen overtakes her, and all that matters is that he is dead. He must be, since she dreamed it so vividly.

He must be in that awful, colorless hell. Her fate, at this point, is inconsequential. She can still smell the rotten odor of that gray mist. A sob tries to break out of her midsection, but she wilts on the crushed glass on the ground, too broken even for tears. She wills the voices outside the wreckage away. She has never wanted to be alone more than she does at this moment.

The quick thud of approaching footsteps breaks through the din of voices to draw her back to consciousness. She can see pant legs moving through patches of glass and violet dawn, but her inebriation coupled with the head injury blur the lines. She drifts back and forth between the car and a cold, silent blackness. When she is in the world of the living, she feels her heart rhythmically pumping blood through the hole in her head. With each contraction, she feels lighter, emptier.

Karma takes short, quick breaths in an attempt to ward off the sensation of dying. She hears a creak as the surface toward the sky disappears. The full force of the morning air flows into her prison as a head pokes through the space where the door had just been.

She can make out the shape, but not the details, of a face that asks her repeatedly if she is okay. The whimpering nearby has stopped dead, and she knows this question is aimed squarely at her. She doesn't know how to answer truthfully, so she makes a moaning sound and lifts her head. The sharp smell of spilt gas gives way to the overwhelmingly bright scent of copper. She feels blood soaking her side adjacent to the ground, but she does not know if it is hers.

Any fate would be better than drowning in this growing pool of blood. "Help me. Help me!" she whimpers, as loudly as her broken body will allow. Another head appears in the hole to the sky. The two figures turn toward each other and confer in words she cannot decipher. She remembers the pills and wonders if they are the root of this miserable experience. When her supposed rescuers disappear, she wriggles the bottle out of her pants and manages to hide it in the pocket of the seat two inches from her face.

The whirl of approaching sirens grows. Karma is alternately sweating and shivering. The wisps of the pale dawn threaten to smother her as she struggles to keep taking those shallow breaths. The pain in her head dulls to numb as she passes out into blackness again. In here, she feels nothing but the freezing cold.

The shouts of "Ma'am, ma'am" bring her back to the light. When she moves her head slightly, the voice continues on by asking her if she is able to move. In response, she lifts her arm and wriggles her fingers at the questioner. "What about him?" the voice inquires. Karma does not understand so does not answer. "Please, ma'am, stay awake," the voice pleads with her.

Karma chuckles at being called "ma'am," and the laughter keeps her in the car. She tries to stay awake, whatever that means, but she has forgotten how. The darkness tugs at her, and newly written rules dictate that the cold always wins out over the pain. The voice continues calling out to her, and she tries to hold her eyes open, but after a few moments, she falls back into the cold blackness.

As she shivers in the void, a speck of light, the same soft hue as the dawn, appears. The speck grows until it dominates everything. The light is much warmer than the void, and she has finally found a place where she can rest comfortably. Karma prepares to close her eyes for the last time.

Before she can leave the world permanently, gravity drags her rudely back into it. People she cannot see have righted the car, and the sudden movement reactivates the untenable throbbing in the side of her head. Blood pours down over one eye, so through a crimson filter, she sees a brown body slump to the right over the gearshift.

Its muscles are elastic, and of this she is jealous. She wills her eyes back closed because the place with the soft, empty light is far preferable to this wretched wreckage. She inhales in the car and exhales in the comfort of an all-consuming white light.

She basks in the gentle warmth for a moment before a woman with long dark hair, arms outstretched, appears before her. The woman sobs quietly, and Karma asks her why she is upset. "I don't know what else I can do for you, my child," the woman says with strength and resignation in her voice.

"Please, pray for my soul," Karma answers.

As Karma disappears into the woman's inviting arms, a team of military medical personnel pulls her body onto a stretcher. One medic tries unsuccessfully to find her pulse. He makes his way to the open back of the ambulance to grab tools for her revival, but his partner stops him and shakes his head.

Karma's pale and blood-soaked body lies cold and motionless. Her open eyes stare straight up into the morning sky. Another medic has placed Hafiz' lifeless body onto another stretcher and rolls it next to hers. The two city policemen look down at their feet. The one with Hernandez written on his shirt scowls.

Hernandez notices a metal case a few feet from the wreckage. "Did this come from the car?" he asks aloud. No one answers. He kneels down to inspect it, and when he picks it up, the broken locks on the case disengage. A clear glass vial drops directly into his hand, breaking open on contact.

STAGE SIX

REBIRTH

CHAPTER TWELVE

FULL CIRCLES

My poor children. I send them into the world with endless love and such great hope, only to see them squander it all away on meaningless obsessions. The pain of caring for seven billion people is too intense to bear. I love them all, I truly do. Each and every one has a pure heart, but the ways of the world get so convoluted.

One by one, over the course of time, they return to me, asking for favors and good graces. I try to appease them all, as any adoring mother does for her children, but happiness remains a global impossibility. When the hourglass runs out of sand, I will drown the world in a sea of my tears, and we will start anew.

While most forget the loving embrace of their mother, others build shrines to me and worship these things regularly. For this, too, I weep. These same children, who pray so fervently, hate themselves. They treat their temples terribly. They castigate themselves for the slightest misstep. They expect miracles but refuse to accept them.

The group packed into the truck prays incessantly to me as they cross the border back into Mexico. The little boy Eduardo's feverish tears especially break my heart. On the drive south, he has asked me to watch over his mother no less than two hundred times. The rest are asking for a safe passage home -- a wish I will be able to grant.

After the exclusion and the judgment these poor souls have endured in Texas, they deserve a lucky twist of fate, which is what they will receive in this last-minute escape. As the truck nears the border crossing, each silently asks for safety. They do not know that all cars are being allowed to cross quickly into Mexico without any sort of inspection. Several border patrol officers wait on the opposite side of the road, preparing to turn back any vehicle attempting to head north, but no cars approach them.

The deep devotion of those in Mexico has helped safeguard them at this crucial time. I answered calls for protection by granting the information that chaos and violence had overtaken the United States. I would have done everything in my power to prevent the awful heartbreak beginning to claim lives by the millions up north, but my abilities are nothing compared to the incredible force of hatred in the world.

Lalo has never been to Mexico. His mother told him so many stories of horses and bonfires and dancing, but all of these things exist only in his imagination. His eyes well up again realizing that he has now crossed into Mexico, and his mother is not with him. His little body shakes with fear that he will never see her again.

He burrows into his father's side, and the man absently reaches up to tousle the boy's hair.

So far, everything is quiet in Mexico. Lalo hasn't seen a single horse. The sun begins to rise, and he does see a stray person or two. The buildings are older and shabbier, and the words adorning them are in another language, but as far as Lalo can tell, Mexico is identical to the United States.

He thinks of his uncle Javier, and the tears come again. Lalo's sadness wets the side of his father's shirt, but the man continues to stare ahead blankly. Tia Esme hums a song underneath her breath. The hint of a melody is the only spot of joy in this otherwise abject vehicle. Miguel speaks up and asks how much longer they have to drive.

"We are halfway there," Adolfo answers. "But we made it through the difficult half."

Lalo wonders what was so difficult about driving to Mexico. He experienced only grief and boredom. He doesn't expect either to abate any time soon.

To some, a clear line demarcates the good from the evil, but human nature has never been so simple. The world was corrupt from the beginning, yes, and suffering is a self-perpetuating cycle. As John Hernandez licks the blood from the seemingly innocuous nick on his hand, I weep for him too. Yes, his ways have caused a sizeable deal of pain on innocents, but I will sweep him up soon, as his time approaches. John, although he could have been the one to break the cycle, is a product of generations of war and hatred. He, like his ancestors, could not expel the darkness from his heart.

When he comes to me and has a chance to look back over all he has done, I'm certain he will be devastated about the way he acted. When we set up the arena once again, he will go back and attempt to correct himself. To some, a lifetime done over again is hell, but in this universe, I offer salvation for everyone. Even him. The next time around, though, I will not be so kind as to offer him a great love. Part of his lesson will be the hollow pain of unshakable loneliness.

John Hernandez sucks at the faint spot of blood the broken glass has drawn from the side of his index finger. The motion causes the lines in his face to become more pronounced. The small act of sucking ages him at least a decade. The presence of the two dead bodies, now completely covered by thin white sheets, softens his anger. While most things in this world serve to stoke his ire, death gives him pause. He knows that he, too, is a mortal man.

He tries to will away the shame of all the terrible things he has done. He continues to suck the tainted blood out of his finger, but he does not realize the futility of his attempt. As he tries to curtain over his mind's insistent image of Marian in the bar bathroom, the unseen virus replicates inside of him at the speed of sound. His maker prepares to meet him as John turns his attention to the practical matter of transporting the former people on these stretchers and cleaning the remnants of this yellow car off the road. As more officers arrive, John starts to feel acutely sleepy. A yawn seizes him, and he just wants to go home.

In a land of abundant kindness, why do so many of my children act weak and isolated? Fingers point, then heads roll, leaving a broken landscape of hurt hearts and desperation. Only when one stops expecting others to conform to his ideas of what another should be can real love be attained.

The Phelps family sits in a circle on a rug on the living room floor. They hold hands until Scotty releases his mother's grip and runs his fingers through the plush taupe fibers. The events of the previous day have left him exhausted and confused, but here at home, he feels safe.

When her son lets go, a single tear appears at the wide outer corner of Mercy's eye. Her singular obsession at the moment is Lynn, whom she never found after she called asking for a ride home from the hospital. The fact that Mercy herself made it back to her house and her kids is nothing short of miraculous.

The streets last night were resonant with dread, a feeling replicated in the pit of her stomach when she returned to the house and found it to be lacking her children. Being here with them now comforts her, but if the end is near, she wants to spend it with Lynn, too.

Emma Grace Phelps can feel the cold air settling on her shoulders, which are positioned directly under the vent. She thinks back to the miserable trek to the hospital the day before and that awful encounter at the church. She shivers. She has grown unnaturally tired. Stickiness arises in her throat, and she coughs.

Emma's sad little cough breaks the tranquil nothing Cody Phelps has conjured in his mind. He looks over at his daughter, whose eyes seem strangely hollow. He lets go of her hand and draws her close in to him. Yesterday must have been so traumatic for her.

He hopes that guarding her safely at home will prevent her involvement in the unfolding tragedy.

He thinks of his estranged uncle Edward, who has a large plot of land in West Texas. He weighs the possibility of escaping out there with his family. Perhaps with Lynn, too. Emma coughs again in the crook of his arm. Cody's bones begin to ache.

A mother's love for her children should know no bounds, even when the children in question begin to rebel and recreate themselves in an image opposite of the mother. This process, traumatic to both, is part of the human experience. So many seek to sever the bonds that gave them life in the first place. That sort of intimacy is unnatural to the density of an earthbound body. What you seek to repel, however, finds a way back into the center of your heart. Consciousness and love are the keys. Acceptance.

Lynn Hernandez weeps over the broken, cold body of her mother. Doreen had complained of wild temperature swings as they walked back to her apartment in the heat. Lynn had taken her arm to provide a steady source of comfort, but she had not been able to hold her mother when she fell.

Doreen's significant weight sent both crashing into the asphalt. Lynn tried all possible methods to revive her mother, but none worked. Her phone chose this moment to run out of batteries, and though Lynn tried to flag down several passing patrol cars and a military tank, no one would stop to help the old woman whose life slipped away from the sidewalk yesterday evening.

Doreen was too heavy for Lynn to lift or move, so she kept vigil over her mother's body all through the night. Being in close proximity to death gave Lynn pause to evaluate her own life. She vowed to be more peaceful. She wanted Mercy. She wanted to sleep.

As dawn broke, a strange metallic hue settled over the sky. Lynn had never seen anything like it, and she was not pleased. As she waited (for what, she did not know), she started to feel tired and achy. She rested her head on the dead weight of Doreen's cold belly and fell asleep.

The more comfortable you are with the unknown, the more peaceful you will be in the here and now. One of my precious sons learned this lesson and now serves as a valuable guide in humanity's most dire hour of need.

Christian Cantrell walks down the hallway of Hawthorne Hospital. He is slightly off-balance. His paper gown trails to the floor, and the bandage on his head needs changing. He reaches out to steady himself against the wall, and the lights sear into his brain, but he is utterly unconcerned.

On a normal day, several members of the hospital's staff would have already guided Christian back into his room, but the scene has dissolved into pure chaos. The sounds of coughing and wailing ring off of every surface. The speakers along the ceiling broadcast a constant stream of panic.

The remaining hospital workers run to and fro down the hall in confusion. More and more people, red-faced and runny-eyed, cram into this random hallway. Christian bends down in an attempt to console a young woman. She recoils at his bruised face, but he promises her that everything will be okay. She relaxes some then coughs violently right in his face.

Christian takes the elevator down to the ground floor. He arrives at the same time as a horde of military personnel dressed in thick camouflage. A sturdy bespectacled man shouts that everyone who has not been officially admitted must leave the hospital immediately.

When the suffering throng groans in protest, he explains at the top of his lungs that a triage station is being set up outside. Sullenly, people begin to make their way out into the sweltering heat. Coughing and wheezing fill the air.

Christian joins the outside crowd, placing his hands on as many passing shoulders as he can reach. He has been on the other side, and he tries to share his experience. Each time he begins his story, frightened ears relax at the sound of his happy voice.

What appears to be a crowd of thousands has gathered in every inch of available space outside the hospital. Christian does not see a triage tent. He turns around and sees that the hospital doors have been shut. Gone are the cotton-clad troops. In their place stand two forbidding people in biohazard suits holding automatic weapons.

This realization terrorizes the crowd. For thousands, this one vision signifies the beginning of the end -- the event they have shunned (but secretly courted) since birth. Christian holds his hands up to the heavens and cries tears of joy. His reaction placates some.

It warms my heart. He has learned.

Imprisonment is the inability to accept something that is eternally free. In an environment in which everyone creates her own reality, suffering need not be so prominent.

Flor Hidalgo sits alone in a pitch-black cell and cries because she misses her sons. She lashed out violently at her captors when they brought her here, so they put her in this dark and despicable place, but at least no one raped her.

She prays over and over that they go ahead and send her back to Mexico. At first, the warm darkness was a relief, but the prison has been unnaturally quiet over the last few days.

Flor is growing unnerved. She can't hear a thing. At first, someone pushed sandwiches through the slat in the door, but now she cannot remember the last time someone brought her food. Her mouth contracts from excessive thirst, and she can't bring herself to drink water from the toilet in her cell. The silence is deafening.

After an interminable period of lying on the floor, witnessing her soul slip along the thread connecting her to the earth, she lets go. As Flor travels through a tube of time and space, she expands. She has never been so happy.

Circles. Just like last time.

Marian Smythe has been asleep for nearly five days. In a rushed panic, the nurse had given her more than ten times the recommended dose of sedative. Not a soul has considered the terrorized woman since.

Marian badly needed the sleep. During the ordeal, her mind shut off, leaving her with no task except for to regenerate in the void. Calm cures so many ills, and when Marian finally opens her eyes, she feels renewed. Her first thought upon her return is of her pregnancy. She reaches a tired hand down to her belly and feels a miniscule stirring.

She experiences a fleeting moment of happiness before a nauseous stench slams her nostrils. She gags involuntarily. She calls out for someone to unhook her from these tubes, but no one answers. She can only wait a moment before the smell becomes unbearable. She gets out of bed and stands still for a moment while her muscles readjust to gravity. Sensing that something is horribly wrong, she walks into the hallway and sees dozens of motionless bodies. She screams, begging for help. No answer.

Marian runs to the elevator well, and the button surprisingly lights up. Two camouflaged bodies lie bloated on the floor of the elevator. She holds her breath and pulls them out into the hallway. She rides to the bottom floor, which is a scene of death and carnage. Marian just wants to leave. She cannot even begin to process what might have happened.

She steps over bodies and pushes the door to the outside world. It gives effortlessly at her touch. Seeing the sea of bodies, she wonders if a nuclear attack took place while she was sleeping. She doesn't know what a radioactive world would look like, but other than the obvious, it seems like a normal late-summer day. She yells as loudly as she can in hopes of finding a response. Silence.

Marian Smythe walks away from Hawthorne Hospital, determined to make something of her second chance. While she walks, directionless, she decides to name her baby Atticus.

And so it is that the meek did inherit the earth. Better luck next time.

The end. (until it begins again)

269

Caroline Collier

ABOUT THE AUTHOR

Caroline Collier is an award-winning writer who believes in the possibility of mapping a better world with words. When she isn't writing news stories about counterculture trends or helping worthwhile projects get funded through grant proposals, she is making music or supporting the TCU Horned Frogs. She lives in Fort Worth, Texas with her cats Biggie and Mia Louise Smalls. Visit her website at carolinebyline.com